Dead Winner

Dead Winner

Kevin G. Chapman

Copyright © 2022 Kevin G. Chapman
Reg. # TXu002327413

First Legacy Publishing, LLC
West Windsor, NJ

Edition 1.0 2022

Cover by Bespoke Book Covers
www.bespokebookcovers.com
Publicity by Aurora Publicity

Names, characters, and incidents in this story are either products of the author's imagination or are used fictitiously. Any resemblance to actual events, locations, names, and people, living or dead, is entirely coincidental and beyond the intent of the author and publisher.

Except as permitted under the US Copyright Act of 1976 and except for brief quotations in critical reviews or articles, no portion of this book's content may be stored in any medium, transmitted in any form, used in whole or part, or sourced for derivative works such as videos, television, and motion pictures, without prior written permission from the publisher.

Library of Congress Control Number: Pending

ISBN- Paperback 978-1-958339-06-0
ISBN-Hardcover 978-1-958339-07-7
ISBN-Ebook 978-1-958339-05-3

Other novels by Kevin G. Chapman

The Mike Stoneman Thriller Series

Righteous Assassin (Mike Stoneman #1)
Deadly Enterprise (Mike Stoneman #2)
Lethal Voyage (Mike Stoneman #3)
Fatal Infraction (Mike Stoneman #4)
Perilous Gambit (Mike Stoneman #5)
Fool Me Twice (A Mike Stoneman Short Story)

Stand-alone Novels

The Good Girl (coming in 2023)
A Legacy of One
Identity Crisis: A Rick LaBlonde Mystery

Short Stories

The Car, the Dog & the Girl

Visit me at www.KevinGChapman.com

For Sharon, who keeps me honest, makes me laugh, and makes my characters so much better. All my love.

Chapter 1 – An Unexpected Reunion

"**R**ORY! IT'S AWFUL. TOM KILLED HIMSELF."

Rory McEntyre held his phone at the end of an extended arm as if it were a live cobra. The voice over the speaker sounded desperate, panicked.

"What?" was all Rory could manage as a reply. "Wait." He turned away from his 60-inch television screen, made an apology to his virtual gaming companions, and removed his J-100 surround sound headset. "Monica? Where are you?"

"I'm at our apartment. I don't know what to do. The police are on their way. I need you."

Rory jumped out of his six-hundred-dollar ergonomic chair and fumbled for the remote control to turn off the TV. "Police? Wait. Slow down. What happened?"

* * *

When Monica had walked into his office three days earlier, Rory's heart skipped two beats. He had not given much thought to the entry on his appointment calendar: "New client meeting – Mr. & Mrs. Williams." Her face was the same one about which he occasionally still dreamed.

Rory was out of his chair in eight tenths of a second and halfway across the small space between his desk and the office

KEVIN G. CHAPMAN

door. Then he saw Tom, entering behind her. Rory stopped short and forced his face into a professional smile, holding out a hand toward his old law school classmate. Tom looked better than he had at the wedding, where Rory had been a groomsman and Monica Bettger, the bride. In the intervening eight years, Rory had worked his ass off, first in a Boston firm and then for the past two years at Fitzsimmons, Packman & Kronish. When he saw Monica, he felt like a second-year law student again.

"My God, Monica," Rory disengaged his hand from Tom's and held out both arms. "You look amazing!"

Monica smiled warmly, then stepped toward Rory, engulfing him in a hug that made his toes tingle. After an extended squeeze, Rory leaned back, keeping a hand on each side of Monica's slender waist, and stared at Tom's wife. He did the mental math. It was early June and her birthday was July 14. Since Rory was now thirty-three, she was getting ready to turn thirty. She looked younger, still with the glow of youth he remembered from their school days, when she was an undergraduate at Barnard while Rory and Tom toiled at Columbia Law School.

Monica's three-inch red designer heels matched her dress, which flirted with the tops of her knees. He admired the shape of her bare calves, the curve of her hips, and the peek of cleavage escaping from the dress's neckline. Her long, blonde hair hung in waves around her shoulders and framed her soft face and mysterious eyes. He was instantly lost in those sparkling orbs, as he always had been. Monica stood five-foot-seven, but with heels was as tall as Rory.

"Great to see you, pal," Tom said, breaking Rory out of his stupor. Tom's dark blue pinstriped suit and patterned tie were elegant but understated. Rory instantly remembered why he had always been envious of Tom's six-two physique, broad shoulders, chiseled chin, and bright blue eyes. His sandy blond hair was as

DEAD WINNER

thick and wavy as ever, in contrast to Rory's tight brown curls, which had started their thinning retreat. Rory worked out regularly, rode his bike fifty miles every weekend, and thought he might be in better cardiovascular shape than Tom. But he would always be four inches shorter and lacking Tom's classically handsome features. "Sorry not to call ahead, but Monica wanted to surprise you. I guess it worked."

"It certainly did," Rory said with a forced chuckle as he motioned his visitors to two padded guest chairs. He hustled behind his desk and forced himself to occasionally glance at Tom so he didn't seem to be staring only at Monica. "Now, what in the world brings you two here today?"

Tom, as he always did, took charge and spoke with the confidence of a salesman. Rory had followed his old pal's career. Tom was a superstar money manager at Northrup Investments, LLC. Rory always knew Tom would be wildly successful at whatever he did. Everyone expected it. "We have a situation we need handled with both discretion and alacrity, Rory. It falls into your area of expertise, so Monica immediately thought of you."

"You did?" Rory beamed as he unashamedly turned his head toward the woman he had stared at every chance he got for the entire two years she and Tom had dated.

"I did," Monica smiled, lowering her eyes bashfully. "I mean, who else can we trust as much as you, Rory?"

When she said his name, Rory felt a rush of blood to his face. He picked up a Mont Blanc fountain pen and sat forward in his chair, ready to take notes. "I'm flattered. Well, I can assure you that this conversation is entirely privileged and confidential, based on my ethical obligations as a lawyer and my personal obligations as your friend." Rory was pleased with himself for coming up with such an eloquent response. Tom was always the guy with the fancy words. He saw Monica smile at him with her red lips and noticed her perfect, snow-white teeth. He had not seen either of them in years, yet he fell immediately into the familiar sphere of their long relationship.

"Terrific. We knew you'd be the man for us," Tom leaned forward and put a forearm on the edge of Rory's desk. He lowered his voice, as if concerned about being overheard. "You see, Scout, we need to set up a trust."

Rory bristled at Tom's use of his old prep school nickname. It had grown into a common moniker thanks to Tom, who pushed it to all their mutual friends. Tom said it was a combination of Rory being a Boy Scout and being Tonto to Tom's Lone Ranger—except Scout was Tonto's horse. Rory tried calling Tom "Silver" for a while, but it never caught on. Rory knew the use of "Scout" was Tom's way of asserting his superiority and Alpha male status, like he always did. Rory mentally flogged himself for allowing Tom to belittle him all those years ago. Since Tom was a potential client now, he had to let it pass again. But it still scratched at Rory. "What's the purpose of the trust? You don't have any children yet, right?"

"No. Not for our children. It's for us. We've had a bit of good fortune. You might have heard there was a big New York Lotto jackpot a few weeks ago."

"The lottery?" Rory didn't try to hide his puzzlement.

"Yes. The lottery. There were five winners, splitting a $300 million jackpot."

Rory stared blankly. "Do you know someone who won?"

Tom assumed a condescending expression. Rory knew it well. "I should say we do. It's us."

"You play the lottery?"

"Sometimes I do," Tom replied smoothly. "I like to pick up a ticket from the guy at my local newsstand along with my *Wall Street Journal*. And, well, I got lucky. We—we got lucky," Tom

DEAD WINNER

glanced at Monica as he reached for her hand. She squeezed it, then released quickly.

"Hold on. You're telling me you hit a, what? A sixty million lottery jackpot? Are you serious?"

"Yep. Serious as cancer, bro. That's why we need the trust."

"Tom, a trust isn't going to give you any tax advantages."

"I know. That's not why we need it. I understand we can legally transfer the ticket to a trust, then have the trust claim the prize without disclosing our identities as the winners."

Rory, who was furiously scribbling notes on a yellow pad, looked up with a frown. "I can't say I'm an expert on the rules of the New York State lottery. I'll have to do some research. But why don't you want to be identified?"

Tom hesitated, then applied a serious expression. "Rory, there are some very good reasons why I need to do this confidentially. The men who run my asset management company would not be happy about it. There are some other reasons, but suffice to say we very much need to keep our identities out of the media. Is that sufficient?"

"Of—of course," Rory stammered. "I didn't mean to imply that you didn't have a good reason. It's entirely your business, naturally. I'm pretty sure a properly organized trust could be the legal owner of the ticket and claim the prize money, then the trustee could disburse the funds to the beneficiaries without publicly disclosing the identities of the winners. Of course, the IRS would need to know, and if some reporter really dug into it, the identity of the beneficiaries could be discovered . . . unless we set up a double blind—"

"I told you Rory would know what to do," Monica said, uncrossing her legs and leaning forward. "He'll take care of us, won't you, Dear?"

5

KEVIN G. CHAPMAN

"Ye-yes. Absolutely." Rory again felt a rush of blood to his face and hoped he was not obviously turning red.

"Super. What's the next step?" Tom removed his arm from the desk and sat back, relaxing into a cross-legged posture. "We'd like to get this done as soon as possible."

"Well, I'd say the first thing to do is secure the winning ticket." Rory reached for his desk phone and lifted the receiver.

"Wait," Tom interjected. "Hold on. Who are you calling?"

"Oh, our chief of security, who handles the vault. We're going to want to put your ticket away for safekeeping, especially if the trust we're going to set up will be the owner. We'll obviously need the original to make the claim for the winnings. Do you have it with you?"

"No. God, no," Tom said calmly. "It's in a secure location. In fact, I've already taken the liberty of creating documentation of our ownership." Tom dug into his jacket pocket and pulled out his iPhone. After a few swipes and taps, he handed the device across the desk to Rory, who watched with great interest. On the tiny screen, a video image of Tom explained excitedly that he and Monica had hit the lotto jackpot. The shaky camera zoomed in at one point on a cluttered dining room table, where a small rectangle of white paper lay on a gold placemat. As the camera zoomed and focused, Rory could make out the familiar blue ball—the logo of the New York State lottery—and the laser-printed numbers on the ticket. The initials "TW" were handwritten in blue ink next to the lottery logo.

Rory tapped the screen to pause the video, wrote down the numbers and the date of the drawing, then allowed the video to play to its conclusion. He guessed the film had been made in Tom's and Monica's apartment. Monica appeared briefly in the background.

DEAD WINNER

"That will certainly be helpful to prove you are the rightful owner of the ticket, if there were ever any question," Rory observed. "Even if the ticket were stolen, you would be in a good position to contest anyone else coming forward to claim the money. It was a good idea to put your initials there."

"Thanks. It seemed like the obvious thing to do."

"Most people would immediately post a picture on Twitter," Rory joked.

"True. But we're not most people."

"Ain't that the truth." Rory smiled, making a few more notes on his pad. He thought about all the reasons why Tom was extraordinary. He was a star athlete, and an honor student thanks to Rory. In prep school, Tom had been good in every subject except math. Math was Rory's sweet spot, and so he helped Tom get a gentleman's B. During the tutoring, they became friends. Rory knew Tom viewed him mainly as a useful tool, but he got to hang out with the cool kids, so he didn't mind. After Tom went off to Yale and Rory to Columbia as undergrads, their paths crossed in law school, where they fell back into their old pecking order.

Discussing the formation of a trust was Rory's comfort zone. He was a meticulous estate planner. Over the next ten minutes, Rory obtained all the information he needed. Both Tom and Monica said they also wanted to have wills drafted. Up to that point, they had not worried about estate planning, but this windfall was a solid impetus to start thinking long-term. Rory promised to make the assignment a priority. After having Tom and Monica separately sign client services agreements to fully establish an attorney-client privilege, Rory eventually had to concede that the meeting needed to end.

KEVIN G. CHAPMAN

"I need to get back to the office," Tom looked at his watch. "They don't know I'm here and my assistant, Breonna, is covering for me."

"Are you sure you don't want to store the ticket in the firm's vault?" Rory asked again as Tom reached for his briefcase.

"I'm sure. You're such a worry wart. Always were."

"True," Rory conceded good-naturedly. "That's what makes me a good estates lawyer." They all had a good laugh.

Monica stood. As Rory watched, Tom put both hands on the arms of his chair and pushed himself up. Rory noticed a grimace and a muted groan. Monica gripped Tom's upper arm and steadied him as he gained his balance. Rory suppressed a smile, thinking that he was, indeed, in better physical shape than Tom.

They made their good-byes. Rory handed out business cards and escorted Monica and Tom down the hallway, through the lobby, and past the ten-foot-high windows overlooking the Hudson River. It was an impressive view. He never tired of showing it off to clients. In the expansive client lobby on the thirty-seventh floor, Monica once again treated Rory to a lingering hug as they parted. Rory watched them walk slowly through the glass doors and down the carpeted hallway toward the elevator, Monica hanging onto Tom's elbow. He could still smell her perfume as Monica's red pumps disappeared into the downward-bound car. He remembered how she nearly always wore Christian Dior's *Poison*. Monica had expensive taste, even when she was a starving college student wearing an Indigo Girls t-shirt.

Tom was a lucky man. He always had been. Rory's thoughts wandered as he strolled back toward his office. Tom had the looks, the confidence, the great job . . . and Monica. And now, a huge lottery prize. Some guys had all the luck. Was he jealous of Tom? Sure. Who wouldn't be? In their youth, Tom had always

8

DEAD WINNER

been the popular one, the life of the party and the top of the class. They had formed a certain bond, even if it was Rory's Tonto to Tom's Lone Ranger. Rory was always fine with that. He had never questioned deferring to Tom on everything. Including Monica.

Still, there was a time. Rory met Monica first, when they both auditioned for the Fall Follies show at Columbia at the start of Rory's second year at the Law School. They had gone out for a slice of pizza and stayed up late into the night talking about philosophy and the environment. Monica was a more accomplished actress and singer, which landed her a role in the show, while Rory worked on the lighting crew. They had enjoyed hanging out together when their studies permitted. But then she ran into him while he was with Tom. He was no match for Tom in a romance competition.

Rory had played the scenarios out in his head a thousand times. If he had made a romantic overture toward Monica before Tom had the chance, would she have chosen him? Would Tom have backed off if he knew Rory had already started a relationship? The endless procession of "what ifs" led only to regret. He thought he had gotten over it, but Monica's sudden appearance brought back all the old feelings.

Lost in his thoughts, Rory waved reflexively when he passed Heidi Hottinger, the attractive blonde receptionist on his floor.

"Hi, Rory. Who are the new clients?" Heidi asked brightly.

He stopped, shaking off the cobwebs of his memories. "Oh, they are – old friends. We went to school together."

"Are you riding on Sunday?"

"Sure," he replied automatically. He rode his bike nearly every weekend. He had to think about what organized ride was happening on Sunday. Then he remembered the event, which started at the George Washington Bridge and then followed the

KEVIN G. CHAPMAN

Palisades Parkway north, along the Hudson River. It was an exceptionally beautiful route. He smiled at Heidi. She had always been friendly and cheerful. He had seen her at a few bike races, but never spent more than a minute talking with her. He had always assumed she wouldn't find him very interesting. "I'm looking forward to it. I guess I'll see you at the bridge?"

"I'll be there," she flashed a wide smile, then turned to answer her ringing phone, while Rory continued toward his office.

Back at his desk, Rory navigated to the lottery commission website. He verified the date of the drawing for a jackpot of $308 million. The date matched the ticket on Tom's video. The numbers also matched. It was the real deal. According to the website, only one of the five winners had come forward since the drawing. Rory wondered whether all the other winners were busy setting up trusts.

As he filled out a new client form, he found himself fantasizing about having Monica as a client. It wasn't like he spent much time with his clients once their wills were signed, but maybe this trust would need more hands-on attention than most. He began thinking of ways to make it happen.

* * *

On the following Monday evening, Rory had arrived at his apartment shortly before seven-thirty. The day had been typical, except for the excitement he felt working on the trust and wills for Monica and Tom. He enjoyed a fresh dinner with the aid of a prepared food delivery service: grilled salmon, roasted Yukon gold potatoes with rosemary, and a grilled veggie assortment. Rory was actually a pretty good cook, but buying fresh food at the market to prepare only for himself was too depressing. The

DEAD WINNER

freshly delivered and ready-to-cook meals, aided by the high-tech bar-code-scanning convection oven, was much more efficient and almost as tasty.

He instructed his home assistant device to play some John Coltrane while he ate and sipped on a local New Jersey Chardonnay. Then he processed payments for two bills that had arrived in the mail and surfed through his Facebook feed. Six new posts from friends, all business acquaintances except for one from his prep school days. He automatically clicked the "Like" button for each post, but left no comments. He didn't feel any connection to their lives, and he was certain they felt none to his.

After checking his work email one last time and shutting down his laptop, Rory spent thirty minutes reading a biography of Lyndon Johnson, which was his book club's discussion subject for the month. His sister had suggested joining a book club as a way to meet intelligent women. There were certainly several brilliant thinkers in the group, which was mostly female, but all of them were either married or not interested in male companionship. He remained in the group because it allowed him to have conversations about something other than taxes and funerals. During the last fifteen minutes, he skimmed through several dull chapters. He felt reasonably prepared for that Thursday's meeting.

At eight-forty-five, Rory settled into his deluxe gaming chair in front of his sixty-inch television. Forty minutes into a session of *Counter-Strike*, while leading a team of five players assaulting a terrorist stronghold in the Afghanistan mountains, Rory's cell phone rang. He did not recognize the number, but pushed his headset off one ear to answer anyway.

Before he said anything, he heard Monica's panicked voice. "Rory! It's awful. Tom killed himself.

Chapter 2 – Home, Bloody Home

TWENTY MINUTES AFTER RECEIVING Monica's frantic call, Rory argued with a uniformed NYPD officer outside her apartment door. "Monica Williams called me and asked me to come. I'm her lawyer."

Monica, hearing the disturbance, raised herself from the barstool next to the kitchen and hurried to the door, followed by the female officer who had been assigned to watch her until the detectives arrived. When Monica confirmed that Rory was her lawyer, and her friend, he was admitted past the yellow crime scene tape.

As soon as Rory made it to the entry foyer, Monica melted into his chest, crying. He wrapped his arms gently around her and patted her back, not knowing what to do or say in such a circumstance. Usually, by the time clients arrived at his office, they had made it past the immediate grief of losing their loved ones. After an awkwardly long period of hugging, Rory whispered into Monica's ear, "Why don't we go sit down?"

Monica sniffed, pushed away momentarily, then latched onto Rory's arm and led him toward a cushioned bench by the window next to a small kitchen nook. As they passed the half-wall separating the kitchen from the living room, Rory saw several figures moving about. Two uniformed officers lingered on the periphery, watching as silent sentries. A short woman

DEAD WINNER

wearing blue paper scrubs, booties, a hair net, and blue latex gloves, squatted down next to a lump on the floor covered with a white sheet. A photographer holding a large Nikon D750 with a protruding flash tower was snapping pictures. Two EMT techs, flanking a gurney outfitted with white sheets and a pillow, waited to remove the body hiding beneath the sheet.

When they settled on the window seat, Rory could see the sparkling lights of New York City out the window. A few stars struggled to penetrate the ambient light. Rory spoke in a hushed voice. "What happened?"

Monica's eyes were red from crying. She grabbed both of Rory's hands in hers. "Should I be saying anything with the police here?"

"You're right," Rory agreed, realizing he should have given that advice. "You shouldn't say anything that could be misconstrued."

"You're my lawyer, right? So, things between us are privileged, aren't they?"

Rory turned his head to determine how far away Monica's police chaperone was. "You signed a representation agreement in my office on Friday. So, yes, I'm your lawyer. And, yes, there is an attorney-client privilege between us. But if anyone overhears, then the privilege won't help, so you do need to be careful—not that you'd be saying anything incriminating, right?"

"Of course not." Monica pulled her head back and looked reproachfully at Rory. "Why would you even ask that?"

Rory's face blanched. "No—no. Of course you wouldn't. I didn't mean to . . . I'm not suggesting—"

"Oh, I know," Monica softened her expression and reached for Rory's hand. "I'm sorry. I'm just so freaked out. I came home and found Tom . . . on the floor . . . dead." She lurched forward,

KEVIN G. CHAPMAN

resting her forehead against Rory's shoulder and breathing heavily, fighting back more tears.

Rory reflexively put an arm around her shoulders and rubbed her back softly. "Have the police questioned you at all?"

Monica sniffled and pulled her head back so she could look Rory in the eye. He once again noticed her perfume: still *Poison*. "No. The first officer said somebody else would be coming to talk to me."

"OK," Rory said confidently. His experience with criminal law was limited to one pro bono project he had worked on at his Boston law firm. But he knew the police could not question a witness—or a potential suspect—who was represented by counsel without the lawyer's consent. Because he was acting as Monica's lawyer, he could shield her from any intrusive questioning. He was her defender. She needed his protection.

Rory removed his hand from her shoulder, where it was still resting, and reached for Monica's left hand with both of his. "Listen to me. I'm here for you. I'm not going to let any policeman bully you."

"Oh, Rory, thank you so much for being here. I don't know what I'd do . . ."

Before Rory could say anything else, two men wearing jackets and ties strode purposefully across the kitchen, accompanied by a uniformed officer. One was slightly taller and thinner than the other, and was the first to speak. "Mrs. Williams?"

"Yes?" Monica said, looking up. Rory raised his head without speaking.

"I'm Detective Steve Berkowitz," he had a thick New York accent. "This is my partner, Detective George Mason." Berkowitz gestured toward his shorter and rounder partner. "I'm sorry to

DEAD WINNER

have to do this, but we need to ask you a few questions about what happened here. Is there somewhere we can talk in private?"

Monica looked at Rory. "Um, I'm not sure . . ." She squeezed Rory's hand, digging a polished nail into his sensitive flesh.

Rory snapped to attention, pulling his hand away and rubbing his scratched skin. "Detective Berkowitz, my name is Rory McEntyre and I'm Monica—Mrs. Williams' lawyer. I should be present for any questioning."

Berkowitz looked at Mason and shrugged. "Fine. Do you mind if we do it here?" When both Monica and Rory nodded, Berkowitz continued. "I understand you're the person who found the deceased, is that right?"

"Uh huh," Monica monotoned, not looking at the detective.

"What time did you arrive home?"

Monica looked at Rory, who nodded for her to answer. "Um, it was around nine o'clock, I think. I came back from Long Island on the train. I'm pretty sure it was about that time."

"How long were you away from home?" Berkowitz continued.

"All day, I suppose. I went to work this morning. Then, after work, I took the train out to visit my mother. I go every week, usually on Mondays. She's in a nursing home."

"Can you tell me, in as much detail as you can, what you did when you came home?"

Again, Monica looked at Rory, who didn't speak, but nodded encouragingly. "I came in, and . . . it smelled strange. I called to Tom, and when he didn't answer, I went into the living room and . . ." Monica dissolved into tears.

"I'm sorry, Ma'am. I know this is difficult." Berkowitz motioned to his partner to get Monica a tissue from the box on a nearby shelf. When Monica finished dabbing her eyes and

KEVIN G. CHAPMAN

blowing her nose, the detective pressed forward. "Was anyone else in the apartment when you arrived?"

Monica dropped the soiled tissue on the small kitchen table. "No. No, it's just me and Tom here. There's nobody else."

"OK. Was your husband's body lying where it is now, when you found him?"

"Um, yes, I guess. I mean, when I saw him . . . I ran over. I wasn't sure what had happened." Monica put her head down and sobbed.

"Was the door locked when you arrived?" Berkowitz asked.

"Yes. I used my key to get in, like always."

Berkowitz looked down at Monica's black pumps. Her legs were crossed underneath her chair; her soles smeared with blood. More blood marred the sleeves of her blouse and the hem of her skirt. A large dark blotch under her left knee told Berkowitz that Monica had knelt next to her dead husband's body. The floor around the kitchen nook showed faint footprints from her stained shoes. "You touched the body?"

"Yes. I-I-I did."

"You picked up the gun?"

Monica nodded.

Detective Mason spoke for the first time. "It's understandable, Mrs. Williams. Do you know whether the gun belonged to your husband?"

"Yes, it did," Monica replied, this time without seeking Rory's permission. "He bought it a few months ago. He had it all registered and everything. He wanted it for protection. That was the gun on the floor."

"How can you be sure?" Mason pressed.

"There's an inscription on the bottom. I saw it."

Berkowitz tilted his head toward the living room. Mason walked away and returned a moment later with a plastic evidence

16

DEAD WINNER

bag containing a black Beretta M9 pistol with bloody streaks on its hilt. He held it up to the light, peering through the plastic at the butt. "T. Williams," he read the script inscription.

Monica nodded.

Berkowitz, who had been making notes on a small pad, scribbled something. "Can you tell us whether your husband had any reason to kill himself?"

"No. No. No," Monica said, choking back tears. "Everything was great. His job is terrific. We're happy. There's no reason he would . . ." She dissolved into tears again, burying her head in Rory's shoulder.

Berkowitz handed Monica another tissue. "I'm sorry, Ma'am. I know this must be the worst possible time. But do you recall your husband acting unusual, or saying anything to suggest he was having any problems lately?"

Monica dabbed away the fresh tears. "He was really busy at work. I know he was kind of nervous about a big new client he was working on. I don't know anything about it."

The detectives exchanged a glance before Berkowitz asked the next question. "Mrs. Williams, were you two having any problems in your marriage?"

"Wait!" Rory broke in. He wasn't sure exactly what to say, but he knew this question was not about Tom's suicide. He felt a constriction in his throat, but managed to croak out, "Hold on, now. I mean—what has that got to do with Mr. Williams' suicide? I don't think that's a very appropriate question, I think. So, I don't think Monica should answer."

Again, Berkowitz and Mason exchanged a glance. "Will you consent to taking a test for gunpowder residue on your hands?"

Rory again jumped in, gaining confidence in his criminal defense attorney instincts. "That is offensive, Detective. Besides,

17

KEVIN G. CHAPMAN

she admitted to touching the gun, so any residue would not prove anything. Monica—Mrs. Williams—is not a suspect, is she?"

"Nobody is a suspect yet," Berkowitz said. "And you can't get powder residue from touching an already-fired gun."

"Well," Rory hesitated, not knowing one way or the other if the detective's statement was true, "we're not taking your word for that." Monica stayed silent, but made eye contact with Rory, flashing an approving if momentary smile. Rory felt a warm glow in his gut.

Berkowitz put away his notebook. "OK, that's fine. We're going to look around the scene, Mrs. Williams. If we have any other questions for you, we'll come back. We'll ask you to please stay here and keep out of the way of the officers and the medical examiner. OK?"

Monica nodded and squeezed Rory's hand. Rory couldn't remember if he had taken her hand, or if she had reached for his. It was warm and soft and wet from her tears. The two detectives walked away, around the corner into the living room where Tom's body lay under the white sheet. The police photographer had completed her work and was packing up. The EMTs were lowering the gurney in preparation for the removal of the body.

Rory whispered to Monica, "Why didn't you tell the detective about the . . . the subject of the trust we're setting up? That would certainly seem to be a rock-solid reason why Tom would not kill himself."

Monica leaned in so her mouth was next to Rory's ear. He felt her warm breath as she spoke, which sent shivers up the back of his neck. "Tom said it was very important that we not be identified as being in possession of . . . the item. It was critical. I don't want to say anything. You'll help me keep it secret, right?"

When Monica pulled away, Rory looked into her pleading eyes and said, "Of course. But, under the circumstances, don't

DEAD WINNER

you think the police should know? I mean, what if somebody—" Rory then hushed his voice even further, "—killed Tom?"

Monica looked shocked at the thought. "But, how? The door was locked when I got home. I used my key. There was nobody else here. I can't see how it's possible."

"Are you certain there's no chance somebody could have been inside the apartment when you got home, and slipped out after you came in?"

"I don't see how. I would have heard the door close. I came out to get my phone in the foyer and stayed there until the first officer arrived. No. There's no way." She fell back against Rory's shoulder, breathing heavily as if she had no more tears to cry.

A few minutes later, Detectives Berkowitz and Mason returned to the kitchen nook. "I'm sorry, Ma'am. I need to ask you, when was the last time you had any communication with your husband? A phone call, or email, or text?"

Monica looked up, blinking rapidly to hold back more tears. "I ... well, I'm not sure. I think we exchanged a text this afternoon, when I was at work."

"Do you mind showing us?" Berkowitz asked gently.

Monica walked to the foyer table to retrieve her phone. She navigated to her text messages while she walked back into the kitchen. As she approached the two detectives, she stopped short. "Oh, my!"

"What is it?" Rory called out.

Monica stared at her phone in wonder. "There's a text here from Tom from four hours ago. I never saw it."

"What does it say?"

Monica made eye contact with Rory, who nodded. A text from Tom was something Monica should not withhold from the cops. They could probably get it with a subpoena to the phone company anyway. She scanned the text, then her arm dropped.

19

KEVIN G. CHAPMAN

The phone slid from her grasp and clattered onto the marble tile floor.

Rory jumped up and rushed to Monica, who slumped into him as he put his arms around her. Berkowitz grabbed the phone without asking permission. He read the text:

I'm sorry. I love you.

Berkowitz shouted to the living room. "Carson! Check the stiff—er—Mr. Williams' pockets to see if he has a phone." He then handed Monica hers. "Ma'am, can you check your phone to see if there are any calls from your husband from today?"

Monica started sobbing again. Rory patted her back awkwardly, like he was burping someone else's baby. He didn't know what else to do as Monica pressed herself against him. She gathered herself and took the phone from the detective, then checked her telephone records. She showed Berkowitz two missed calls from Tom's phone, at 5:45 p.m. and 6:21 p.m.

Before Berkowitz could ask, Monica explained that the nursing home where her mother lived asked guests to turn off their phones while visiting. She said she didn't check phone messages when she was on the train home. Instead, she was listening to an audiobook, a true crime story called *The Case of the Righteous Assassin.*

Erin Carson, the coroner's assistant whose job was to secure the body, yelled back a moment later, "Got an iPhone, Detective."

Mason went to the living room to retrieve the iPhone and brought it back, wearing blue latex gloves and holding the unit by its edges. Berkowitz said to Monica, softly, "Mrs. Williams, do you know the unlock code to your husband's phone?"

Monica nodded and entered the code. The detective navigated to Tom's text messages. In the sent messages, time-

DEAD WINNER

stamped at the same time as the incoming text on Monica's phone, was the same message: *I'm sorry. I love you.* Berkowitz grabbed an evidence bag from the pocket of his suit jacket and deposited the phone inside. He didn't ask Monica for permission. Rory said nothing.

"We're going to have to retain this phone as evidence."

"Yes, of course," Monica said in a monotone. "Rory? Is that alright with you?"

Rory had no idea whether retaining the deceased's phone was appropriate. His only thought was to protect Monica, and it didn't seem like there was anything on Tom's phone that could get her in trouble. There wasn't any real trouble for her to get into. He was thinking about the lottery ticket, and how Tom's death was going to affect the trust. It certainly wasn't going to adversely affect Monica. When she said his name, he snapped out of his internal musings. "Um. No. I don't think there's any problem."

"Fine," Berkowitz said, handing off the evidence bag to the uniformed officer standing in the kitchen, whom Rory had not noticed. "We'll let the medical examiner evaluate whether there's anything suspicious about the body or the cause of death. There's no sign of forced entry here, and no sign of a struggle or anything out of place. Mrs. Williams, did you notice anything missing when you arrived? Any jewelry or other valuables?"

"I—I don't know. I haven't thought to look."

Berkowitz looked at Mason. "Walk the lady around the apartment and have her take a look."

Detective Mason followed Monica as she patrolled the apartment, looking for anything out of place. Rory trailed behind. She found Tom's wallet on his dresser, with a few hundred dollars in cash and a pile of credit cards inside. She looked into an elaborate jewelry box and did a quick inventory of

KEVIN G. CHAPMAN

her diamonds, rubies, and gold bracelets and necklaces. Everything was present, as far as Monica could tell at a glance. After ten minutes, Mason was satisfied that there was no sign of a robbery.

Mason and Berkowitz huddled for a minute, then handed out business cards to Monica and Rory and left the apartment. The coroner finished and packed away her equipment bag, motioning to the EMTs to take away the corpse. When the last of the uniformed officers finally left, Monica closed the door and engaged the deadbolt. She collapsed into a sitting position on the floor of the foyer, hugging her knees to her chest.

Rory held out his hand to help her up, but she wouldn't reach. He lowered himself to the hardwood to join her, curling his brown loafers under his legs. He sat next to her, unable to find any words.

Chapter 3 – Reminiscing

AFTER FIVE MINUTES ON THE FLOOR, Rory coaxed Monica to the sofa in the living room. He fetched her a glass of water and sat with her in the dining nook next to the kitchen, looking out the picture window on the far side of the living room at the lights in the high-rise apartment buildings and office towers of the city.

Remnants of police activity littered the floor under the window. Thin shards of plastic, yellow post-it notes marking the location of Tom's gun and his corpse, and lines of yellow chalk silently spoke of recent death. Dried blood seemed to be everywhere: on the walls, on the window treatments, on the furniture. The blond hardwood retained congealed puddles of scarlet with oozing fjords jutting out along the seams of the floorboards. The air felt thick, with a pungent metallic odor mixed with those of hand sanitizer and fingerprint powder.

Monica still wore her blood-stained clothes. Rory thought of Jackie Kennedy after JFK's assassination. He was considering how to broach the subject of changing into something clean when Monica spoke. "I'm so lucky you came to help me tonight." She looked more composed than at any time since Rory arrived. It was nearly midnight.

"I really didn't do much," Rory protested.

"You did! Don't be so modest. That was always your biggest problem, Rory. You never gave yourself enough credit. You always let other people grab the glory instead of you. You were

KEVIN G. CHAPMAN

wonderful tonight. It looked for a moment like those detectives thought I might have had something to do with Tom's death, but you stopped them from asking any questions about our marriage. That was smart. I watch enough crime drama on TV to know they always suspect the wife, right?"

Rory nodded. His knowledge of how homicide detectives worked was also mostly based on television and movies. His law firm had a white-collar criminal group, but they dealt in financial fraud and tax evasion, not murder. As he thought about Monica's comment, his eyes widened. He hushed his voice, even though they were alone. "Oh my God. Is that why you didn't say anything about the lottery ticket? Because they might think you killed Tom so you could keep all the money?"

Monica rose and walked behind Rory's chair. "You're a smart guy, Rory. You're absolutely right. While I was sitting here, waiting for the police, I started thinking about how it was going to look. I was the only one here. I found him. I've got blood on my hands and clothes. I picked up the gun, so it has my fingerprints on it. If they thought I had any motive, they'd suspect me. The more I thought about it, the more frightened I got. I don't have to tell them, right?"

"No. No. Of course not. You don't have to answer any questions."

"Oh, Rory, I can't believe he's gone . . ." Monica turned her head away from Rory and stared toward the window. "I'm so scared, Rory. I don't know what I'm going to do. Tom always took care of everything. The bills and the finances, everything is in his name."

Rory stood and approached Monica. He longed to place his hands comfortingly on the sides of her shoulders. Instead, he took a step to the side so he could see her face better and adopted a voice he frequently used with clients going through the loss of

24

DEAD WINNER

a spouse. "I know things have happened suddenly, but you are a strong, smart, independent woman who can take care of herself. I've been through sudden deaths like this for other clients. Usually they're much older and much less capable than you and they all make it through. It's hard, but you'll do it. Tom has life insurance, right?"

"I guess. Yes, I think so—through his company. But does life insurance pay off if he killed himself?"

"Actually, yes, in most cases. As long as he has had the policy in place for more than two years. Tom has been with the company much longer, so it should be good. Do you know where the policy information is?"

"I don't know. I don't know how much coverage he has, or where the policy is. Oh, I'm hopeless."

"Don't talk like that. You are a fantastic person."

Monica turned toward Rory. Her eyes pleaded for something Rory wanted desperately to give. "I'm so happy you're here." She stepped to the side and leaned her head onto Rory's shoulder. He could smell her shampoo; something with orchids.

Rory searched for something to talk about, hoping to take Monica's mind off the evening's events. He needed to get her to focus on the future, including the immediate future of whether she was going to stay in the blood-stained apartment or find a hotel room for the night. He would have his secretary send over a cleaning crew in the morning. Such cleansing operations were, unfortunately, a regular part of his practice. Far too frequently, when people who lived alone died, the bodies were not discovered for many days. Cleaning up the homes was a service the firm often arranged.

"We should contact Tom's parents," Rory suggested softly. "Do you have a phone number for them?"

25

KEVIN G. CHAPMAN

"No," Monica lifted her head. Rory immediately felt the absence. "I mean, they're both dead. His mother died a year after we were married. Then, about two years ago, his dad was diagnosed with pancreatic cancer. It was really fast at the end. He had no symptoms at all until it was too late. He suffered terribly for the last few months. It was hard on Tom."

"I'm so sorry," Rory said sincerely. He knew Tom had no siblings. "Are there any other relatives you need to call?"

"Maybe. But I can't do it now," Monica replaced her head against Rory's shoulder. He was doing a terrible job of taking her mind off her grief.

"That's OK. I understand." He stiffly put an arm around her shoulder, keeping his hand away from the exposed skin on her neckline, and waited through a minute of silence. "I'm sorry I haven't kept in touch with you and Tom."

Monica raised her head. "I'm sorry, too. We knew you were back in New York. Tom saw a mention in the alumni magazine. He was impressed to read about the paper on forensic accounting you delivered at the ABA conference in Cleveland."

"Really?" Rory was surprised and flattered. "I didn't think anyone paid much attention to those things."

"Tom did. He said he knew the law firm you work for. But we never reached out—never invited you over for dinner. Even when your father died."

"You knew about that?"

"Tom heard. I'm not sure from whom. I remembered that you weren't that close to your dad, but we still should have called." Monica hung her head, but only for a moment. "You remember that weekend when you invited us out to your family house? I was so impressed! What ever happened to that girl you were with? I forget her name."

26

DEAD WINNER

Rory couldn't help cracking a smile. "Her name was Angelica, and if you recall she dumped me a week later."

"Oh, sorry. I didn't remember that." Monica reached out to pat Rory's elbow. "Did you get the house when your dad died? That must have been worth a king's ransom."

"No. Neither my sister nor I wanted to go back there, so we sold it and split the profits. Dad would probably have yelled at us both for letting the family castle go, but it wasn't someplace that held a ton of fond memories for me."

"Well, I wish we had been there for you. Losing a parent is a time when you need friends by your side."

"Thanks. I appreciate the sentiment. I don't have many friends here in New York. I could have contacted you, but I suppose I was always a little jealous of Tom. I should have been able to put that aside once I came back to the city."

"It would have been nice. But at least you're here now. I think I'm really going to need that trust, huh? Are you sure the police won't find out about the ticket?"

"Well, if the police had a subpoena they would be able to find out who the beneficiary of the trust is. We can't keep it secret if they come asking. But it's still a good thing you'll have it ready to go."

Monica took a half-step backwards, prompting Rory to let his arm fall to his side. "And you can't tell them, right? Because you're my lawyer and that makes it confidential, right?"

"Yes. Of course. It's privileged. I can't tell anyone." Rory paused, wondering if he should even ask the next question. His curiosity overcame his worry about upsetting Monica. "Why was Tom so concerned about not divulging your identity as the winners?"

KEVIN G. CHAPMAN

Monica now walked a few steps into the living room. "It was because of his company. He didn't explain it to me, but he was terrified that someone from there would find out."

"Why would his company care?"

"I don't know. He manages other people's money. Maybe they wouldn't want him to have too much of his own. He had been unusually nervous and jumpy the last month or so. I asked him about it, but he never told me why." Monica sank down into the sofa, turning her head toward Rory. "Do you think it's possible that somebody killed him?"

"I don't know," Rory admitted. "The cops seemed satisfied that it was a suicide. I'm no expert, but I agree with you. It's probably best if you don't tell the police about the ticket. At least for now."

Rory took a step toward Monica, thinking about returning his arm to the warm place around her shoulder. She leaned down and grabbed the remote control from the end table next to a plush maroon sofa, reflexively clicking on the television. The late replay of the local news was on. A smiling woman wearing a bright blue dress spoke into the camera.

"Ali Bauman here in Brooklyn Heights, where Mr. and Mrs. Tyrone Green have come forward as the holders of the second of the five winning tickets in the big three-hundred-eight-million-dollar Mega Millions jackpot. Mr. Green, a sanitation department employee, made a statement a few minutes ago."

When the picture cut to the taped statement by the obviously very happy Mr. and Mrs. Green, Rory said, "I hate to even mention it, but we should secure that ticket. Where is it?"

Chapter 4 – Hiding Places

MONICA WALKED TOWARD A HALLWAY that led away from the living room without a word. Rory wasn't sure whether he should follow. He figured the hallway led to the bedrooms. Should he follow her into her bedroom? Was it appropriate for a lawyer to go into his client's bedroom without a specific invitation? Before he made a decision, Monica stopped and turned. "Please come with me, Rory. I don't want to be alone."

He followed her to a small room on the left side of the hall. On the opposite side, a section of the master bedroom was visible through a half-opened door. The smaller room served as an exercise space and a home office, with a desk and a twin bed pushed against the wall. He figured it was also used as a guest bedroom. A silver laptop computer rested on the desk next to a New York Mets Tiffany-style lamp. Monica crossed the room, opened a closet door, and stretched toward a high shelf.

When Monica turned around, she held a dark wooden box in her hands. Monica carried the box to the desk and put it down. She sat in a leather chair where Rory imagined Tom doing his work, making stock trades and increasing his clients' wealth. Monica pushed aside a bronze latch and opened the mahogany case as Rory watched. Inside, a black foam insert lay across the top, with an indentation in the shape of a gun.

The box had to be the case where Tom kept his gun, the one the police had taken away in a plastic bag. Monica lifted the foam rectangle out of the box, revealing two small cardboard boxes of bullets and a velvet pouch. Rory assumed the bag contained cleaning implements. She lifted out all the items, setting them haphazardly next to the laptop, then extended her index finger and used her manicured nail to pry loose the wooden bottom of the gun case, which was covered with green felt. As she pulled up the thin plate, Monica gasped.

"Oh, no!" she whispered.

"What?"

Monica lifted the felt-covered bottom piece entirely out of the box and examined the underside, running her fingers all along the smooth wood. Then she reached into the box, searching the bottom with her hand. She looked at Rory with wide eyes. "It's not here."

"The ticket?"

"Yes, the ticket!" Monica's voice cracked with anxiety. "This is where Tom put it. The gun case lives inside a locked safe in the closet. He once hid a necklace there, under the bottom of the gun box. He told me he was putting the ticket there to keep it safe. It was locked away and hidden. Nobody would find it." Monica was becoming more and more agitated as she spoke. "I mean, the safe wasn't locked just now, because . . ."

"Well," Rory tried desperately to think of something soothing and encouraging to say. "If Tom took out the box in order to get the gun, and he knew he was going to kill himself, he might have expected the police to retrieve the box to confirm it was his gun."

"It was his gun. I could tell by the inscription," Monica said dismissively.

"Sure, *you* could tell that, but if somebody else found him, the police wouldn't know it. They would want to check. If Tom figured that and didn't want the ticket to be found, or taken away

DEAD WINNER

along with the gun case, maybe he moved it—put it somewhere else."

Monica's face brightened. "That makes sense. I'm so glad you're here. I was starting to panic."

"Where else might he have hidden it?"

Now Monica's face fell again. "I'm not sure." She opened the center drawer of the desk and peered inside. The ticket was not there, nor was there any container where it was likely to be hidden.

Rory reached out and slid the drawer closed. "There's no use trying to search the entire apartment right now. Maybe tomorrow we can look for it."

"You'd help me?"

"Of course." Rory froze, looking into her pleading eyes. "But before we tear the place apart looking for it, maybe he left you a note—let you know where he moved it to."

"Maybe," Monica mused. "But there weren't any texts from him, or emails. You think he would have written a note on a slip of paper?"

"I don't know. You know him better than anybody. What do you think?"

Monica tossed the box bottom back toward its container. "I don't know. I can't think. I'm so tired."

"OK." Rory took her arm and nudged her in the direction of the door. "I should have figured that. It's been a terrible day. You get some sleep and we can work on this in the morning. Will you be alright here, by yourself?" As he said the words, Rory felt his throat constrict. Did he just ask her if she wanted him to stay?

"Oh, God. I can't stay here. I can't. I can still smell the blood and the chemicals the police left behind. I'm going to have find a service to clean everything." She slumped into a plush chair next

KEVIN G. CHAPMAN

to the door and put her head into one hand. Rory thought she was going to cry again.

"I'll take care of that for you tomorrow. Nothing has to happen right now. Is there someone you can call? Someone you can stay with tonight?"

"No. It's past midnight. There's nobody I can call at this hour. I'll get a hotel room."

Rory cleared his throat. "Uh—I can make a call for you, unless . . ."

"Unless what?" Monica raised her moist eyes.

"Well. I mean, I don't want you to take this the wrong way, but my apartment isn't far from here. It's closer than any hotel. I have a guest room. It's not the Ritz, but if you want to I could put you up for the night."

Monica smiled momentarily. "You're so sweet. You wouldn't mind?"

"No. Not at all." He smiled back. "You put together what you need for the night. We can come back here tomorrow, when it's light. I'll have my secretary make some calls in the morning and get a cleaning service for you. We do that, well, pretty regularly." He walked to the door and motioned for Monica to follow him, as if he knew where she kept her overnight bag and he was going to lead her to it.

She rose slowly and reached out to take Rory's hand. She went into her bedroom while Rory, at her suggestion, went to the kitchen to find a bagel or a banana—something for her to eat, to keep up her blood sugar. He envisioned the state of his apartment and how embarrassed he would be leading Monica inside without having a chance to straighten up. It couldn't be helped. He had already volunteered.

As he waited for Monica, Rory wandered around the living room, avoiding the blood stains on the floor. On an end table, out

32

DEAD WINNER

of the line of gory fire, he noticed a photograph in a silver frame. Tom and Monica stood in front of a boat, a fairly large one from the look of the prow. Tom was smiling like a new dad. Monica's head was turned toward Tom, looking at him, but not smiling. Around the rest of the room, there were no other pictures of the occupants.

The space was large for a Manhattan apartment, befitting a tycoon money manager like Tom. A faux fireplace with a gas flame dominated one wall. It had no real chimney, but sported a mantle displaying various personal items. A Lucite "tombstone" was inscribed with the details of the launch of a hedge fund called The Imperial Fund. Rory suspected it might have been Tom's first, but he hadn't kept close enough track of his old friend's business conquests to be sure. A crystal vase held a delicate blown glass rose. Rory recognized it. He had one of his own, which was a gift to the members of Tom's and Monica's wedding party. The rose matched a small tattoo on Monica's left ankle.

Next to the rose, Rory admired a bobble-head doll of a baseball player, a pitcher wearing a New York Mets uniform with the number forty-one. Tom Seaver. The Hall-of-Fame pitcher was sculpted in mid-delivery with his left leg extended and his right knee dragging on the brown plastic of the pitcher's mound. Next to Seaver, a painted ceramic bulldog crouched next to a similarly sized lion in mid-roar. A sleek, detailed model of a boat dominated the center of the mantle, with a tall, delicate mast and two silk sails. On the prow, in thin script letters, he saw the name: *Couples Therapy*. It looked like the boat in the photo on the end table.

Before Rory had a chance to examine any more of the room's knick-knacks, Monica appeared at the threshold and announced her readiness to depart. Three minutes later, Monica locked the deadbolt behind them as they walked silently toward the elevator. Rory carried her Louis Vuitton overnight bag. She held only her purse and a black laptop bag. Rory had suggested they take Tom's laptop with them so she could search it the next day in case Tom left a note for her. He was also hoping Tom had left information about his life insurance policy and other assets that would have to be accounted for when settling the estate. It was his instinct as a lawyer, and advice he had given to hundreds of clients over the years, so it didn't seem weird to him.

When they arrived at Rory's apartment, it was after 1:00 a.m. The adrenaline of the evening had worn thin and Rory was feeling tired. He apologized for the slovenly state of his home. The living room was dominated by the flat screen television mounted on the wall opposite two huge west-facing windows with a view of the Hudson and New Jersey. Beneath the screen, a glass-and-chrome shelf unit housed boxes of black, white, silver, and purple, each with wires snaking away toward a central console that looked like a computer. Monica recognized the outlines of game controllers from several brands of video systems. A plastic-and-leather throne sat directly in front of the TV, with small wooden tables on either side housing cup holders. One had a deep trench containing several remote controls.

While Monica meandered through the living room, scrutinizing the memorabilia and family photographs, Rory hurried to remove several expandable files of client documents, his guitar case, and a pile of books from the bed in his home office and guest room. He had not had an actual overnight guest since he moved into his new place, close to a year earlier. When his father died, Rory had moved back to New York to be near his mother. He took the job with Fitzsimmons, Packman & Kronish, bringing along his father's estate issues as well as a book of other clients. His father (who never trusted his two children with their own finances, even after Rory graduated from law school and his

DEAD WINNER

sister got her MBA) left their inheritance in a trust, with their mother as executor. Then, his mother had developed a staph infection following minor surgery and passed six months later, leaving Rory with full control of the ten-million-dollar trust. He liquidated it and distributed half to his sister.

He had invested in the condo at a solid new construction discount. He opted for the two-bedroom model both because it was easier to flip later and because it would be a suitable home for several years if he ever got married. He was pleased to have a use for the guest room. The balance of his inheritance was parked in a low-risk bond fund. He had not touched a penny. His father told him repeatedly that he would never be successful in life unless he learned to take risks. But his sister had already squandered more than half of her share of the inheritance, while Rory had managed his finances prudently. Who was more successful now?

Monica waited patiently for Rory to fuss with the guest room. She said she was bone tired after the events of the day and would have happily slept on the sofa. Rory insisted on making up the spare bed.

When Rory emerged and declared the room ready for occupancy, Monica was lying on the couch, her overnight bag at her feet. Rory couldn't immediately tell whether she had fallen asleep. He knelt down to get a better angle at her face, to see if her eyes were open. They weren't, but as he stared at her, her lids fluttered. She smiled at him, which made his gut turn a somersault. She sat up, reaching out her hand toward Rory and pulling him from his knee onto the couch next to her.

"I've got the guest bed ready for you. The bathroom is across the hall. I have my own, so you don't need to worry about me walking in on you."

35

KEVIN G. CHAPMAN

"Thank you, Rory. You're being so sweet to me. I don't know how I could have gotten through today without you."

Rory blushed and lowered his chin. "It's my pleasure. Really. I can't even imagine what today must have been like for you. It's a wonder you're still functioning."

"Barely," Monica quipped, letting out a somber chuckle. "My world has been turned upside down. I feel like it can't be real. But I know it is. It's the worst dream ever." She slumped toward Rory, putting her forehead on his shoulder. He was becoming accustomed to the aromas from her body: her perfume, her shampoo, her perspiration mixed with whatever deodorant she used. It was an intoxicating olfactory cocktail.

Haltingly, he reached his opposite arm across his body and placed it on top of Monica's hand, which was resting on her thigh. She let out a heavy sigh, then squeezed Rory's hand as she sat up, wiping away a tear with her other hand.

"Thank you. For everything," she said, leaning in and kissing Rory's cheek softly. He felt her warm breath.

Rory searched his brain for an intelligent and empathetic response. "Well, if it turns out today isn't a bad dream, I'll be here to make you breakfast in the morning. Now, my recommendation, as your lawyer, is that you get some rest. We'll deal with whatever we need to in the morning."

Monica nodded and rose from the sofa, grabbed her bag, and headed toward the guest room. At the threshold, she turned to Rory, who was a few paces behind. "You're a gem." She blew him a kiss, then entered the room and closed the door, which latched with what Rory perceived as an extraordinarily loud click.

Rory adjourned to his own room, thinking about what appointments he had on his calendar for the next day and how best to reschedule them. Monica was going to need him, and he was not going to let her down.

36

Chapter 5 – Wake Up Call

THE NEXT MORNING AT 7:15 a.m., Jackson "Jack" Northrup stepped off the elevator on the 52nd floor of the First Union tower, home to the offices of Northrup Investments, Ltd. It was his habit to wake early and be the first executive in the office. Occasionally, some underling would be in even earlier trying to impress the boss. If they were smart, they would park near his reserved spot in the underground garage so he would notice. Most of them stopped the charade when he chastised them for being "late" the next time they came through the door after he was already pouring his first cup of coffee. He loved busting the balls of the young Turks.

One of the few who kept up the early morning arrivals was Tom Williams, at least before he made Vice President. Jack smiled to himself at the thought. He had to hand it to Tom. He had set his sights on a goal and worked tirelessly to achieve it. Then, he slacked off a bit. It was probably Tom's plan all along. Work extra hard, impress the boss, get the big promotion, then take it easier and enjoy time with his smoking-hot wife. Well, fine. Men like that would never sit in the CEO's chair. To get to the very top, you could never slack off. Jack never had.

The early morning sun glared off the glass façade of the office tower across the river in Jersey City, creating a beam of golden light inside Jack's spacious office. He always felt like he got the sunset twice every day. He scrolled through emails before pausing on one from an unusual but familiar name. Delroy was

KEVIN G. CHAPMAN

a good man, but he never sent emails to the CEO. He scowled at his screen, figuring this was not going to be good news. He was right.

The email message, copied to the company's head of security, was a model of succinct efficiency. At 9:27 p.m. the prior evening, an EMT unit arrived at an apartment building owned by Northrup called the Winchester Tower. A few minutes later, a police officer arrived, followed later by three more uniformed officers, two detectives, and a crew from the medical examiner's office. They were responding to a 9-1-1 call to the apartment rented to Tom Williams. Mr. Williams' wife, Monica, had arrived a short time before the EMT crew. At 12:08 a.m., the medical examiner's team wheeled out a covered body. Delroy gave one of the attendants fifty dollars to confirm the identity of the deceased as Tom Williams and that the apparent cause of death was a self-inflicted gunshot.

Jack re-read the message. He was pleased with his strategy of buying the apartment building. It was a solid investment and he encouraged his key employees to live there by giving them discounted rent. He had the building security staff on the company's payroll. Keeping tabs on his employees—especially his insiders—was always helpful. In this case, the information worried him, but he was happy to get it so quickly.

He grabbed his phone and punched one of his twenty speed-dial buttons. His day had just gotten off to a terrible start. Tom Williams was a loyal soldier, and had been part of the inner circle at the firm for two years. Losing someone from the family was always difficult, but a suicide? This had the potential to create some serious problems. Jack knew he had people who would take care of it, manage the damage, and alert him to any unforeseen risks. Knowing that didn't make him any happier. He needed to wake a few people.

Chapter 6 – Code Red

RICHARD "BUSTER" ALTMAN JERKED his head up, coming out of his sleepy fog and only vaguely hearing the music coming from his phone. As Van Halen's "Jump" blared out from the night table, Buster groped in the darkness with his left hand until he made contact. He sat up, dragging the sheet from the curvy body of the red-haired woman sleeping soundly next to him. The phone's screen illuminated Buster's hairy chest as he clumsily swiped to answer the call and quell the music. Buster was darkly featured, with bushy black eyebrows above brown eyes, a bulbous nose, and a square jaw covered with morning stubble. In the darkness, his broad shoulders and muscular chest and arms made him look as much like a gorilla as a man. When he spoke, his breath echoed the scotch and cigarettes he had consumed the night before.

"Yeah?" Buster knew who the caller was before he spoke. Most callers in his address book were silenced if they called before eight o'clock. The boss was the only person who got "Jump" as his ringtone.

"We have a situation." Jack Northrup was not one to mince words or make small talk, especially on a call this early.

"OK. Gimme a sec." Buster fully extracted himself from the bed, looking admiringly down at his slumbering companion. He padded across the hardwood floor toward the bathroom and slugged down a paper cup of water to chase the cotton balls from his mouth. Leaning his naked buttocks against the marble

KEVIN G. CHAPMAN

countertop, he unmuted the phone. "OK, boss. What's the emergency?"

"Tom Williams. Blew his brains out last night in his apartment. The one in your building. Delroy called it in."

"Not good." Buster lifted the toilet lid and sat on the throne, releasing a stream of urine that splashed loudly into the bowl. The boss either didn't hear or didn't care.

"Fucking right it's not good. I need you to make sure it's not awful. I'm surprised you weren't already aware."

Buster cursed under his breath. He had been out late. Very late. When he and his red-headed companion came through the front doors, one of the doormen said Buster should make sure to check in at the front desk with Delroy. He had blown off the recommendation. He tried to deflect his responsibility. "I guess Delroy didn't call my cell."

"I guess not. You know now. We're going to need a complete scrub job on this."

"Got it," Buster said with a grunt as he squeezed out a final gush and hung up at the same time. He knew Jack didn't need any more chit-chat, and he knew what he had to do without further instruction. It was his job, and the reason he was living in the high-end apartment owned by Northrup Investments. The investigation would not require travel. He headed to the house phone on the wall in the kitchen, not bothering to throw on a robe. Eddie at the front desk answered. Buster knew Delroy would be long gone, but Eddie would have started his shift at midnight. He instructed Eddie not to leave until they talked.

Buster enjoyed exercising authority. Six years earlier, he had been a New York City cop taking the detective's exam. His sergeant told him he had a bad attitude, was too easily prone to violence, discharged his weapon too frequently, and would never make detective. The sergeant was right. Buster wasn't cut out to

40

DEAD WINNER

be a cop, although he did enjoy it. He appreciated all the perquisites, like never having to pay for a beer at his local bar in Queens and getting into any club in town, which impressed the girls. They were also impressed by his big gun.

Fortunately for him, several opportunities surfaced shortly after his resignation from the NYPD. When one of Jack Northrup's lieutenants reached out, Buster was intrigued. When he heard the offer, which was more than three times his former salary, he was in. Over the next several years, he proved himself loyal, resourceful, and able to pull in favors from some of his old colleagues on the force. Now, he was Jack's head of security, with thirteen people working for him in four offices on three continents. He left the cyber security and data privacy issues to the tech nerds. He handled the personal security and the confidential files.

On the force, his name had been Richard. He never let anyone call him "Dick." Over the years, he had developed a reputation as a ball-buster. Pretty soon, some of his friends started calling him Buster. He didn't love it at the time, but when he went private and put his cop self in the rearview mirror, he decided to go all-in on "Buster."

This morning, he was in charge of damage control. He knew the drill. Whenever one of the firm's insiders retired or died, it was critical to prevent any confidential information from leaking out the door along with the departing employee. A death was particularly risky. A sudden and unexpected death was a fire alarm, since the deceased may have left unexpected bits of data lying around in unsecured locations—places where an outsider might stumble upon them.

A suicide was DEFCON 1. Somebody getting ready to check out voluntarily was liable to do anything. Buster's job was to identify and assess the risks, then sanitize them. He enjoyed the job.

This was the first suicide since Buster rose to the top of the security team. The cobwebs clouding his brain ten minutes earlier had dissipated. He felt an adrenaline rush. He had done cocaine only twice in his life. This felt better.

"Up and at 'em, babe," he slapped the sleeping woman on her bare thigh, making her lurch sideways.

"What the fuck?"

"Time to go, sweetheart. Emergency. I need to leave and you can't stay here without me." Buster was at his closet, picking out the proper suit for the day's activities.

A half-hour later, after debriefing Eddie in the lobby of the Winchester Tower, Buster strode confidently toward his office on the opposite side of the 52nd floor from the executive suite in the First Union building. Within five minutes, his two deputies, Matt Galante and Clarence Major, joined him. Clarence held a Starbucks cup. Matt had two and handed one to Buster.

"OK, guys. This is not a drill. Tom Williams took the big dive last night. We don't know why and we don't know what he left behind. Let's get after it."

Chapter 7 – A Feeling

HOMICIDE DETECTIVE STEVE BERKOWITZ and his partner, George Mason, walked into Captain Edward "Sully" Sullivan's office at 9:30 Tuesday morning. They reported on the prior night's visit to the posh downtown apartment building formerly occupied by one Thomas Williams. It was pretty clearly a suicide, assuming the wife was being honest about finding him dead when she came home. There was no sign of forced entry, no sign of a struggle, and the door had been locked from the inside.

"Any concerns about the wife?" Sully asked casually, looking down at the summary report Berkowitz had sent by email earlier that morning.

"Don't think so," Steve responded quickly. "We'll check out her story about visiting her mother during the day. Williams was a bigshot money guy at a pretty big Wall Street financial firm. We'll check that out also, but it seems like he was her meal ticket, so not much motive to knock him off."

"What about life insurance?"

"We're not sure yet, Captain. It's always possible. She seemed genuinely broken up about the guy blasting off his head in her living room."

"Anybody hear the shot?"

"No. At least nobody we talked to yesterday." Steve hesitated, realizing the gaping hole in his response. "But the

KEVIN G. CHAPMAN

uniforms weren't able to interview all the neighbors. We'll finish canvasing the building today."

"Do we have a time of death yet?"

"The assistant M.E. on the scene said she couldn't be sure, but the blood was coagulated and the corpse looked like it had been there for a few hours at least. We won't have an official TOD until we get the autopsy back, but it didn't seem likely the wife shot him after she came home at nine o'clock. The stiff wasn't that fresh."

Sullivan looked up from the report at his two detectives and blew out a breath. "You look like you got something else to say, Steve."

George glanced at his partner, then shrugged. Steve said, "It's just a feeling, Cap. We decided not to put anything in the report, but the wife's behavior at the scene was . . . a little unusual."

Sully dropped his head and said into his desktop, "OK, out with it."

"Well, this was a pretty bloody scene. It looks like the victim put the gun in his mouth and blew out the whole back of his head. The wife said she found him and rushed to the body, rolled him over, stepped on the bloody floor, and picked up the gun. So, her prints are all over the gun, her footprints are all around the body, and it's basically impossible to tell whether she was there when the shot was fired or came to the scene later. It seems unusual to me. What kind of fresh widow rushes over and touches the body? It's not like there was any chance he was still breathing. But, like I said, she was pretty broken up and emotional last night, so her behavior while we were there wasn't particularly suspicious."

Sully scowled. "Did you test the wife for powder residue?"

"No. She had a lawyer."

"A lawyer? At the crime scene?"

DEAD WINNER

"Yeah. It looked like they knew each other. He was looking at her like he wanted to spend some time alone with the widow. Don't worry, Sully, we'll cover our bases here. If there's anything fishy, we'll let you know."

"OK, but don't chase shadows here. Let the M.E. confirm it was self-inflicted. If there's no smoke, get it closed. We've got actual homicides for you to chase down."

Steve understood that the meeting was over, so he and George left without another word. Out in the bullpen, a young female detective named Patterson called out to Berkowitz, "So, you think the wife iced her husband for the insurance money?"

"Why do you ask? You have some inside information?"

Patterson cocked her head to the side, causing a strand of straw-colored hair to fall across her face. "I always assume it's the wife—or the husband."

"Well, it doesn't look like there's anything like that going on this time." Berkowitz walked past while Patterson gave him a look clearly indicating her continued skepticism.

The two detectives paused at George's desk. As he sat down, George said, "Let's look carefully at the couple's finances. If it looks like the wife had a motive, we'll press things further."

"Unless the M.E. gives us some reason to doubt the shot was self-inflicted," Steve added. They exchanged a nod, then Steve walked to his own desk, where several message slips awaited him.

Chapter 8 – Breakfast at Rory's

RORY HAD A SPATULA IN HIS HAND when Monica staggered into the kitchen, drawn by the smell of bacon and coffee. She was wearing a knee-length sleep shirt with the logo of the New York Road Runners Club. Even without makeup and with pillow hair, Rory thought she looked like a movie star. "Good morning!" he said brightly, truly meaning it. He immediately realized his mistake. "Oh, crap! I'm so sorry. I'm an idiot. I can't even imagine how you must feel today. Did you get any sleep?"

Monica gave him a yawn and a thin smile. "Some. That coffee smells great."

Rory clumsily dropped the spatula, spattering bacon grease on the sparkling ceramic cooking surface of his high-end stove. He knocked a wooden spoon from a wire rack in his haste to grab a mug and pour a cup. "How do you take it?" he turned and held out a thick mug bearing the logo of the Fairway grocery store.

"Milk and Sweet n Low, or any no-cal sweetener." She did not reach for the mug. "Please."

"Oh, yes." Rory turned toward the refrigerator, sloshing a little hot liquid on the floor. "Crap!"

"It's OK, Rory. There's no rush." She sat on a cushioned bench built into the wall next to a window in the alcove adjoining the kitchen. She waited patiently while her host reached deep

DEAD WINNER

into the back of a cupboard and rummaged around before retrieving a pink sweetener packet. He added a dollop of milk, and brought the cup to her. He set his own matching mug on the butcher block dining table.

Rory stood over her as she took the first sip, waiting for her reaction to his freshly ground gourmet beans. Before Monica could provide the positive reinforcement he craved, the smell of burning bacon drove him back to the stove. He watched her with half his attention while he finished preparing the breakfast.

Monica surveyed the living room, which had been cleaned up since the night before. The impressive gaming chair was relegated to a corner; the video system controllers had disappeared. Rory smiled to himself at his efforts. The apartment appeared less like a post-adolescent man cave and more like the proper living space for a respectable attorney.

Later, after they had enjoyed Rory's scrambled eggs with bacon and cheese and engaged in small talk about the coffee, the eggs, and what a nice day it was, Rory asked, "Have you looked at the laptop yet?"

Monica closed her eyes. "No. Not yet. Do you think it's important?"

"Yes. If I were Tom and I wanted to leave you a message, and I didn't want to do it via text or email, I'd leave it on the laptop. Plus, there's probably financial information there and information about his life insurance and such. We need to get that information." Once again, Rory fell into his professional demeanor, handling the details of a deceased person's estate.

"Alright. I suppose you're right," Monica sighed, holding in her emotions. "I'll log in, but I'm not sure I can deal with searching around in his files. Can you do it for me?" Her eyes pleaded.

KEVIN G. CHAPMAN

Rory never considered saying no to her. "Of course. I can do it. I've already called my office and canceled my appointments this morning. I've also asked my assistant to make arrangements for a cleaning crew to go to your apartment. Can you call the building and give somebody permission to let them in?"

Monica nodded and pulled out her phone. Before she dialed, she opened Tom's laptop, which she had left on an end table next to Rory's leather sofa. She typed in a password and handed the small unit to Rory, then walked to the next room to make her call.

Rory navigated around Tom's laptop. He searched the files for keywords, starting with *Monica*. When he didn't find any note from Tom to his wife, he searched *account, password, investment*, and *financial* and browsed the most recent web searches and internet bookmarks. He found two recently edited spreadsheets protected with passwords. He attempted to open them without success. He left the Excel files bookmarked for later consideration while he searched for links to Tom's banking and investment accounts. When he found a market account hosted by Northrup Investments, his attempt to log in resulted in an electronic demand for a two-factor verification code sent as a text message to Tom's phone.

"Monica?" Rory called out toward the other room.

Monica rounded the corner, clicking the END button on her phone call. "What is it?"

"Do you have a separate log-in to Tom's Northrup Investments account?"

She paused to think, then said, "I think so. I'm pretty sure it's a joint account, although Tom handled all the finances. He also has a separate account they call the *bonus* account, where the company puts all his long-term incentive money."

"Do you have access to that?"

48

DEAD WINNER

Monica shook her head. "No. Tom didn't have access to it directly either. The company controls it and we have to request withdrawals after the money vests."

"Do you think you can recall your login credentials to the joint account, or do you have it recorded somewhere? It's asking me to verify a text to Tom's phone, but obviously we don't have it."

Monica sat down next to Rory, who pushed the laptop across the small table to her. She took her time typing in a login ID and password for the account. The first attempt resulted in an error message, as did the second. On the third attempt, the website prompted her for a texted code sent to her phone. While they waited for the text, Rory asked whether Monica knew the password Tom used to protect work files. She suggested a few possible passwords, which Rory used in an attempt to open the protected spreadsheets. On the third try, they both opened. The sheets contained financial records for many different clients, each identified with a four-letter acronym he didn't recognize. He scanned the information, which he immediately thought was potentially significant.

Before he had much of a chance to scrutinize the spreadsheets, Monica received the text code from Northrup Investments and completed the login. The account came up, listed as Thomas and Monica Williams.

"This isn't right," Monica said, puzzled. She tilted her head sideways at the screen.

"What?"

"The account summary. It says there's only twelve thousand dollars in the account. It should be two hundred thousand." Monica pushed the laptop in his direction, saying, "This must be a different account."

49

KEVIN G. CHAPMAN

Rory frowned as he scanned the page and clicked into the account history. "Oh, crap!" he exclaimed, then turned to Monica. "This shows a transfer of one hundred ninety-nine thousand dollars dated yesterday."

"That's impossible! Yesterday? But that's when Tom . . ."

Rory's arm twitched as he thought about reaching out for Monica. Would she think it inappropriate? He wanted to comfort her, to ease her pain. But he didn't know what to do, so he turned back to the screen. "The withdrawal was a wire transfer. I can't tell what this account number means. It's tagged at 4:32 p.m. yesterday. Wouldn't Tom have been at the office then?"

"Not necessarily. He sometimes worked from home in the afternoon if he had meetings out of the office. I'm not sure where he was yesterday."

"Why would Tom transfer all your money? Do you recognize the account number?" Rory adjusted the laptop's screen to make it easier for Monica to read.

"I don't know!" Panic built up in Monica's voice. "Tom took care of the money. I don't know what that account is. We have an account at the Citibank, and his investment account, and I have my own checking account for my paychecks. I think that's all we have, except for the bonus account I told you about, but I don't know for sure. Does this mean all the money is . . . gone?" Monica's face was ashen.

"Now, let's not get excited. Maybe Tom had another account set up. Maybe he wanted to move the investment account money because of the lottery winnings coming in soon. There are plenty of explanations." Rory, as he always did when he had emotional clients, took on an aura of calm control. "Let's take things one step at a time. Are you sure there aren't any other accounts?"

"No. I don't think so. Why do you think there would be?"

DEAD WINNER

"Well, I don't mean to jump to any conclusions, but it seems, given Tom's income level, that you would have more money put away in savings than just a few hundred thousand."

Monica dropped her eyes to the floor. "Yeah, well, we talked about that sometimes. We spent a lot. Even with the deal we get on this apartment, the rent is pretty high. And we like to travel. And we like to eat out. And Tom had some extra expenses recently. But, we have the bonus account, which Tom says has plenty. And it's not like we're planning for retirement or anything. We live a nice life. We're not really worried about savings."

"OK. I get it. But there's no reason to worry. I'm sure Tom has life insurance, too. For now, I'll look for any other references to this account number on Tom's laptop. You call the customer service number for the Northrup account and ask them to give you the details of this transfer."

"What do I ask?" Monica's voice cracked.

"They won't talk to me without your permission, so you get them on the phone and tell them it's OK to talk to me so I can ask the questions. Don't worry. I'm right here." He reached out and patted the palm of Monica's hand. She responded by digging a nail into the back of his as she squeezed back. He winced, but was proud of himself for not crying out at the sudden pain. "Look here, there's a customer service phone number. Use your cell and call. You'll probably be on hold for a while. I'll get back to the laptop."

"OK," Monica said blankly, squinting at the screen and punching the numbers into her phone.

Rory first keyed into the search bar the number for the account into which the funds had been transferred, then small pieces of the number, hoping to find a match. No results. Then he opened Tom's Gmail account and searched for the account

51

KEVIN G. CHAPMAN

number, then for Northrup, which produced hundreds of useless hits. Then, he switched to All Mail and combined "Northrup" with the first four digits of the joint investment account.

The first search result made Rory sit forward. "Here it is," he said, then realized Monica was talking on her mobile. He hadn't noticed while he was concentrating on his searches.

"I'm going to put you on with my attorney, Rory McEntyre. He is authorized to speak to you on my behalf." Monica handed the unit to Rory, who spent the next five minutes meticulously tracing the account activity with the assistance of the customer service representative. Monica sat pensively next to him, exchanging worried glances while he made notes on a legal pad.

When he thanked the agent and ended the call, Rory turned toward Monica and forced his face into a calm expression. "You said you have your own checking account, right?"

"Uh huh."

"How much money do you have in there?"

"Um, maybe three or four thousand. I use it for my expenses and a few bills for accounts in my name."

"OK, that will buy groceries until we can find the lottery ticket."

Monica's face fell into despair. "What do you mean? What about the money in the joint account?"

"Since the wire transfer was sent to a bank in Bermuda, they don't have much visibility into it. It can't be reversed. If it had been an ACH transfer within the U.S., we might be able to stop it and reverse it, but you can't cancel a wire. I found the confirmation email from Northrup, which includes a verification code. That's like the two-factor identification from the login, except it went to Tom's email, not his cell. But the email isn't in Tom's inbox. It only came up in a search that included his trash folder."

52

DEAD WINNER

"What does that mean?" Monica shook her head, trying to make sense of the information.

"It means that, after he used the verification code and got the confirmation email, he deleted them."

"Why would Tom do that? And yesterday, of all days?" Monica stood and walked quickly toward the little window next to the kitchen, holding a hand to her face.

"Let's not jump to any conclusions. Lots of people routinely delete emails from their inboxes."

"Yes, but not Tom. How many emails are in Tom's inbox?"

Rory clicked back to the inbox. There were more than eleven thousand emails. "Well, there are a bunch."

"Tom thought if everything was in his inbox, he would never lose anything. I don't think I ever saw him delete anything except spam."

"I don't understand it," Rory admitted. "If I didn't know any better, I'd say it looks like somebody hacked into Tom's accounts, including his email, and transferred almost all the money to an offshore bank account."

"That would be a pretty incredible coincidence," Monica said flatly. "I mean, the same day Tom . . . killed himself? Somebody just happened to hack his account?"

Rory looked into Monica's eyes, trying to remain calm. He didn't want to say anything that might upset her further. His mind was racing. It was possible. It was crazy. He couldn't say what he was thinking without driving Monica off the deep end.

She did it for him. "Rory . . . do you think Tom gave away all our money to somebody before he . . ."

"I don't know. Can you think of anybody he would want to do that for? I mean, I hate to even ask this, but, um, were you and Tom having any . . . problems?"

Monica looked at the floor and said, "We were fine."

KEVIN G. CHAPMAN

"I mean, is there any chance Tom was . . . involved with somebody else?"

Monica went silent.

"I'm only asking," Rory haltingly continued, "because sometimes I've seen men try to siphon off money from their estates for the benefit of people—mostly people they were, um, involved with—right before they died, as a way of taking care of them outside of an estate. It's a way to keep it quiet, especially when the surviving spouse and other heirs are well taken care of by the rest of the estate's assets. So, I'm thinking that could explain things. Maybe."

"No," Monica responded sharply, pacing away from the table. "No. No. No. I can't believe that. And why would the money go to some offshore account? Tom doesn't know anyone in Bermuda."

"It's a way of shielding it from taxes, and keeping the owner of the account secret. So, it's not entirely unusual." Rory was glad Monica was not freaking out about the discussion.

Monica, who was now standing by the window, turned toward Rory. "I'd almost feel better if Tom had been murdered, and somebody forced him to drain his account and then killed him, but that didn't happen."

Rory's eyes went wide for a moment before he spoke. He choked out the first few words. "You know, Monica," he cleared his throat, "as crazy as that idea is, if somebody had forced Tom to disclose his account password and transfer all your money into an offshore account, then that person could have forced him to give up the location of the lottery ticket."

Chapter 9 – There's Always More

RORY RUSHED TOWARD MONICA, taking her left hand in both of his. "We will find that ticket," he assured her. "I was just speculating. I can't believe somebody murdered Tom. I mean, can you even think of anybody who would want to kill Tom? Somebody who would know about his investment account, and maybe about the lottery ticket?"

"Nobody knew about the ticket," Monica snapped. "We agreed we wouldn't tell anyone. Tom was crazy nervous about somebody finding out. He wouldn't have told anyone. I'm sure." She put her palms flat against Rory's chest and looked into his soul. She seemed to be pleading with him to believe her.

"Of course. Right. I know." His arms encircled Monica's back. He pulled softly and she melted into him, pressing her cheek against his chest. "It's far-fetched. Someone would have had to get Tom to let them into the apartment, then force him to give up his account informa-tion and his laptop password and use his laptop to transfer the money. There can't be a lot of people who could have done that."

"Oh, I can't think about it!" Monica cried out, now sobbing softly.

Rory lifted a hand to stroke her soft hair. "It's OK. Don't worry. It's fine. But we should probably tell the police about the money being moved out of your investment account."

KEVIN G. CHAPMAN

Monica abruptly pushed away and stepped back, her eyes wide. "Why?"

"Well, if somebody stole the money from Tom's—your—account, then it makes the possibility that he was murdered more likely. Even if it's not likely, it's certainly relevant. I think they should know. And maybe they need to know about the lottery ticket. If it was stolen, then we need to report it. Tom made that video, right? And he initialed the ticket. So we can make a claim that it's your property so nobody else can try to put in a claim with it."

"No!" Monica raised her voice, but then she put a hand to her mouth and whispered. "No. No. Rory, please. You can't. We can't."

"Why not?" Rory responded. He was not trying to be argumentative. He could not think of any reason why Monica would have such a strong opinion.

"Oh, Rory. Don't you see it? If they think somebody might have killed Tom, they're going to think it might have been me!"

"You would never do that."

"Of course I wouldn't! But the cops don't know that." Monica paced around the small room with her head down, her heels clacking on the hardwood. "The police *always* suspect the wife—or the husband. I was there. God, I touched the gun! My fingerprints are probably all over it. I touched him. I had his blood on me."

Rory sat down on the sofa, trying to think. He was way outside his comfort zone. He dealt with deaths all the time, of course, but generally not suicides or murders. He processed wills and managed estates. He made sure the money intended for beneficiaries made it to the right people. Since Tom and Monica were his clients, he would do the same for Tom's estate, although the money from Tom's investment account was apparently gone.

DEAD WINNER

"Wait!" Rory sat forward and held out his hand toward Monica. "I know what you're saying, except you have no motive. You didn't steal the money from the investment account. It was *your* money. There's no reason for you to take it. Plus, there's the lottery winnings."

"Exactly!" Monica's voice got more frantic. "The lottery ticket. If they knew about it, they'd think I killed him so I could have the money all to myself."

"But the ticket is missing."

Monica stopped pacing in front of the sofa and looked down at Rory. Several blonde strands of hair hung down around her cheek. "They don't know that. If we tell them about it, they'll think I'm lying about it being missing. Oh, God!"

"Wait—Wait. Monica, even if we don't mention the ticket, we should let them know somebody transferred all your money. They can trace it, maybe find out what account it went into. I know I said it was hard, but if there's any chance of getting it back, you have to act quickly."

Monica made a fist and raised it to her mouth, biting down on a clenched finger. "Rory—" She turned away, moving back toward the window. The dark water of the Hudson River reflected the morning sun. "If the police start digging, they might find something."

"What?" Rory had lost Monica's train of thought.

She turned her head, but not her body, in his direction and said softly, "A reason why I might want to kill Tom."

"What are you talking about?" Rory's mind was racing through scenarios.

"Tom was having an affair."

"Are you sure?"

"Yes, I'm sure. He admitted it after I found out. It was his assistant, Breonna. It had been going on for several months. I don't think anybody else knows, but I'm not sure. If the police find out Tom was cheating on me, and then the lottery, and now he's dead. Who benefits more than me? They're going to suspect me." Rory jumped from the sofa and Monica fell against him again, wrapping her arms around his neck. "Rory, you can't let that happen. Promise me."

"Of course. Of course. I promise."

"You're my lawyer, right? You have to keep my secrets, don't you?"

Rory couldn't see Monica's face, so he spoke into the top of her head. Her hair smelled like his Pert Plus shampoo. "Yes. I'm your lawyer. You can trust me. Of course. But, if somebody did kill Tom, and maybe has the lottery ticket along with most of your savings, we can't let them get away with it."

Monica pulled herself away from Rory's embrace, still keeping her arms around his neck. "We?"

"Huh?"

"You said *we* can't let them get away with it. Like, you and me."

"Well, um, I mean, sure. I'm here to help, so it's you and me. I'm here for you." Rory squeezed his hand against Monica's lower back, then released it, letting his hand fall to his side. "It's far from certain that anybody killed Tom, or that if somebody did, they have the lottery ticket. Tom might have moved it beforehand. If we can find it, then the investment account money won't mean anything."

Monica leaned back into him. Rory could feel the pressure of her cheek and her body heat through his dress shirt and the white t-shirt underneath. "You'll help me, won't you, Rory?"

"Of course I will. Of course."

"And you won't talk to the police?"

DEAD WINNER

"No. Not unless you want me to. So, where do you think Tom might have moved the ticket? Is there anywhere else he might have left you a message about it?"

Monica turned back to the window. Rory noticed the curve of her body, silhouetted against the outside sunshine. "I've checked my phone. I suppose he might have left me a note somewhere in the apartment. We weren't really looking for one. Or maybe, like you said, on his computer."

"I'll keep looking on his laptop. If we don't find anything there, we'll probably need to go back to the apartment. Do you think you'll be OK going back there?"

"I don't want to go alone." Monica's lower lip quivered.

"Yes, of course. OK. We'll go together. I'll bring the laptop along. We'll look for a note. I've got all morning for you. Alright?" Rory worked hard to keep his voice even as his mind raced through the concept of accompanying Monica back to the apartment where her husband so recently spewed his brains all over the walls. He was also running down his memory about meetings he had scheduled for later that day and the work he had planned to get done. But helping Monica was most definitely his first priority.

Before they reached the door, Monica's phone sang out the first bars of "Takin' Care of Business" by Bachman Turner Overdrive. She retrieved the phone, looking ashen. "That's the ring tone for Tom's office." She answered. Rory silently listened to Monica's side of the conversation. "Hello . . . yes, Breonna . . . Thank you, I appreciate it. . . They are? . . . Why? . . . OK, I will. Bye."

"What was that?"

"Tom's assistant, *Breonna*." Venom dripped from her voice as she said the name.

"Oh. Wow. Well, why was she calling?"

KEVIN G. CHAPMAN

"She said the Northrup security guys are cleaning out Tom's office and if I want to retrieve any of Tom's personal stuff, I should get there fast."

"Why would they clean out his office so soon?" Rory said, not expecting a response. "Do you think it's possible Tom might have hidden the lottery ticket in his office, or left you a message there about it?"

Monica's eyebrows raised together. "Maybe."

Chapter 10 – Cleaning Day

BUSTER ALTMAN AND HIS CLEANING CREW arrived on the 48th floor of the Northrup building at 9:03 a.m. A few of the more energetic analysts and money managers were sipping their first lattes of the morning when Buster burst through the glass doors in the reception area. He was wearing a blue pinstriped suit with shiny black loafers and no necktie. Behind him, three men followed who could hardly have looked more different. Matt Gallante wore black jeans, a tight-fitting black t-shirt, and black Michael Jordans. Matt dwarfed the other two members of the squad. At a muscular six-three and tilting the scale at more than 275, he looked like he could suit up and play defensive end for the Jets.

Behind Matt came Dexter Friedman, who had less than half the bulk of his burly companion. Dexter looked every inch the part of the computer whiz, with a starched white button-down, a thin black tie, and three pens hanging off his shirt pocket. Black-rimmed glasses and a tussled mop of black hair completed the stereotypical look.

Walking next to Dexter, Walter Vogt looked like he could be the computer nerd's father. His gray hair covered a small portion of the sides of his otherwise bald head. A salt & pepper moustache and an emaciated appearance made him look even older than his sixty-three years, but he had clear, steel-blue eyes and a "don't mess with me" expression. The three mis-matched

KEVIN G. CHAPMAN

companions strode confidently down the carpeted hallway with Buster, stopping at the threshold of Tom Williams' office.

Breonna Nelson, Tom's personal assistant, was already at her desk putting together Tom's schedule for the day. She was a striking Black woman, five-eight, with long arms and legs. Her dark curls dropped just below her ears. Gray slacks and a loose-fitting cream blouse hid her athletic body. She stood quickly upon the arrival of the four men. She was not the type to be intimidated. When she moved from behind her work station, Buster could see a plaque hanging on the cubical wall with a banner reading "US Olympic Judo Team" next to a framed poster from the Broadway production of *Chicago,* covered with autographs.

"Excuse me, gentlemen. Can I help you?" Breonna stepped between Buster and Tom's office door.

"No, thanks, Sweetie," Buster said, looking Breonna up and down as if she were a dress on a department store mannequin. "We have this covered." Buster unclipped his cell phone from a belt holster and punched a button. A moment later, he handed the phone to Breonna, then turned to Dexter and motioned him forward.

When Breonna spoke into the phone, Jackson Northrup's executive secretary, Gwen, told her the news about Tom. Breonna leaned backward against the half-wall separating the hallway from her work station. "Oh, my God! I can't believe it."

Gwen explained that the firm was keeping the news private for the moment. As the personal assistant to the CEO, Gwen was the de facto supervisor for all the other executive assistants. What Gwen said came straight from the big boss.

"How is Monica?"

"I don't know. I understand she found him last night in their apartment."

DEAD WINNER

Breonna stared at the printout of Tom's schedule for the day. "So, I suppose I should cancel all his appointments?"

Gwen told Breonna to leave Buster and his crew alone while they did their jobs and to follow Buster's orders. She also instructed her to tell nobody about Tom's death. As far as anyone in the office was concerned, Tom was home sick. That was the official story.

Breonna looked to Buster for direction. "What do you need me to do?"

"Not a thing, Honey. Just sit there and look pretty. If anybody calls, tell them your boss is out, and keep people away from us." Buster turned around and entered Tom's office, which Dexter had unlocked with a master key card. Buster and his crew went inside and closed the door. Buster silently motioned to Dexter, who pulled two long, thin wands from his shoulder bag. He flipped switches on each and spent several minutes carefully scanning every square foot of the room. Then he unplugged all the electronic equipment and snapped the cord out of the desk telephone. He nodded to Buster.

"Alright, gentlemen. You knew we had a high alert when you got the call this morning. As always, your professionalism is outstanding. Now that we know we're clear to talk, the clean-up job here is for Tom Williams. Last night he blew his brains out in his apartment. Very unexpected and, of course, concerning. This is, obviously, his office. Dexter and I will handle his apartment later. Right now we need to secure all his sensitive files and scrub the office. While you do your work, be looking for anything that's missing. If you see any gaps, or anything unusual, flag it for me. Any questions?"

Buster looked around at three nodding faces. Then, the crew went to work. The process was pretty standard, although not generally conducted under such time pressure. When a company

KEVIN G. CHAPMAN

insider left the organization, Buster's job was to ensure no stray information or documents escaped from the company's secure possession. The worry was always that the person checking out might not have all their records carefully stored and, whether intentionally or inadvertently, could compromise the operation. He worried always about the wives and girlfriends, since confidential information tended to slip out during intimate moments or when somebody had to justify long hours or an inability to discuss certain topics.

The men who retired knew where the bodies were buried, but the company made sure its life-long umbilical cord stayed connected. Long-term incentive payments that vested over many years, life insurance policies for their beneficiaries that could be canceled, and the threat of possible criminal prosecution, kept people on the straight and narrow path. The profits from the operation were kept in accounts that required Jack's personal authorization before a withdrawal was permitted. If the insider stepped out of line, Jack could make the money disappear. Fear of a sudden death also helped.

The biggest risk was someone who could not be controlled because they had nothing to lose—such as because they were already dead. The sudden suicide of a thirty-eight-year-old man was a three-alarm fire. Each member of the team started into his assignment.

Buster had barely scooted his chair into a comfortable position when he heard a knock at the door. He had an annoyed scowl on his face when he jerked the door open. Seeing Breonna standing calmly, he snapped, "What? I told you not to disturb us."

"Actually, Sir, you said to keep people away from you. I didn't think that included me. Here." She held out a stack of file folders. "These are some of the files I was working on for Tom, to

DEAD WINNER

organize them and catalogue them in the master index. I thought you would want them." Breonna fixed a defiant stare at Buster.

The former cop ran a hand absent-mindedly across the buzz cut on his head, then took a step back. "Fine. Thank you, Doll. I'll take them."

"Can I get you boys some coffee?" Breonna offered with a smile, raising her voice enough for the men inside the office to hear.

"No, thanks," Buster said, using a foot to nudge the door closed since his hands were full of files.

"I wouldn't mind some coffee," Walter called out as the door clicked shut.

When Buster re-opened the door, having dropped the folders on the floor with a thump, Breonna took two coffee orders. Dexter wanted green tea with lemon.

When she delivered the drinks, Buster allowed her inside the room. Dexter was sitting at Tom's desk, pointedly typing on the keyboard connected to Tom's desktop computer. Matt knelt next to a full-sized file cabinet with the bottom drawer open. A garbage can next to him was already stuffed with papers and folders. Walter sat at the round table next to the window buried in a pile of printouts, his shirt sleeves rolled up. Buster had his own laptop open on the table next to Walter, a spreadsheet visible on the fifteen-inch screen.

"While you're here," Buster snapped Breonna out of her observations, "I need to talk with you about your former boss."

Buster led Breonna out of the office, leaving his crew behind to do their work. He paced down the hallway to a small, empty conference room and stepped inside, closing the door after Breonna. She waited until the big man motioned to her to sit.

"I need to know about Mr. Williams' activities."

65

KEVIN G. CHAPMAN

"I'm not sure what I can tell you." Breonna was calm, not showing any sign of nervousness. Buster wondered if an Olympic athlete would ever show fear.

"You're still an employee of the company, Breonna."

"I'd prefer to be addressed as Ms. Nelson." Her eyes flashed defiantly; her face remained calm and confident.

"Like I said, *Breonna*, your loyalty here lies with the company, not with your dead former boss. I need you to be completely honest with me. My job is to protect the company and its confidential information. If I think for a minute you're withholding information, then that disloyalty will get you fired without severance pay. You understand?"

"Sure," Breonna replied casually. "Ask me anything."

"Did you know Tom Williams was an insider?" He let the question hang in the air, watching for any sign of understanding.

Breonna's expression turned to puzzlement. "He was an EVP, and a member of the Executive Committee. Is that what you mean?"

Buster smiled. "Yes. Of course. Did you ever see the minutes or reports from the Executive Committee meetings?"

"Sure. Tom had a file for them, and I kept the files organized."

"Did you ever read those summaries?"

"Yes." Breonna held Buster's gaze, unrepentant about looking at the documents.

"You realize that was a breach of confidentiality?"

"No. It wasn't. I'm Tom's confidential executive assistant. I saw lots of sensitive information. I knew what deals he was watching and what tips he was getting from his guys on Wall Street. I knew which of his clients he called first when he had a hot lead and which ones he called when he needed to unload some high-risk shares. I knew which AmEx bills were for the lap

DEAD WINNER

dances at the strip club and how to code them so Finance didn't raise an eyebrow. There was nothing in those ExCo reports any more confidential than what I dealt with every day." She finished with a forced smile. Buster could tell it was more of a "Screw you."

"Did Tom ever have you work on the account statement reconciliations?"

Breonna tilted her head. "The what?"

"Never mind. I need to look at Tom's calendar and address book."

"I have access to them at my desk."

"Let's go." Buster led the way out the door and stopped at Breonna's work station. After she pulled up Tom's appointment calendar, Breonna grabbed a three-ring binder from a shelf and handed it to Buster. The folder was labeled "Daily Schedules."

"Those are Tom's daily schedules for the past six months. He liked to have a paper printout every day." She hopped onto the desktop against her cubicle wall. Buster sat in her chair, perused Tom's contacts list on her computer screen, and thumbed through the daily schedules.

"What's this?" he barked, pointing to an entry from the prior Friday.

"Tom and Monica—his wife—had an appointment with this lawyer. Rory McEntyre. I think an old friend of theirs. They were going to have him draft new wills for them." She stopped talking, catching her breath. "Oh, dear! He wanted a will, and then—"

"Yeah. Looks like he was planning ahead. You don't happen to know what's in his will?"

"No. I didn't type anything up for him."

"Did he mention anything?"

"No, not that I remember. It was all kind of . . . sudden."

67

KEVIN G. CHAPMAN

"Yeah. I bet." Buster searched for Rory McEntyre in Tom's electronic address book and wrote down his information. He recognized the law firm of Fitzsimmons, Packman & Kronish. Harry Packman was the outside counsel Jack Northrup used when he needed a lawyer. Buster made a mental note. "Keep this information to yourself. Say nothing to anyone about any of Tom's clients. You do that and you keep your job. I'm sure the company will be replacing Mr. Williams. The replacement will need an assistant who knows her way around. Understand?"

"Sure. I get it." Breonna jumped off the desktop nimbly and stood at attention, waiting for Buster to vacate her chair.

When Buster reentered Tom's office, he said to his crew, "Talk to me."

Dexter, still sitting at Tom's desk, spoke first. "Not good. The guy purged all his files. His desktop is reset to factory specs. Hard drive is wiped clean. Not so much as a picture of his dog. He knew he was kicking it and he left nothing for us to find."

Buster showed no reaction. "What about his company email account?"

"His last sent email was at 4:13 yesterday afternoon. So far, I haven't found anything significant."

"Search for a lawyer named Rory McEntyre. See if there's anything about him making a new will. What about the files on his corporate server?"

"Those files look to be all fine. It's like he didn't want to mess up any actual accounts and clients, but he wanted to erase anything personal."

"Go figure," Buster said, looking out the window at a barge slowly chugging upriver. "Can we get back the files from his desktop?"

"Negative. Those are gone. Hard drive is reformatted. No chance."

68

DEAD WINNER

"Great. Walter? What about you?"

Walter straightened himself and held up several sheets of paper. "It's a slow process, Boss. Everything looks in order so far. The important files are supposed to be kept electronic only, as you know. So far, I haven't found anything to suggest the guy deviated from protocol. So far."

"OK. Keep looking." Buster turned to Matt. "How you doin'?"

Matt grunted, but didn't say anything. He was sitting on the floor next to Tom's desk, the bottom drawer open. Two black garbage bags on the floor were partially filled with the contents of the drawers Matt had already searched and purged. He continued the job, searching for anything suspicious and trashing everything else.

Buster sat down across the little table from Walter and picked up a folder.

Outside, Breonna put Tom's appointment schedules in the shredder and sat at her desk, staring blankly at her computer screen. Five minutes after Buster left her, she opened the bottom drawer of the little file cabinet next to her desk. She pulled out a 5x7 padded envelope and slipped it into her purse. Then, she picked up the handset on her office phone and used Tom's line to call Monica.

Chapter 11 – It Must Have Been Awful

MONICA HAD VISITED TOM'S OFFICE many times. She was no longer impressed by the décor and the view. She approached the overly made-up receptionist, leaving Rory to hurry behind her to keep up. She had changed into a business suit with a tight blue pencil skirt and matching jacket with a white blouse. She looked like she belonged in the high-powered office.

"Erica, Hi."

"Monica? Tom's not here. He's home sick. What are you doing here?"

"Breonna called and said I should come in to get some, um, files from Tom's office. I assume it's alright if we go find Breonna, right?"

"Who is he?" Erica gave Monica a side-eye glance toward Rory.

"He's—Tom's lawyer."

Erica shrugged and nodded toward the hallway leading to Tom's office. Rory's head spun from side to side, taking in the interior of the offices and catching glimpses of the spectacular views across the expansive open space. Desks full of traders or account managers sat in front of multiple-monitor setups in rolled-up sleeves. Rory and Monica padded across thick

DEAD WINNER

carpeting, the smell of coffee and perfume filling the recirculated air.

Monica rounded a corner and stopped, causing Rory to pull up suddenly. He nearly lost his balance trying to avoid bumping into his escort. Breonna was standing between her work station and Tom's office door, which was shut. Rory supposed Erica at the reception desk had buzzed ahead to let her know visitors were on the way. Monica made eye contact with Breonna, who stared back with an emotionless face. After ten seconds of silence, the two women moved together and hugged briefly before stepping back.

"It must have been awful," Breonna said with genuine sympathy.

Monica lowered her head. "It was much worse than I ever could have imagined." She forced herself to look up at Tom's assistant. Breonna didn't look away. "Thanks for calling."

"No problem. The cleaning crew swooped in early. They left a few minutes ago. There's not much left inside."

Monica pushed through the office door. Rory followed without an introduction to Breonna. Inside, Rory had to pull up short again. Monica had stopped only a few feet inside the threshold. Rory was shocked to see the interior of a professional office looking like it was vacant. He recalled his own office on his first day: the spotless desk, empty shelves, and bare walls. Now, after two years at the firm, his office walls were adorned with art, diplomas, professional certificates, photos, his framed map of Middle Earth, and an autographed R. A. Dickey Mets jersey, worn by the pitcher the day he won his 20th game on his way to a Cy Young Award. Legal reference books and personal mementos crowded his bookshelves. His desk was strewn with magnetic toys, note pads, pens, and work files. Tom's office looked like

KEVIN G. CHAPMAN

nobody had ever worked there. Breonna lurked in the doorway behind them.

"Why would the firm clean out an executive's office less than a day after he died?" Rory said aloud, although more to himself than as a question for Monica. "It's not like somebody else from the firm is going to come in and steal confidential information if Tom's not here to defend it."

From behind him, Breonna spoke softly. "Tom had some special files in a locked drawer. He never gave them to me to work with. And he had some folders in the computer system protected with a password. But it doesn't matter now. They took all the files, and his computer." Rory and Monica turned toward her. Monica locked eyes with Breonna, who retreated back to her work station.

Monica moved slowly, as if in a trance. She sat behind the desk and opened the empty drawers. She opened the cherry-wood credenza, where Tom kept his bar supplies, but even that was stripped bare. It was clear there were no secret notes from Tom. Rory had speculated that they should check on the backs of the photos and artwork on Tom's office walls, but everything had been stripped, leaving only naked picture hangers. They exited back to the hallway. Rory saw Breonna motioning to Monica, who walked around the half-wall into the secretarial bay.

Breonna reached into her purse and pulled out a yellow padded envelope. Monica took it and handed it to Rory, without opening it. She said to Breonna, "They even took our wedding picture. The one he kept on his desk. Why would they do that?"

"They probably thought he hid the secret code on the back of the photo."

"What secret code?" Rory asked innocently.

"Oh, sorry," Monica responded. "It's just a term Tom used. He said there was a mythical algorithm that could magically

72

DEAD WINNER

guarantee Tom's clients would make money. He probably meant any kind of inside information or hot tip that would let him get a jump on the market. Sometimes we played a game where I would search in his office for the *secret code*. It was really a piece of my favorite candy, Almond Roca. It was silly."

"It was sweet," Breonna said, reaching for a tissue.

"Oh. Right," Rory said. He was thinking about the spreadsheets he had noticed on Tom's laptop. He looked down at the envelope in his hand. There was no address or label. "What's this?"

"Tom gave it to me yesterday," Breonna said, "before he left for some client meetings. He said it was important. I was supposed to make sure Monica got it. I thought it was a little weird that he gave it to me, when he was going home at the end of the day. I guess, now, it makes some sense, although I still don't understand why he didn't leave it for you at the apartment."

"Tom never trusted the security at home," Monica said.

"Why not?" Rory held up the envelope, squeezing its padded sides and feeling something hard.

It was Breonna who answered. "Northrup owns the building. It's a sweet deal for the executives because they get submarket rates on the rent as long as they work here, but the staff is all paid by the company. Tom always joked that the old man could walk into his apartment whenever he wanted."

"Is that true?"

Monica tilted her head with a scolding expression. "Of course it's not true—probably. It was just Tom being paranoid. Let's go." She started walking back toward the elevator lobby. Rory hustled to catch up, stuffing the envelope into an outer pocket of his soft-sided briefcase.

When he caught Monica, he asked, "Aren't you going to open the envelope?"

73

KEVIN G. CHAPMAN

"Not here," she said in a loud whisper as she continued walking. She glanced behind her and saw Breonna, watching her walk away. When they exited out to the street, Monica maneuvered through the pedestrian traffic to a concrete park across from the Northrup building. She sat on the edge of a fountain where a bronze bull and bear engaged in a struggle in the center, water spurting from their mouths and ears. When Rory joined her, she said "Let me have it."

Rory found the envelope. Monica ripped it open and reached inside, extracting a two-inch-long steel rod with a flat end like a flag: an old-style key. She tipped the envelope upside down, allowing a slip of paper to fall out. The wind caught it and sent it sailing across the paving stones with Rory scuttling behind excitedly. He planted his loafer on the wayward sheet and grabbed it, returning it to Monica like a Golden Retriever with a freshly killed duck. She studied it with a frown, then handed it to Rory.

It was not the lottery ticket. He read the handwritten block letters on the plain square. *C-104.*

"What does it mean?" Monica posed the obvious question. "I've never seen this before. What's C-104? A mailbox? A storage locker?"

Rory took the key and rolled it in his fingers. "Do you guys have a local bank branch?"

"Sure. The Citibank on Church Street."

"I think this might be a key to a safe deposit box."

"You think?"

"Yes. My older clients often keep their most valuable items and important papers in safe deposit boxes. The firm has a bunch of keys like this tucked away with the wills in our vault. We sometimes have to accompany the trustees to the bank to open

74

DEAD WINNER

the boxes and retrieve the valuables. Did you know Tom had a safe deposit box?"

"No," Monica shook her head. "Why would Tom have one and not tell me?"

Rory reached out and gently put his hand on Monica's forearm. "I can think of one extremely good reason."

Chapter 12 – High Security

BUSTER AND DEXTER STOPPED in front of the security desk at the Winchester Tower. Buster had called ahead. The dayside shift supervisor, Julio, had the key ready. "Make sure nobody goes up to the Williams apartment until we come back down," Buster instructed.

Upstairs, Buster handed the key to Dexter while he turned his back and reached into a pocket. He extracted a small tube and squeezed a dab of yellowish gel onto his index finger. While Buster rubbed the yellow goo onto his upper lip, under his nose, Dexter unlocked the apartment door and pushed it open.

The stench of congealed blood and decaying body tissue hit the computer expert hard. He reeled around with a hand over his nose and mouth, dropped to his hands and knees, and gulped in the unsullied air from the hallway. He retched, but managed not to spew vomit on the expensive carpeting.

Buster laughed heartily. "What'sa matter, Dex? Never been to a blood-soaked crime scene before? Heh, heh." He tossed the tiny tube of menthol gel to the ground near Dexter's head. "Here, use some of that under your nose. It'll mask the stench." He steeled himself against the smell and went inside. Dexter followed a minute later with a thin scarf wrapped around his face, leaving his eyes visible. "Get to it," Buster said softly, trying to breathe through his mouth. "I'll clean out his study. You're sure the laptop isn't here?"

DEAD WINNER

"Not unless the guy hacked the GPS system," Dexter replied, choking slightly on the combination of menthol and death. "Trust me. It's not here." Dexter set down a black canvas computer case on the kitchen counter and extracted three small boxes. He then traversed the apartment, looking for the best locations to place the tiny surveillance units. They were practically invisible once installed, and Dexter knew how to hide them.

Buster found Tom's home office and examined the contents of his drawers. He took his time, leaving no obvious signs that the contents had been disturbed. He then searched the bedroom, under the bed, inside the storage bins, and in the compartments of the headboard. He searched the closet, noticed an empty space where three suitcases were lined up on the floor, then opened all the shoe boxes and plastic bins lining the shelves above the hanging suits. He found a box of dark walnut, which obviously once held a pistol. A box of ammo and a cleaning kit rested under the foam insert that had cradled the gun. He made a mental note of the wall safe at the back of the closet, which was locked. The safe was not standard issue for apartments in the building, so Tom must have had it installed. He could have a locksmith get that open another day. It was too small for a laptop computer. After twenty minutes, he called out to Dexter. "You finished?"

"Just done," came the reply.

"Let's get out of here." Buster washed his hands in the bathroom sink, then met Dexter in the kitchen. "All set?"

"It's wired into the building security wi-fi. The server's in the basement. It will send the files to the company's cloud and we can access them from there."

"Good. I'm not sure how fast the widow will be coming back, but you never know."

77

KEVIN G. CHAPMAN

Dexter packed up his computer case, making sure to include all the boxes, wire clippings, and other trash from the camera installation. "You find anything?"

"Nah," Buster grunted. "Nothing important. We need to find that laptop. I want you to track it and let me know if it shows up back here."

"No problem. I'll alert you. Anything else we need?"

Buster shook his head and walked toward the door.

When they crossed the lobby, three women wearing blue and white maid's uniforms and carrying buckets and cleaning supplies were sitting on a padded bench near the front desk. As soon as Buster handed Julio the key, the supervisor handed it off to one of the front desk attendants, who motioned to the cleaning ladies.

Chapter 13 – Hidden Numbers

TWO HOURS AFTER Buster and Dex had left it, Rory and Monica stood at the door of the apartment in the Winchester Tower. Monica had barely spoken in the cab. She waved a quick hello to Eddie, the doorman, in the building lobby as they breezed through. Rory had half-expected to see crime scene tape covering the entrance, but then recalled that he and Monica had been the last ones to leave the night before. It had been less than fifteen hours.

Monica handed Rory the key. "I can't."

Rory accepted the heavy key hesitantly. His hand was shaking as he turned his wrist and heard the clunk of the deadbolt giving way. When the door pushed back, the smell of industrial cleaning solution hit them both hard.

"That's wretched," Monica said, holding a hand to her nose.

"The cleaning crew has been here. That's good. Trust me, this smell is a great improvement over decaying flesh and congealed blood." Rory instantly regretted his insensitive words. Monica did not seem to react.

Inside, Monica walked around the space as if it were a foreign country. They both grew accustomed to the antiseptic odor.

"I tell you what. You look for any place Tom might have left you a note. While you're at it, why don't you pack a suitcase with some more clothes and things you'll need so you can get out of here for a few days. I can have my assistant get you a hotel."

KEVIN G. CHAPMAN

"I can't stay with you?" Monica said, disappointed.

"Well, I mean, you'd be welcome, of course. I just figured you'd be more comfortable in a hotel room."

"I'm comfortable with you."

Rory felt his face flush. "I'm glad to hear that. I'm very happy I can be here to help."

Monica grabbed a tissue from a flower-patterned box on the marble counter. "I don't want to be all alone."

"Yes. Of course. You can have my guest room for as long as you need it." Rory smiled warmly at Monica for a moment, then turned aside and put down his briefcase. He extracted Tom's laptop and set it on the table in the nook next to the kitchen. He started the machine using the access password Monica had provided.

As he listened to Monica in another room, opening drawers and moving from place to place, he focused on Tom's files. He trawled through his file trees, eyeballing files recently revised or created in case there was anything with a coded name that would not come up in a search. He checked his work email on his phone every five minutes to make sure he wasn't missing any urgent matters on a day he had not planned to be away from his office. He fired off a quick email to his assistant, thanking her for getting the cleaning crew there so fast.

After twenty minutes of futile searching, Rory was closing down several open windows when he came upon the financial spreadsheets he had opened back in his apartment. They did not contain any messages about the missing lottery ticket or any notes about plans to kill himself, so Rory had not spent much time on them, but they had sparked something in the back of his brain. Both files had been recently modified, contained financial information about several companies, and included a collection

DEAD WINNER

of four-letter codes. His interest piqued, he spent another ten minutes perusing the files, including multiple tabs and tables.

He was absorbed in the spreadsheets when Monica came back into the kitchen nook, carrying a small suitcase. Rory didn't immediately acknowledge her, so she placed a cool hand on the back of his neck, massaging the muscles at the edge of Rory's hairline. Rory startled momentarily, but then melted into the massage, leaning his head back and letting out a deep growl.

"Mmmnnnn. That's nice. Did you find anything?" He knew if she had found anything important, she would have called to him.

"No note. Nothing like a note. The key seems to be the only message, which I guess only I'm supposed to be able to figure out. You really think the safe deposit box is at our Citibank branch?"

"It's most likely. We'll start there. We can go first thing in the morning. If Tom left it in a safe deposit box, he would want you to find it. That's why he gave the key to Breonna, so you would be sure to get it."

"I'm surprised she gave it to me and didn't keep it for herself," Monica said bitterly.

Rory took a moment to compose his response, not wanting to upset Monica. "Listen, even if Tom was . . . involved with Breonna, and even if she knew what was inside the envelope, she has no way to access a safe deposit box in Tom's name, so she had to either give you the key or throw it away. What good would that do her?"

Monica fell into a chair next to Rory. "I don't know. You're probably right. I hate that I didn't catch on to their affair. I knew Tom was distracted and distant, but I thought it was just work pressure. Now, I'm not sure whether our marriage was over. I guess I'll never know."

KEVIN G. CHAPMAN

Rory stared at Monica's face. She had lowered her eyes. He had no idea what to do, so he tried to change the subject. "Is there any reason to stay here longer?"

Monica looked up. "No. I packed a case. I'm ready to get out of here. It doesn't feel like home anymore."

"OK," Rory said, giving Monica a quick, reassuring smile. "But first, let me show you something. Take a look at this spreadsheet from Tom's laptop. Have you seen this before?"

Monica leaned over Rory's shoulder to see the screen. He felt her warm breath next to his ear. "No. I don't think so. I never paid much attention to Tom's business work. I'm sure he had spreadsheets like that on his screen all the time."

Rory nodded. "Sure. I understand. Well, let me try to explain. You see these two sheets with financial account information? The companies on the two sheets are the same, so the information is parallel—except for one extra company that's on the second sheet. So, when you look at the numbers and analyze the expenses and earnings numbers for each of them—"

"Rory," Monica interrupted, "I assume there's some point here, but I don't understand the financial or legal issues. Is this going to help us find the missing ticket?"

Rory hung his head, realizing his failure to communicate. The senior partners at his last firm told him repeatedly that he was brilliant, but he lacked the ability to explain things to people who were not experts in his field. He had written a paper for a bar association conference about forensic accounting and how to detect fraud when examining financial statements. His peers in the field agreed that the algorithm he wrote was amazingly useful. When he made a presentation about it to the other lawyers at a firm-wide meeting, half the room fell asleep.

"Sorry. I do that sometimes. The bottom line is that these sheets show somebody altering the financial statements for these

82

DEAD WINNER

companies and, I think, transferring assets from all of them into the account of this one different company on the second sheet. It's embezzlement. Have you ever heard of a company called New Haven Express Services?"

"No. I don't think so. It kind of rings a bell, but I'm not sure. It may be something similar to something else. Why does it matter?"

Rory adopted a concerned but compassionate face. He had been in this situation a few times with estates clients whose now-dead spouses had canceled life insurance policies or taken loans against retirement accounts without their knowledge. "It matters because it may indicate that Tom was involved in some fraud. He may have been doctoring the investment records in order to siphon off money from the earnings on investments from all these companies and transfer them to this other company. Did he ever explain any of this to you?"

"Me? No. No. I don't—you mean you think Tom was doing something illegal? Really? Are you sure it was Tom?"

"Well, I can't be sure. He had these sheets on his laptop. I'd have to know whether he managed these coded accounts. Did he ever talk to you about his clients? Did he mention any that were particularly difficult to deal with, or mention the name of any client he particularly liked or went out to a ball game with or anything like that?"

"I'm sure he did sometimes, but I don't remember right now. Can we talk about this later? I want to get out of here." Monica pushed her suitcase forward. It rolled on well-lubricated wheels across the kitchen floor toward the front hallway.

83

Chapter 14 – The Walls Have Ears

BUSTER GOT THE CALL from Dexter at 3:15 p.m. The laptop was on the move, and it had arrived back at the Winchester Tower. Within fifteen minutes, Buster was connected via a secure VPN to the cloud storage server to which the surveillance cameras uploaded their feeds. They had planted three cameras, each with a high-sensitivity microphone. The system was motion- and voice-activated, so it wouldn't record footage of a silent, empty apartment. With three cameras to watch on one screen, he had to toggle back and forth between the audios. He figured he was about sixty minutes behind real time by the time he started actually listening. His attention was piqued when Monica made a reference to a note from Tom, and then a key which was somehow a message, and a safe deposit box. More concerning were Rory's comments about a spreadsheet on Tom's laptop and a company which Buster had never heard of. It looked like Tom might have been freelancing.

When he finished watching Monica and Rory leave the apartment and the videos all shut down due to lack of motion or sound, Buster whistled softly. He pulled out his cell phone and punched a button to call Jack Northrup.

"Boss, I just watched some interesting surveillance. We may have a problem on the Tom Williams front. I'm going to put a tail on his wife. I'm thinking she may have killed him, but no matter

DEAD WINNER

what, the lawyer found some evidence on Tom's laptop that he has identified as embezzlement . . .No, I'm not sure if it's only Tom or not. He may have been siphoning funds into his own private company . . . I'll find out. Plus, there was a reference to a key and a safe deposit box . . . No, I don't know, but I'm going to find out. . . I'm not sure yet . . . And it's possible that Tom might have been banging his secretary . . . I'm not sure. It might not be important. . . . Of course. I'll be all over it."

Buster hung up and called Matt Gallante to arrange for twenty-four-hour surveillance on Monica Williams. At the moment, they had a GPS track on Tom's laptop in Monica's possession, which would make it simple to get a location on her—until she left the computer somewhere. If Tom left any compromising information behind when he died, Buster wanted it back. And if his widow did kill him, Buster wanted to make sure her motive was simple jealousy, or that she wanted his money—not something worse for the company.

85

Chapter 15 – Nothing Is Ever Routine

DETECTIVES STEVE BERKOWITZ and George Mason spent their day Tuesday on a messy, complex double murder. The Tom Williams suicide was quickly pushed to the back burner. The Conjoined Corpses, as the two detectives immediately dubbed them, were found lying side-by-side in a pool of blood in the basement of an Upper West Side apartment building. They had languished long enough that the smell attracted attention. The blood had congealed, leaving the two bodies stuck together. The M.E. didn't want to rip them apart in case there was evidence in the middle, so they transported them both to the morgue on side-by-side gurneys, strapped together with yellow crime scene tape. The uniformed officers on the scene started circulating a set of photos.

Steve and George spent four hours interviewing building residents and staff to identify witnesses who saw the two dead guys earlier in the day. Half a dozen residents openly admitted wanting to tear them both new assholes because they were selling drugs to the building's teenagers. The superintendent had refused to fix anything in their apartment because of the drug paraphernalia inside. Nearly everyone the detectives talked to wanted to throw a party to celebrate their demise.

While they were busy uptown, Berkowitz sent four uniforms to the Winchester Tower to canvas Tom Williams' neighbors and

DEAD WINNER

see if they could find someone who heard a gunshot. The timing of the shot could potentially eliminate the wife as a suspect, unless she somehow got in and out of the building without being seen, then came back in at nine o'clock, without any visible blood on her, and pretended to find her dead husband. George put the odds of that scenario at about equal to the odds of a New York rat carrying away a whole pepperoni pizza.

At four o'clock, Steve got a report from the lead officer. None of the neighbors heard anything. The residents of several adjoining units were out of town, and in New York City, the sound of a distant gunshot does not create huge attention. The doormen confirmed that Tom Williams came home earlier than normal the day he died. It wasn't unprecedented. He often had client meetings outside his office and sometimes came home rather than going back to the office. Mrs. Williams was out for the day. Nobody visited Tom Williams—at least nobody who checked in at the front desk. Of course, anybody who lived in the building could have knocked on his door. The hallways had no security cameras. But, aside from rampant speculation, there was no evidence of anything suspicious.

Berkowitz and Mason made their way back to the precinct house on west 94th Street and commandeered a small conference room so they could call the Medical Examiner. Nicole Jansen, the assistant ME, answered.

"Hey, Nicole," Steve chirped sweetly into the silver speaker box in the center of the pock-marked wooden table. "Did you manage to separate the Conjoined Corpses?"

Nicole, a petite Asian woman whom Steve could picture standing in her green scrubs next to a stainless-steel tray of surgical implements, answered in a tired voice. "Yes, Detective. It wasn't that difficult."

87

KEVIN G. CHAPMAN

"Anything you can tell us off the cuff that might help with our investigation?"

Nicole sighed, without trying to cover her microphone. "Detective Berkowitz, you know I have not completed a proper autopsy, but I can tell you that both of the corpses display what appear to be gunshot entry wounds in the backs of their heads. I can't be certain about the cause of death yet, but there's a high probability they didn't shoot each other simultaneously."

"Thanks, Nicole. We appreciate it." Steve reached for the button to end the call, but George grabbed his arm.

"Say, Nicole," George called out in an extra-loud voice, as if the ancient speaker box might not hear him otherwise, "how about our other stiff with a gunshot to the head—Tom Williams? Have you taken a look at him yet?"

The line was quiet, except for the sound of footsteps. After a prolonged pause, Nicole said, "He's third in line for take-off. I took some blood and tissue samples for the lab, but I won't get to the full autopsy until tomorrow at the earliest. I assume you want the twins done first?"

"Oh, yes. For sure." George nodded to Steve, who nodded back. "But just off the top on Mr. Williams, do you have anything to suggest it wasn't the suicide it appears to have been?"

"You can't quote me, boys, but on initial cleaning and inspection of the body, I did not see anything to suggest that the gunshot that blew off most of his head wasn't self-inflicted. Is that what you want?"

"Yes. Thanks. We don't have anything in the investigation to the contrary, either. So, get to him when you can, but it's fine if he's at the end of the line. You have a great day. And give our regards to Dr. McNeill." George ended the call and stood up to leave the room all in one motion.

DEAD WINNER

When Steve's butt made contact with his desk chair, Captain Sullivan's office door opened. "Berkowitz! Did you finish looking into your Wall Street stiff?"

"No, Sully. We've been chasing the Conjoined Corpses all day."

Sully hung his head and scowled. "The public communications office has been getting calls from the press. Apparently this Tom Williams guy was a real mover and shaker or some shit. So we need to lock that down. Get out a subpoena for his financials and his phone records and find out if he was raping any pension funds or fucking some mobster's wife. If not, let's get that one off our plate. Fast!"

The office door closed behind Sully before either Steve or George could respond. Steve struggled to a standing position and ambled to George's desk in the open floor the cops called the bullpen. "Did you ask the DA to line up a subpoena for Tom Williams' records?"

"No, Steve. I guess you didn't, either?"

"Shit," was all Steve could say. "Fine. I'll get on it. We should also talk to his coworkers. Can we squeeze that in tomorrow morning?"

"Sure. I'll call narco and see if anybody over there had our twins on their radar for dealing. Maybe that will lead us to an unsatisfied customer, or a rival business group."

"Good. Fine. Our suicide worked at Northrup Investments. I know where the building is down near Wall Street. Let's meet there at nine tomorrow. We'll kick out our interviews by lunch. Maybe by the day after tomorrow we can get the financials and close things down."

Chapter 16 – After Hours

ONICA AND RORY HAD DINNER at a Mexican restaurant on 6th Street that had outside tables. They drank margaritas and nibbled on fresh tortilla chips while waiting for their entrees. A parade of New Yorkers provided a live floor show on the sidewalk inches away.

"You think it's OK to talk here?" Monica said in a hushed tone.

"It's New York City, nobody cares about what anybody else says." Rory laughed at his own comment, but stopped abruptly when he noticed Monica not joining in. "Seriously, it's fine to talk, especially out here. We can't stay inside my apartment all day and night."

Monica reached for her glass and licked several large crystals of salt from the rim before taking a small sip. Rory, realizing his mouth was open, grabbed his own drink, which sloshed over the rim and into a pot of salsa. That made Monica smile briefly. She reached across the little table and placed her hand on a mosaic tile, inviting Rory to join. After a moment of indecision, he set down his glass and brought his other hand to the table top. Monica gently put her fingertips on the back of Rory's hand.

"There's only one reason why Tom would get a . . . one of those boxes and leave the key with Breonna. He must have needed a safe place for something valuable. I'm *sure* about this."

DEAD WINNER

"Let's hope. By not identifying the bank, he made it hard for anyone but you to find the box. Unless he left a second note somewhere else, disassociated from the key."

"You think? Maybe something on his phone?"

"If he left something on his phone, he wasn't thinking clearly." Rory shook his head. "He had to know the cops would take his phone after he left his suicide note in a text."

"You're giving him a lot of credit for thinking clearly in the hours before he killed himself."

Rory felt the pressure of Monica's fingers gripping his more tightly as she finished the sentence. He returned the squeeze. "I'm sorry. I—I didn't mean to say anything about Tom. He was a—well, he was an amazing guy."

"It's nice of you to say that, Rory. We both know you don't mean it, but it's nice."

"I—I mean—" Rory struggled for words. He removed his hand and took a sip of water to buy some time. "I'm not going to say anything bad about Tom. It wouldn't be fair to you. I mean, you loved him."

"I did." Monica pulled her hand back to her lap. The clinking of silverware on ceramic plates mingled with the chatter of happy diners all around them. In the midst of such bustle, Rory and Monica were completely alone. "I fell in love with him, and I did love him. But I'm not a fool. I know Tom wasn't faithful. And I'm not innocent." Her face was pained. "I remember how Tom treated you. He took advantage of you, and you were so sweet. You let him boss you around and never complained."

Rory turned away, embarrassed by the memories. "It was always like that, even back in prep school. I was happy to hang out with Tom and the cool kids. Then, in law school, I got to hang out with . . . you." Rory forced himself to look at Monica. He felt

91

the blood rushing to his face and heard a high-pitched whine in his ears.

Monica smiled warmly. "You were always so nice to me. I loved hanging out when we were working on that silly Follies show. I sometimes wondered how things might have been different if you had asked me out before Tom."

Rory did a double-take. "You did?"

"Sure. I mean, Tom was so impressive and handsome—and rich. What girl wouldn't be swept off her feet?"

"Yeah. Tom was good at that." Rory let out a mirthless chuckle.

"We had some great times. It was quite a ride. But sometimes I think about how things might have been different if I'd married somebody else."

Before Rory could think of an intelligent comment, their waitress arrived with heavy plates. Rory's was piled high with rice, beans, and bubbly cheese. Monica's was an elaborately decorated salad. They spent a few minutes digging into their dinners. They were both hungrier than they had realized.

In between bites, Monica put down her fork and said, "I know Tom was ambitious. He loved all the money and power-brokering of his job. The last few years he spent more and more time working and less time with me. And he got paranoid about things."

"What things?"

"Secrecy and confidentiality about his clients and accounts. He was worried that somebody was hacking his computer and his phone. He never told me what he thought *they* were after."

"Did you ever ask?"

"No." She turned to look at the street as an ambulance screamed by. When the siren's noise faded, she said, "I think I

DEAD WINNER

didn't truly want to know. I was happy to spend his money, and I knew he wouldn't tell me anyway."

Rory sat forward in his chair, leaning across the little table. "Do you think that had anything to do with his—"

"I don't know."

"No—not . . . that," Rory held up a hand, holding a butter knife. "I was going to say, do you think his paranoia about somebody hacking him had anything to do with those spreadsheets I found on his computer? If he was embezzling money from his clients, that would be a good reason to be paranoid about secrecy."

Monica chewed a forkful of green peppers and onions slowly, apparently deep in thought. When she swallowed, she whispered, "Do you seriously think Tom might have been involved in something illegal?"

Rory pursed his lips. "I don't want to accuse him of anything. I can't be sure yet. But I have to say it's possible."

Monica dropped her fork onto her plate with a clang, drawing glances from the adjoining tables. She apologized, then turned back to Rory, using a hushed voice. "What would happen if the police found out about what Tom was doing?"

Rory sat back, surprised by the question. Without thinking about the implications, he launched into a short summary he had nearly memorized because he said it to so many of his clients. "Criminal activity on the part of a deceased person represents a potential risk to the estate. In some situations, the authorities can seize assets through a process called forfeiture. Whether estate assets can be captured depends on whether they can be linked to the criminal activity, but the feds have been known to attach liens against property like real estate or stocks if they were purchased with the profits from the criminal enterprise. They can't reach a trust that's set up for the benefit of third parties,

KEVIN G. CHAPMAN

and they can't reach pension funds." He stopped the robotic dissertation when he saw the terror in Monica's face. "But really, it's very unlikely that this is going to be a problem for you. I mean, I'm not even one hundred percent sure there's any illegal activity involved here. And even if there were, I doubt any law enforcement authorities would uncover it quickly enough to interfere with the closing of Tom's estate. So, you're going to be fine."

Monica downed a gulp of her frozen margarita, then winced with a moment of brain freeze. When she opened her eyes, she said, "What about the . . . ticket? Could they make any kind of claim against that? I mean, worst case?"

Rory shook his head, but didn't immediately respond. After a few seconds, he looked up and smiled. "I don't think so. Especially if we have the trust established. It would be extremely difficult for the authorities to even uncover your relationship to the trust. And even if they knew, the proof that the assets are linked to the criminal activity would be tenuous. I don't think it would be an issue."

Monica relaxed in her chair. "Good. That's good. But we should make sure the cops don't start investigating, right?"

"Right," Rory said, as confidently as he could muster.

Monica again reached out her hand and squeezed Rory's. "I'm so glad you're here for me, Rory. You're going to protect me, aren't you?"

"Of course," he quickly answered. His clients were often grateful that Rory was there to protect their inheritance but he had never felt so personally responsible. Protecting Monica was something he would do even if he weren't her lawyer.

Then Monica's face took a sudden dark turn. "Rory, if Tom was involved with something criminal, do you think somebody

DEAD WINNER

could have wanted to . . ." she lowered her voice, ". . .kill him over it?"

"I don't know. That seems like something out of a spy movie."

Monica looked down. "I'm not sure what to think anymore. Rory, I'm scared."

She lifted her head. Her eyes were moist and pleading. She needed to be comforted. Supported. She needed to be made to feel safe and secure. If only he knew the right words to say. He looked across the table, over the salt-encrusted rims, and said, "I'm scared, too."

Chapter 17 – Warm Reception

AFTER TWO MARGARITAS EACH and feeling emotionally drained, Rory and Monica wobbled through the door of his apartment. She sloughed off her sweater, leaving it hanging on the back of the sofa as she plopped down and kicked off her shoes. With both arms raised above her head in a languid stretch, she called out, "Rory? Where'd you go?"

Rory padded in stocking-covered feet across the ceramic tiled kitchen floor and into the living room, holding two tall glasses of water. He held out one toward Monica, admiring her lithe, muscular arms. "I thought we could both use some non-alcoholic liquid."

She accepted the glass, took a long sip, then set it down on the coffee table as she scooted toward the middle of the sofa, making room for Rory to sit. "Come here." She patted the maroon leather.

Lowering himself into the pillow-like cushion gracefully while holding his glass of water proved impossible. He lost his balance, which was already compromised by the earlier tequila. As he hit the leather, water sloshed out of his glass and onto Monica's lap. "Shit!" he cried out.

"Oh!" she chirped, sitting forward and swiping at the liquid with her hand.

"I'm so sorry."

"It's fine," she soothed, regaining composure. "It's nothing. Just water." She rose and unzipped her skirt, allowing it to fall

DEAD WINNER

around her bare ankles. Rory was transfixed by her lace-fringed panties, matching the blue color of the skirt. Smooth skin above the frilly waistband still bore a mark from where the tight skirt had clung to her above the slight bulge of a hip bone. A crease of flesh defined the curve of her bottom above her smooth thigh. Then Monica kicked the wet skirt aside and lowered back onto the sofa, crossing her legs gracefully. She removed the glass from Rory's hand and placed it on the table, then leaned her head against his shoulder, sliding an arm under his elbow and squeezing his. "I don't know what I'd have done the last few days without you." She let out a purr and closed her eyes.

Rory awkwardly shifted toward her, not knowing where to put his free hand and eventually allowing it to settle on his thigh. He couldn't help but stare at her bare leg, one knee elevated. His angle did not allow a view of the blue panties. He could feel the pressure of a mounting erection and was instantly embarrassed. He shifted again, trying to loosen his pants. "I'm just, um, happy to be here for you."

"Why didn't you ever ask me out when we were in school?" Monica kept her head snuggled against Rory's shoulder.

It didn't take Rory long to answer. It was a question he had pondered regularly over the past ten years. "Because Tom had dibs on you. He asked you first, so as long as you two were dating, you were off limits."

"I understand. You wouldn't want to get Tom pissed off at you."

"Or you, for not respecting your relationship. Besides," Rory craned his neck, trying futilely to see her face, "I would have never had a chance against Tom."

Monica disengaged her arm and leaned away from Rory so she could look at him. "You'd have been surprised."

"What?"

97

KEVIN G. CHAPMAN

"You think Tom was every girl's dream. He was confident and handsome and smart, and rich, of course. But you were sweet and kind. You cared about other people. You wanted to change the world. I always wondered what it would have been like with you." She held his eyes with hers and leaned slightly toward him. Her lips parted. She reached out a hand and rested it on his leg, generating a tingle in his swelling groin.

Rory stopped breathing. He stared into Monica's face and leaned into her. Their lips met and he exhaled, causing Monica to pull away. She laughed, then moved back toward Rory's face, pressing her mouth into his. She parted her lips and allowed Rory to devour her.

As he kissed the woman he had fantasized about kissing for most of his adult life, his mind raced. He used his left hand to reach out and touch her arm. As soon as he squeezed her toward him, she rolled on one hip and swung her right leg over his. Before he was aware of what was happening, she was astride him on the sofa, her hips pressing on his full erection. He wrapped both arms around her, maintaining a lip lock.

She moaned softly. He felt the velvet of her tongue brush his, sending a fresh tingle down his body. His hands moved down her back toward the exposed skin below her blouse, feeling the texture of the lacey fringe of the blue panties that were burned into his memory. He cupped her cheeks, pulling her forward as she broke their prolonged kiss and leaned back, grinding her hips into him.

As he squeezed her cheeks, slipping two fingers under the silky panties, she slowly unbuttoned her blouse, allowing it to fall away and fully revealing her blue bra, which perfectly matched the panties with which his fingers were dancing. He couldn't speak. He watched silently while Monica reached behind her back and disengaged the bra. The thin straps slowly slid down

DEAD WINNER

her shoulders. She lifted her arms above her head as the cups fell away, exposing breasts more perfect than he had imagined. Dark nipples, tight with excitement, hypnotized Rory. He couldn't look away. His hands ceased massaging her cheeks and slid upwards, feeling a sheen of sweat in the hollow of her lower back.

"You see?" she said in a breathy whisper, sliding her arms around his neck and pressing into him. She put her mouth next to his ear, gently licking the sensitive skin and softly exhaling. "You always had a chance with me. But you never asked." She moved to his mouth again, hungrily probing her tongue toward his. She breathed more heavily now and pressed into Rory's lap.

Monica slid off the sofa and stood, naked except for the blue panties. Rory stared, then forced himself to look into her eyes. She raised her eyebrows slightly and held out her right hand. Rory reached for her, but then shook his head to tamp down the libido-and-tequila-induced haze.

He pulled back his hand and pulled his legs up onto the sofa. "Wait. Monica—I mean—I'm your lawyer. You just lost Tom. We both had a lot to drink. I so want to keep going, but I'm—I can't. I don't want to take advantage of the situation. It wouldn't be right. I'd hate myself in the morning."

Monica looked disbelievingly down at Rory, whose continued arousal was painfully obvious. She lowered her hand. "Wow. That's maybe the nicest thing any man has ever said to me. I'm disappointed, and I'm very clear that you would not be taking advantage of me. Are you sure?"

Rory dropped his eyes to Monica's smooth belly and the lacy top of her blue panties. "Yeah. Really. I need to not do this. At least—not now." He watched her expression flash from disappointment to what he thought was frustration – or even anger. Then her eyes softened and the edge of a smile curled her lip for a moment.

KEVIN G. CHAPMAN

"OK. Thank you, Rory, for being such a gentleman. It's pretty rare." She turned, grabbed up her skirt, blouse, and bra, and walked slowly to the guest bedroom. Rory couldn't stop himself from watching.

Chapter 18 – Following Up

THE RECEPTIONIST AT Northrup Investments didn't seem phased by the appearance of two NYPD detectives in the 48th floor lobby at nine o'clock Wednesday morning. The lobby desk attendant had called upstairs to warn her. She motioned them toward the hallway, where Breonna Nelson was walking briskly in their direction. She flashed a smile, as if they were prospective clients.

"Hello. I'm Breonna. I'm—I was Tom Williams' personal assistant. What can I do for you?"

Steve Berkowitz pulled out a leather billfold containing his badge. After introducing George Mason, he asked if there was a place they could talk in private. Breonna spun around and led them into Tom's office.

"This is Tom Williams' office?" Steve looked around at the barren interior.

"Well, a few days ago it looked much more . . . lived in." Breonna sat behind the little round table next to the window in front of the spectacular view of New Jersey. She folded her hands on the tabletop and fixed a comfortable gaze on the two detectives.

George leaned against the empty desk, glaring grumpily, while Steve sat in the chair opposite Breonna and handled the questions. "We were hoping to have a look at Mr. Williams' office, examine his personal effects and such, maybe look for notes or correspondence that might give us a clue about why he killed himself. Is this seriously his office?"

"Yes, it is. Well, it was."

Steve turned his head as he scanned the space. "Was he always this neat?"

"No," Breonna said, without any amusement, "the company cleaned it out."

"Is it normal for an office to get cleaned out this thoroughly so soon after someone leaves his employment?"

"Actually, it is." Breonna was wearing a pants suit with a cream jacket and black pumps. She crossed her legs, looking relaxed. "The account managers deal with highly confidential information about their clients and somebody else needs to pick up those accounts right away. I'm told missing a minute, let alone a day, can cost our clients millions. So, the cleaning crew came in Tuesday morning and took away all his files. They wiped his computer and removed everything from the office, as you can see."

"As we can see." Steve and George exchanged a resigned shrug and a what-can-you-do expression. "I won't ask you about his clients or about confidential company information. But can you tell us whether there was anything unusual about his behavior in the days leading up to his . . . death?"

Steve watched Breonna's face carefully. He prided himself on being able to pick up on tells indicating a witness was withholding the truth. Breonna responded immediately. "I've been thinking about that a lot. Was there something I missed? Was he crying out for help, but I didn't notice? I can't think of anything. He was under a lot of stress, but he was always under stress. He thrived on it. I only wish I could have done something for him."

DEAD WINNER

Steve observed no indications of dishonesty. Breonna held his gaze, didn't look away, didn't hesitate, and spoke in a calm, even voice. If anything, he thought the response seemed almost rehearsed, but she did say she had been thinking about it. "Did he have any new clients or unusual things happening at work? Without revealing any confidential information?"

"Not really," Breonna said, but then hesitated. "He had some clients I didn't know about, though. He had a confidential client file that he kept password protected and he never had me work on it. He was very careful about data privacy. So if there was something happening for one of those clients, I wouldn't know. It did seem like Tom was preoccupied with something last week. He didn't say anything was wrong. I've worked with him long enough to notice, but I don't know what it was."

"OK. Thank you," Steve said absently, buying time. "Are there any colleagues of Mr. Williams we could talk to who might have a better idea of what issues he might have been having with his clients?"

"I'm not sure the company would want me to reveal that information," Breonna said. "You'll have to talk to the legal department. Here, let me get the name of the contact person." Breonna stood abruptly, nearly jumping out of her chair. She was at the office door before Steve or George moved. Across the hallway in the secretarial bay, Breonna sat at her computer and searched for the information. Steve and George arrived at the edge of her cubicle and watched silently.

"Judo, eh?" George said, his first words since arriving. He pointed to the plaque hanging on the half-wall next to Breonna's work station, identifying her as a member of the US Olympic judo team.

"Yeah. Been doing it all my life. Comes in handy when jerks don't keep their hands to themselves." She winked playfully, then

103

wrote down the name and phone number of the company's general counsel. "Here. You can find him up on fifty-two. Would you like me to take you there?"

"That's OK," Steve replied, "we can find our way back to the elevator."

A deep voice behind them said, "I'll escort them, Miss Nelson." Steve and George spun around to see Buster Altman with his arms crossed across his chest. He was wearing a black dress shirt with gray slacks and a blue sport jacket. His crew cut was freshly trimmed and bristled atop his squarish head. Steve immediately pegged him for corporate security, and probably an ex-cop, although he didn't look familiar.

"Detective Steve Berkowitz. This is Detective George Mason."

"Richard Altman. NYPD 2010 to 2015. Now head of security for Northrup. I'll be glad to escort you upstairs. I'm sure Breonna told you that we take security and confidentiality very seriously here at Northrup, didn't you?" He glared at Breonna, who stared back.

"Yes, she did," Steve confirmed. "But we'd like to speak to some of Mr. Williams' colleagues, to see if anyone noticed anything about his behavior in the time leading up to his death, or if he had any particular problems with any of his clients."

"I can't promise anything, detectives. I'm just security. I'll let the lawyers make those calls." Buster motioned down the hallway the same way Berkowitz and Mason had come in. Steve and George said good-bye to Breonna.

Over the next two hours, they interviewed four people identified by the company's lawyer as close associates of Tom Williams. None of them had anything helpful to say. As they exited the building, along with a stream of office workers on their

DEAD WINNER

way to lunch, Steve said what George had been thinking. "That was all much too clean."

"Yeah. I know what you mean. Nobody saw anything or noticed anything. All his accounts were perfect. Everyone was shocked."

"Except Breonna, his assistant," Steve noted.

"Yeah. She was very calm and honest. What she didn't seem to be was surprised."

"Or upset."

George shrugged. "Maybe it's the judo training. She controls her emotions."

"Sure. Could be. Let's see what comes up in his financials and we'll look at his phone records. I doubt we'll find anything. And if the M.E. says it was self-inflicted, then that'll do it. Sully will be happy."

"What about you?" George asked.

"I'll live with it."

Chapter 19 – The Morning After

MONICA AWOKE WEDNESDAY MORNING and reached out a hand under the blanket, searching for Rory, but he was missing. Then she remembered what had not happened the night before. When she arrived in the kitchen, wearing a long sleep t-shirt, her host was slicing bagels on the counter. The aroma of just-brewed coffee filled the air, mixing with the doughy scent of the fresh bread.

"Hey there, sleepyhead. I popped out for breakfast. I hope you don't mind plain cream cheese. I got lox and tomatoes too."

"Mmmm, sounds great. But first, I would *love* some of that coffee."

Rory plucked a mug bearing the logo of the law firm of Fitzsimmons, Packman & Kronish from his cupboard and poured. He added a Sweet n Low from a fresh box he had picked up at the bagel store and a dollop of milk, then handed the cup to Monica's waiting hands.

"You remembered how I like it," she smiled.

"I try." Before Monica could take her first sip, Rory awkwardly said, "Hey, listen, Monica, I'm sorry about last night. I know we were both a little drunk. I'm your lawyer, and I violated a bunch of ethical rules. I mean, you just lost your husband, and you're vulnerable and I took advantage of you. I should never have kissed you. I totally understand if you hate me

DEAD WINNER

this morning. And if you want to forget it ever happened, I totally understand." He finished the speech he had been rehearsing in his head all morning, then froze, his heart pounding.

Monica sipped the coffee with her head down. Then she put the cup on the counter, took two quick steps forward, and put her arms around Rory's neck, resting her cheek against his chest. "I don't regret it, Rory. I wanted it. And you didn't take advantage of me. You did the total opposite. There aren't many men who would have turned down having sex last night. Now that I have slept on it, you did the exact right thing." She stepped back and looked up into Rory's eyes. "Maybe, sometime when we're not drunk, you'll make a different choice."

Rory said, "What about Tom? I know he loved you."

Monica dropped her head back to Rory's chest as she replied. "I know he did, but we were married a long time. He was so driven and busy. I guess I didn't excite him like I once did. I know he was cheating on me. So, it has been a while since somebody really wanted me. I'm still a little disappointed that you left me hanging, but I understand and appreciate your motives."

Rory continued to hold her close for a minute in silence. He had no idea what to say. His heart was beating at double its normal rate. Without releasing Monica's soft body, he said, "I called in to take a personal day. When I go back to the office, I'll make arrangements for one of my partners in the department to take over handling your trust – and handling Tom's will. For today, we'll have time to work on the safe deposit box key. Together."

Monica stepped back. "What if I want you to handle my needs?"

Rory wasn't sure how serious the question was. "I really can't be your lawyer if I'm going to be . . . well . . . if we're going to have a personal relationship."

107

KEVIN G. CHAPMAN

Monica pouted momentarily. "Well, let's not worry about that right now. We need to find out what that key opens. But I want to have one of those bagels first. Let me take a quick shower and get dressed and I'll be right back." She turned toward the guest room before Rory could respond. He saw her scurry across the hall and into the bathroom, wrapped in a maroon towel.

Rory finished preparing the bagels and fixings, poured himself a coffee, and sat at his small dining table. He caught a peek of Monica, wrapped in her towel and glistening with moisture from the shower, casually walking from the bathroom to the guest bedroom.

When a fully-dressed Monica joined him, he spread the cream cheese on her bagel for her. When they were nearly finished eating, he cleared his throat. "I've been thinking about those spreadsheets on Tom's computer. I do think they are evidence of somebody embezzling money from Northrup clients." Rory drained the last dregs from his coffee cup. "After we find the ticket and get you set up with the trust, I really do think I have to disclose this embezzlement to the authorities. People's money is being stolen. As an officer of the court, I can't keep it to myself."

Monica's face fell. "Are you sure? Didn't you say that the cops could take my assets—the forfeiture thing?"

"I've been thinking about that, too. I'm pretty sure the lottery ticket winnings would be outside any possible forfeiture. Once we have the trust set up, you should be safe."

"Should be? Are you positive?"

Rory puckered his mouth. "I'll have to do some research before I'll be sure, but I'm pretty sure."

"Well, let's not do anything until you're absolutely sure!" Monica's tone showed how afraid she was of the prospect that Rory might be wrong.

DEAD WINNER

"Of course. Of course. Yes. We won't say anything until we have the trust set up with the sixty million, or whatever the after-tax number is, and I've made certain it's safe from forfeiture. OK?"

"Alright," Monica relaxed. "Fine. Let's go find a safe deposit box."

Chapter 20 – A Rat in the Fold

BUSTER POURED ORANGE JUICE from a decanter on the credenza in the 52nd floor conference room. He then selected an apple turnover from the large plate of pastries and bagels, walked back to the head of the long, polished table, and sat down next to Dexter. As Buster calmly bit into his breakfast, lounging backwards in the soft leather board room chair, Dexter fidgeted. He was on his third cup of coffee of the morning. While Buster had donned a fresh purple dress shirt to go with his slacks and suit jacket, Dexter's white button-down was wrinkled, with sweat stains under the arms. He looked like he had been up all night.

The frosted glass door opened and Jack Northrup walked in, accompanied by a somber-looking man in a slate gray suit. Buster recognized him as Douglas Melton, Northrup's general counsel. Dexter jumped from his chair as if a member of the royal family had entered the room. Buster remained seated and took another large bite of his turnover. Jack Northrup was his usual dapper self: Italian suit, French cuffs on his powder blue Custom Shop shirt, gold cuff studs, and a perfect black pompadour. Jack always looked like he needed a shave, even at nine o'clock in the morning. He was an imposing six-foot-two with a thick body that held his weight well. His girth was always nicely camouflaged by well-tailored suits. His dark eyes did not betray any emotion.

DEAD WINNER

Jack appropriated the seat at the head of the table with Melton on his right. "Talk to me," Northrup said calmly, without any introductions or preliminaries.

"All of Tom Williams' files and accounts are secure," Buster began, brushing pastry crumbs from his fingers. "His office is sanitized and all his clients have been reassigned to other managers. We don't have his phone, which is in the custody of the police. We've activated the remote software to remove any company files, email, and information from the device the next time it's turned on. We are not yet in possession of his personal laptop."

"Do we know where it is?" Northrup interrupted the report.

"Yes. We're tracking its GPS location. His wife has it. She has been pretty constantly in the company of a lawyer named McEntyre, who we think wrote a new will for Williams. We think the lawyer may be a friend, but we're working on that. Dex?" Buster turned to his companion, expecting a reply.

Dexter swiveled toward Northrup, sitting even more forward on the edge of his seat. "Um, sure. Yes. Rory McEntyre and Tom Williams both went to Columbia Law school and graduated eight years ago. They also both attended the Phillips Academy, which is a prep school in New Hampshire."

"I'm aware," Northrup said when Dexter paused.

"Um, yeah. So, it seems likely they knew each other. Beyond that, I haven't found anything. No photos of them together on the internet or references to them both in the same story or post. The wife, Monica Williams, graduated Barnard College the same year McEntyre and Williams graduated from law school, so all three of them were at Columbia at the same time. That's where Tom and Monica met. They were married two months after they both graduated." Dexter finished by trailing off, as if there might be more to say, but then turned to Buster, handing back the floor.

111

KEVIN G. CHAPMAN

"So, we think McEntyre and the wife probably knew each other through Tom. Our problem is that it looks like Tom might have been collecting documentation about his, uh, business activities." Buster glanced at Melton, who sat calmly in his seat.

Northrup, seeing Buster's concern, said, "Don't worry about Douglas. He's our lawyer, which makes everything we say here privileged. You can speak freely."

"Right. Well, like I was saying, it looks like Tom was collecting and downloading information about his key accounts. He was running the program according to the game plan, but the downloading activity is unusual."

"What, specifically?" Northrup pressed.

Buster nodded to Dexter, who pulled a note pad from his shoulder bag and began a recitation of what they found when reviewing Tom's files and emails. Tom had downloaded several key files, including a master spreadsheet containing the ledger entries for all the accounts that were part of "the program," as they referred to it. Dexter couldn't tell exactly where the files had gone after they were downloaded from Tom's work desktop to a removable storage device, probably a thumb drive. Tom had also downloaded about a hundred emails from his company account, but Dexter could not tell where they went. He speculated they were probably on Tom's laptop, since he had remote access to the firm's email servers from that machine. From there, he could have saved them to another removable storage device, or printed them out, or both.

"Was he siphoning off our money into his own account?" Jack asked when Dexter paused.

"Well, Sir, that's another problem. When we checked Tom's account, it turns out almost all the money was transferred out the day he died."

DEAD WINNER

Northrup was silent as he absorbed the new information. "What do you think *that* means?"

"We're not sure." Buster hated not having all the information, and he squirmed in his chair under the boss' obviously perturbed gaze. "It's possible he moved it to hide it from us, if he was planning on leaving. Or maybe he wanted it moved so we couldn't freeze it after he shot himself. We're also checking his other accounts, to see if he was freelancing with some smaller accounts that weren't in the program."

"So, you're thinking he might have been planning to rat us out?"

"We're concerned, but so far there's no indication that he sent anything or published anything that we should be worried about."

"Do we think Tom's assistant is involved? What's her name? Brittany, or something?"

"Breonna. She's been cooperative. We haven't found anything so far to suggest she knew anything about what Williams was doing. But we did overhear Tom's wife say she thinks Tom was sleeping with her, so you never know. It's possible Tom was moving his money so he could run off with his secretary. The problem is, whether he was planning to go to the feds or just take off with the girl, none of it explains why he would kill himself."

Northrup nodded. "You think the wife might have iced him? If she found out he was fooling around? That would make sense."

"It's possible. That would actually be the least worrisome scenario. We overheard the wife say Breonna delivered to her a key to a safe deposit box."

"What?" Melton spoke up, as if this was the first surprise of the discussion.

KEVIN G. CHAPMAN

Buster made eye contact with Jack and got a go-ahead nod. "It seems there is a safe deposit box. We're not sure from the conversation we overheard, but it doesn't sound like they know what's in it. So, it seems Tom had some secret he didn't even tell his wife about. Her lawyer found documents on Tom's laptop that we think might be records of transactions inside the program. It doesn't look like the wife knows what they are, but the lawyer is suspicious."

"That doesn't sound good," Melton said. "I assume you will be monitoring the situation."

"We will," Buster nodded. "She and the lawyer haven't been back to the apartment. Based on the GPS tracker on the laptop, it's been at the lawyer's place. But I have two men on her today. We'll see if they find that box."

"This could get messy, I'm guessing," Northrup said, looking at Melton, who nodded without speaking. Jack returned his eyes to Buster. "I don't want anyone from the firm to be connected to this situation if it turns ugly. I want you to reach out and borrow some resources from Mr. G. His guys should be able to help contain the situation."

Buster pursed his lips, then controlled his face. He knew his boss was right. If it became necessary to eliminate Monica or McEntyre, there couldn't be any connection back to the company. He had good men, and he hated to relinquish control of an operation, but the situation had the potential to blow up. The company's operation churned out a substantial amount of money. With so much cash involved, there was an opportunity to launder the money, and the Gallata organized crime family was always eager to clean their profits. Jack Northrup had a connection, and so a happy marriage was forged years before. When Jack needed some extra support, or some muscle who

DEAD WINNER

didn't mind getting a little dirty, Alberto "Fat Albert" Gallata was always happy to lend some.

"I'll make a call," Buster said, then the meeting broke up.

As they walked away from the conference room, Dexter whispered, "Who's Mr. G.?"

Buster finished chewing another apple turnover, which he had snatched on his way out, then said, "You don't need to know everything, Dex."

Chapter 21 – Jack in the Box

THE CITIBANK BRANCH on Church Street was four blocks from the Winchester Tower. Rory had called to determine that the manager who could help them access the safe deposit box arrived at ten o'clock. Rory and Monica arrived at ten-fifteen.

Rory had prepped Monica on the process for a surviving spouse to get access to accounts held in the name of a dead partner. It could often take several weeks and they would need an official death certificate. His firm could attempt to get a court order, but that would take some time also. They spent fifteen minutes explaining the situation to the assistant branch manager, a lovely Latina woman named Lucy. They had the box number and the key. Lucy looked up the record on her computer and told Monica that the safe deposit box had been added to the joint checking account she and Tom already had. After verifying Monica's identity and having her sign several forms, she eventually led them through a security door toward the vault. Since Rory was her lawyer and was handling Tom's estate, Lucy permitted him to accompany Monica.

The safe deposit boxes occupied a wall inside the bank's vault, lined up in three rows like the mailboxes in the lobby of Rory's building. The boxes in the top row bore the letter A, followed by a number. The bottom row was the "C" row. Lucy navigated to box 104 in the bottom row and inserted her bank key into one of the two keyholes in the box's front. Monica

DEAD WINNER

produced the key Tom had left for her and inserted it into the other hole. They turned simultaneously, the box produced a distinct click, then Lucy pulled the door open. Inside, Rory could see the brass handle of the inner box, which Lucy slid out and placed on the counter beneath the rows of numbered doors. The box was two feet long, six inches wide, and four inches tall. The lid had a hinge two-thirds of the way toward the back and a latch in the front holding it closed.

Rory motioned Monica toward a door leading to a small, secure room where they could examine the contents of the box. Lucy said she would wait outside the vault for them to be ready to return the tray to the secure box, which required both keys again. The little room was smaller than a changing room in a department store. It was all white, with a bright fluorescent light overhead. A plastic chair sat in front of a two-foot-wide counter against the wall, big enough to hold the metal box. It was designed to be a place you did not want to spend any more time in than was absolutely necessary. Rory stood behind the sole chair, while Monica sat, took a deep breath, and lifted the lid.

The box was stuffed with papers, which bulged upward when Monica opened the lid that had been compressing them. Monica turned to look back at Rory, who leaned in and set down his briefcase. Rory had been hoping to find the small lottery ticket, or an envelope containing their prize. Instead, they had a pile to sift through.

Monica reached in to extract an envelope from the top of the pile. It was upside down, but it bore one word in handwriting Monica identified as Tom's: *Monica*. Ripping open the flap, she dug out a single sheet of paper. She opened the envelope wide and shook it upside down to see if the lottery ticket would fall out. It didn't. Then she unfolded the paper and saw more of

KEVIN G. CHAPMAN

Tom's handwriting, in the blue pen he always used for his work notes.

> *My Monica –*
> *I'm sorry that you must be burdened with this information. I regret letting Jack talk me into his inside operation. I wanted the money. Make sure to withdraw the money from our investment account and convert it to cash or gold, since some of it is the proceeds of Jack's criminal operation.*
> *I wish I had the courage to get out and tell the authorities about the whole corrupt garbage heap. But if I'm gone, now you can do it. Everything you need is here. I explain it all on the video. Get out of New York first, somewhere nobody knows you. Don't fly. Don't leave any paper trail. Then call the SEC, say you are a whistleblower and that you want the bounty. Turn over everything to the feds and lie low. Live off the cash. I'm sorry, but there's no other way. Jack will assume you are involved and will come after you. Trust nobody.*
> *I love you.*

Monica stared at the letter, re-reading it twice before handing it to Rory. While he read, she dumped the contents of the box onto the counter. Printouts of spreadsheets, copies of financial statements, and several pages of handwritten notes spilled out. A silver stick, three inches long and less than one inch wide, slid toward the edge of the table: a flash drive. She sorted through all the papers. There was no lottery ticket.

When Rory finished reading the note, he put a hand against the wall for balance. "What did Tom mean about Jack coming after you? Who's Jack?"

118

DEAD WINNER

"Jack is his boss at Northrup. Why would Jack come after me? He said I should live off the cash from the investment account, but there's nothing left! What am I supposed to do? The lottery ticket isn't here!"

Rory sensed panic building in Monica and tried to calm her, as he had many prior clients. "Don't worry. We'll figure it out. Maybe there's a message buried in here from Tom about where the ticket is."

"You think?" Monica took a deep breath, trying to calm herself. "I mean, maybe. OK. Let's get out of here. This room is making me claustrophobic."

Rory helped Monica carefully pack up all the papers and the flash drive into a large envelope he had brought along in his briefcase.

"What do you think is on the video?" Monica held both hands to her head, as if pressing all the new information inside.

Rory knew Monica needed him to be confident and strong. The absence of the lottery ticket was devastating. "Seems like it's an explanation about what all these documents mean. We'll watch it when we have a computer."

"Do you think I should do what he says? Leave town and then contact the SEC? But he expected me to have the money from the investment account. Now I don't have that."

"It looks like Tom wrote that note before you won the lottery. The lottery money would significantly change the plan. He was worried about his account being seized by the government if you notified them about the embezzlement before liquidating the money. So, that means he was involved."

"Could he have been worried about the Northrup guys freezing his account, once they found out Tom had gone to the feds?"

KEVIN G. CHAPMAN

Rory pondered the idea. "Maybe. Or maybe he was worried about all the Northrup accounts being frozen. The point is, you need to be careful. We can't turn this over to the feds until you are properly prepared. But that doesn't help us find the lottery ticket." He reached out and placed a hand gently on Monica's shoulder. She clutched his fingers. Neither spoke, each lost in thought.

"I was so sure," Monica removed her hand and turned away from Rory. "If Tom was looking for a place to hide the ticket, wouldn't he have put it here? Why would he put it anywhere else besides here?"

"Maybe he didn't have time to get to the bank on Monday," Rory offered.

"But if he was in trouble and couldn't get here, he would have called me, or left me a message!"

"He did call," Rory reminded her. "There were two missed calls on your phone, remember? You were visiting your mother and turned off your phone and you missed his calls."

"Then he would have sent me a text, or left me a note."

"He wouldn't have sent a text if he was trying to keep it confidential. Anybody with access to his phone, or yours, could have seen it. The police can get the texts from your phone company if they issue a prompt subpoena. I understand why he wouldn't want to send you that kind of information by text. The last text on his phone was the note to you, which didn't contain any information."

Monica spun around so she could see Rory. "Do you think somebody forced him to send that text? Or sent it from his phone, just pretending to be Tom? That would mean—"

"I don't know." Rory put both hands on Monica's shoulders. "We can't figure it out here. We need to go."

120

DEAD WINNER

They checked and double-checked the box and the counter to make sure they had not missed the lottery ticket. After stuffing the envelope back into his case and closing the box, Rory led the way out of the tiny room. After Lucy returned the now-empty box to its alcove, the three paraded back through the security doors and into the bank's lobby. Outside on the busy Manhattan street, Rory suggested they return to his apartment to take stock of what they had learned, watch Tom's video, and plan their next move. Monica nodded her agreement. Rory took her by the elbow as they crossed Broadway and headed west.

Chapter 22 – A Rude Interruption

WALKING ACROSS LOWER MANHATTAN toward Rory's apartment, Monica was quiet. Rory figured she was trying to process all the information they had received from her dead husband. It was a little creepy for Tom to be sending messages from the grave. He must have been anticipating the possibility of his untimely death. They certainly weren't going to have a deep discussion about it on the sidewalks of Manhattan.

At 11:15 a.m., pedestrian traffic in the financial district was about as thin as it got, with the office workers all tucked in for the morning and the lunch crowds not yet released from captivity. Still, Monica and Rory had to switch from side-by-side to single file frequently to pass slower travelers blocking their forward progress. They cut across Exchange Alley toward Trinity Street, where the sidewalk was narrow but there were few other pedestrians.

Monica said, "It's like Tom was planning for this. I can't believe he didn't tell me."

Rory reached out and put an arm around Monica's shoulders as they walked, which slowed them down a bit. "We'll figure it out."

Before Monica responded, a male voice called out from their left across the narrow lane, "Monica Williams?"

DEAD WINNER

Rory and Monica stopped and turned toward the voice, which belonged to a tall Black man with a shiny bald head, wearing a blue dress shirt with no tie, dark slacks, and polished black shoes. He was walking toward them across the cobblestone street, as if he was a friend of Monica's and wanted to say hello. They stopped, waiting for the smiling figure to approach.

When the man reached his last step before the curb, Rory felt a gripping pain on his left shoulder and was jerked backwards. The back of his head knocked against the concrete wall of a building as he fell. When he opened his eyes and tried to stand, a large White guy with a crew cut had most of the front of his shirt clenched in his massive hand. Rory could smell cigarettes and garlic as he stared into the surprisingly calm face.

"Please, have a seat," the man grunted as he pushed Rory back down. Still feeling pain in the back of his head, Rory slid down the wall until his butt collided roughly with the sidewalk. His briefcase, clutched in his hand, lay on its side on the ground. Rory could see Monica struggling in the firm grasp of the man who had called to her from across the street.

The man who stood over Rory reached down and ripped the briefcase from his hand. "Hey! That's my property!" Rory pushed his back against the wall in his struggle to stand up.

A sledgehammer of a fist slammed into his right shoulder, sending Rory slumping back to the ground. "I told you to sit down!" Crew Cut growled. He had a thick body like a football lineman.

The man handed the brown leather case to his companion. The bald Black guy kept one arm wrapped around Monica's shoulder. To a passerby, it might have looked like they were exchanging friendly greetings. Bald Guy accepted the briefcase and leaned his face down next to Monica's ear. Rory could see she was terrified. "What was in the box, Sweetie?"

KEVIN G. CHAPMAN

"What box?" She turned her head away, but the guy dropped the case and used a meaty paw to grab her face, pulling her eyes back toward him. Monica lowered her chin and bit down on the skin between the man's thumb and index finger. He howled and released the hand, but kept his other arm firmly locked around her shoulders despite Monica's squirms. When he raised his bitten hand, it was bleeding slightly.

His companion darted behind Monica and grabbed her by both arms above the elbows, holding her arms against her body and locking her in place. "You scream and I'll snap your arm, doll. We don't want to hurt you. Just give us whatever you took outta that safe deposit box."

Crew Cut squeezed Monica's triceps hard enough to make her squeal, but she otherwise kept quiet. Bald Guy ripped a gold chain off Monica's shoulder, which supported her small purse, and tore open the purple leather. The contents tumbled to the pavement when the purse went upside down. Nothing about the cosmetics, hairbrush, lip balm, mints, tissues, and other small items from Monica's purse looked significant. The guy re-hung the now-empty purse on Monica's shoulder.

"It's gonna be much simpler if you just tell us," the purse-snatcher said softly. "I'm not really excited about having Bruno breaking your arm, but I will if you don't cooperate. You shouldn't care about any of that stuff."

"Who the hell are you?!" Rory shouted. He had managed to get to his feet on wobbly legs while watching the two thugs manhandle Monica.

When the two guys turned their heads toward Rory, Monica kicked her black heel backwards, but scored only a glancing blow against Crew Cut's shin. He spun her sideways, turning his back on Rory. The Black guy had retrieved the briefcase and was fumbling with the latch. In another moment, he would have the

DEAD WINNER

case open and would easily find the large envelope with the contents of the safe deposit box.

Rory couldn't figure how these two lugs knew about the box, or what was in it. He swiveled his head left and right, looking for a cop or a bystander who might provide some help. He saw pedestrians walking across the open end of the Alley on the Trinity Street side, which was the closest, but nobody paid any attention to the four figures on the sidewalk. He could have shouted, but that would have only drawn the attention of their attackers. For the moment, both men were ignoring him.

Seeing Monica in the clutches of the man called Bruno, Rory jumped, launching himself onto Bruno's back and throwing his arms around the man's neck. The attacker released Monica in order to bring his arms up, reaching for Rory. Having never wrestled and seldom gotten into fights, Rory had no coherent plan for what to do once he had his opponent in a neck lock. He grasped his right wrist in his left hand and pulled with all his might.

Unlike Rory, Bruno had been in plenty of fights. He calmly thrust himself backwards toward the wall of the nearby building. Rory, not at all prepared, absorbed the full impact with his back as the much larger man compressed him into the stone. The air expelled from Rory's lungs, leaving him gasping as he released his grip and fell backwards in a heap. He pushed to his hands and knees, struggling to inhale. His eyes watered. He heard Monica cry out, "Rory!" Rory's vision blurred. He wheezed, unable to fill his lungs. He heard the clicking sound his briefcase made when the latch sprung open. Monica said, "Stop!"

A crinkle of thick paper accompanied their attacker extracting the envelope. Rory sucked in two short half-breaths as he wobbled back to a crouching posture. The two men paid him no attention as they both peered into the briefcase, pawing

125

through his legal pads and his copy of *The Wall Street Journal* to see if there was anything else that could have been removed from the bank's vault. Finding nothing else, Bruno tossed the briefcase against the building a few feet away from Rory, who clearly posed no threat.

"Let's go," Bald Guy said. He roughly pushed Monica against the wall, where she lost her balance and landed on her ass, a splotch of red marring her bare knee.

Rory, breathing in shallow gasps, staggered forward toward the two thugs. He reached out, trying to grab the envelope from Bruno's hand. Bald Guy saw the movement, turned, and planted a straight left jab into the middle of Rory's face. The lawyer dropped to the sidewalk like a bag of groceries, a stream of blood gushing from his nose. He rolled onto his side, moaning in pain and holding both hands against his face while flashes of light scattered over the insides of his closed eyelids. When he managed to open one eye, he saw the feet of the two attackers walking briskly toward Trinity Street.

Monica rushed to Rory's prone form. "Rory! Oh my God, are you OK?"

She got only another moan as a reply. She gathered up her package of tissues, formerly in her purse. Wadding up three pieces, she held them against Rory's bleeding nose while pulling him into a sitting posture. She pushed his head back, telling him to keep pressure on the bleeding. A middle-aged couple who saw them on the ground rushed to offer assistance.

"Who were those guys?" Monica didn't expect Rory to have a good answer.

"Ah dohn know," Rory tried to respond without moving his head or removing the tissues stemming the flow of his bodily fluid.

DEAD WINNER

The good Samaritans offered a handkerchief to replace the blood-soaked tissues and helped Rory to his feet. Monica thanked them, then led Rory in the direction of the Emergency Room at the Lower Manhattan branch of New York Presbyterian Hospital.

Chapter 23 – On Camera

TWO HOURS LATER, a bandage over a plastic nose brace covering Rory's face, he and Monica exited a taxi at Rory's building. Once past the concerned lobby staff and upstairs, Monica, sporting her own bandaged knee, collapsed onto the sofa. Rory sat next to her and tilted his head back.

Monica's hair fell in disorganized strands around her face. She stared at the ceiling, taking deep, slow breaths. "This is awful. How did those guys know we went to the safe deposit box?"

Rory had been pondering the same question ever since they were accosted. He had a dozen more questions, all of which he kept to himself until they had some privacy. From the moment they arrived at the hospital, there was always somebody listening. Now, they were finally alone.

The doctor had given Rory a Tylenol with codeine for his pain. Fortunately, his nose was not broken. The pain was a dull throb and would continue for a day or two. Dark rings were forming under his eye sockets. He looked worse than he actually felt, but his physical injuries were the least of his concerns.

"Monica," Rory began, not looking directly at her. He was afraid of what he might see in her eyes, "did Tom ever show you any of those documents that were in the box?"

"No. Never. But he seemed to have things all planned out. He wanted me, or somebody, to use those documents. Now those plans are ruined."

DEAD WINNER

Rory paused, not sure about the next question. "It seems like Tom stashed away those documents, and the note to you, with an expectation that something might happen to him. He wanted you to liquidate your investment account, which you obviously can't do now, except for the remaining twelve thousand. We should do that, but that's not our biggest problem. If Tom was anticipating his death, and if he was involved in some kind of criminal operation, he might have been worried that somebody might want to kill him. He set up this trove of documents so that you could turn them over to the feds and claim a bounty. He must have been anticipating his death. Maybe that he would kill himself, or maybe something else."

"Um, what's a bounty?" Monica's face was a blank. Rory realized that he knew what Tom's note was talking about, while Monica did not.

"If somebody has information about criminal activity connected to securities or investments, like insider trading or a Ponzi scheme, they can go to the Securities and Exchange Commission – the SEC – and be a whistleblower. If the SEC uses the information to prosecute the criminals and recovers money from the criminals, the whistleblower gets a bounty – like a reward. It can be up to thirty percent of the government's recovery. So, in a big case, it can be millions of dollars. Tom wanted you to take those documents and whatever video he had on that flash drive to the SEC and blow the whistle on Northrup so you could collect the bounty."

Monica shook her head, confused. "I don't understand. Why me? Why wouldn't Tom do it himself. We could have taken that money and run away together."

Rory reached out and held Monica's hand gently. "If Tom was a participant in the criminal activity, which he said he was in his note, then he could not have been a whistleblower. They don't

KEVIN G. CHAPMAN

allow a criminal to profit from their own wrongdoing by turning themselves in and claiming a bounty. But if he gives the information to you, then you can do it. Or anyone else who was not involved in the crimes."

Monica looked away. "Those men who stole the documents. They must have known what Tom did. Jack must have sent them. That means they knew about the key, or they knew Tom stashed the documents in that box." Monica's voice grew more anxious as she spoke. She got up and paced across the room, not looking at Rory. "Tom said they would come after me."

"Well, now they have recovered the documents, so they may not consider you a threat."

"But now we have nothing!" Monica lamented. "We have no documents to prove that Tom's bosses were criminals. Nothing to take to the SEC for the bounty thing. They took the flash drive with Tom's video, so we don't even have that. This is terrible."

"And no ticket," Rory said, reaching out a limp arm toward where Monica was standing, hoping she would come back to the sofa. "I'm sorry I wasn't able to protect the documents from those thugs."

"Don't be sorry. You were . . . valiant. You tried to protect me from those two animals. You had no chance, but you still tried. I love your courage. It means a lot to me. I'm so sorry you got hurt. I'm so sorry you got dragged into this." She slumped onto the sofa and laid her head in Rory's lap.

Rory placed a hand on Monica's hair, softly stroking it. Her eye makeup was still in place. It was fate, he thought, that brought her to his office, and fate had thrust him into the position of her protector. He had not done a very good job protecting her, but Monica seemed to appreciate the effort. A bloody nose was a small price to pay to prove he was willing to do anything for her.

DEAD WINNER

"Don't be sorry. I'm glad you came to me to set up the trust. I'd do it again."

Monica didn't respond, but snuggled her head against Rory's thigh. He was exhausted and drifted in and out of sleep until he felt Monica stir and press against him. "Mmmmmm," she purred, before fluttering her lids and looking up at Rory's face through a sleepy haze. "Hey, you," she said as she stretched her arm off his body. "You feeling OK?"

"Yeah, actually. I'm not bad," Rory sat up. Monica rolled off the sofa and looked down on Rory, who brought a hand to his forehead.

"You're my hero for standing up to those guys. It's nice to know somebody out there will be my champion."

"Isn't that what a guy is supposed to do for his lady in distress?" He smiled, although the face bandage somewhat masked his expression. Rory struggled to his feet and walked slowly to the bathroom. When he emerged, he had removed his facial bandages, the plastic brace on his nose, and the cotton swabbing that had been stuffed up his nostrils. He returned to the sofa, announcing that he felt better without the bandages.

She snuggled against his shoulder, placing her right palm on his chest. "Despite everything that's happened, I'm glad I'm here with you. You're having a positive effect on me. Thank you, my knight in shining armor."

"With a broken sword," Rory couldn't help but go for self-deprecating humor. It was his default. "Did you get in a decent nap, at least?"

"I did. But I keep thinking about Tom's note. He left those documents to be my safety net. Now he's gone. The evidence is gone. I have to move on and make my own plans." She leaned closer. Rory could feel heat rising in his neck. "I'm hoping you'll help me make those plans – together." When Monica parted her

131

KEVIN G. CHAPMAN

lips and leaned even closer, Rory reciprocated, allowing their lips to brush. Rory forgot everything else and became lost in the soft kiss.

When Monica pulled away and laid her head on Rory's chest, he said, "I had another thought, too, while I was napping. We need to find Tom's video."

"What?" Monica sat up, knocking her shin against the coffee table. "Wasn't the flash drive in the envelope with all the documents?"

"Yeah, it was. But Tom had to copy it from somewhere."

Monica looked puzzled. "I don't understand. He copied it onto the flash drive, right?"

"Yeah, but you can't transfer a video from a phone to a flash drive. You have to save it somewhere first. Probably on his laptop."

Monica left Rory leaning against the back of the sofa. She retrieved Tom's laptop from the table by the kitchen and brought it to the coffee table. She set the unit down and entered the password, then pushed it a few inches toward Rory, inviting him to take over. He opened the videos folder from the file directory, sorted the files by the most recent creation date, and read off the names. The second file was labeled "VE4BX."

"That's it!" Rory exclaimed, then winced, having opened his jaw beyond the point that triggered pain from his still-tender nose.

When the file opened, they watched Tom's five-minute recitation of the scheme Northrup Investments used to defraud their biggest clients and the significance of the documents they no longer had. The operation involved skimming profits from the accounts of the firm's largest customers. They siphoned off less than one tenth of one percent of the money earned on profitable transactions, never on losses. The theory was that their clients

DEAD WINNER

would not carefully scrutinize the results of money-making trades if the variances were very small. Over thousands of transactions, the funds added up and were diverted into a special "house" account, which kept all the ledgers balanced while adding millions to the slush fund. This was distributed to all the money managers who were in on the scheme. Tom said the firm's CEO, Jack Northrup, was the mastermind and decided which accounts would be involved. The video referenced numerous documents as proof of the claims: documents from the safe deposit box they didn't have.

At the end of the lengthy explanation, Tom's voice said, *"When you go to the SEC with this, you need to have everything in order and be ready to drop out of sight. As soon as the SEC issues a subpoena for the company's account records, Jack will blow up the whole operation. He has a plan in place to withdraw assets from the slush fund and replace all the money taken from all the accounts in the program for the last six months. He'll be able to present clean account records that won't show the fraudulent transactions. That's why you need the spreadsheets and the account transaction details. The feds will need to go deep into the electronic records to find the real transactions. Without that, they may not be able to make a case, and there won't be any recovery. And Jack will know it was me who gave you the information. He'll come after you, just like he came after Al Reilly. You need to be far away and safe somewhere he can't find you. Remember what we talked about."*

The video ended with Tom saying, *"I regret, now, agreeing to go in on Jack's scheme, but I guess I wanted the easy money. I'm sorry. I hope I can make it right without hurting anyone else. I wish I had the guts to cooperate with the authorities, but I just couldn't do it. The documents I'm leaving with this video should get the job done and take care of you, even if Jack locks*

133

down the bonus account, which I expect he will. Make sure you keep this video and the documents safe. Tell no one. I love you, and I'm sorry."

When Tom's video from the grave was finished, Monica asked, "Is that enough? Without the documents, will this get the feds to investigate Jack and the company?"

"I'm not sure. It's not my area of expertise. But without the documents, it's only an allegation. The feds would need to use the video to get a search warrant, go in and seize the company's computerized records, then do an analysis of the accounts Tom referenced in order to identify the funds that were being skimmed and build a case from there. It's a bunch of work. It's possible. But if what Tom said is true, about them blowing up the scheme and putting the money back, it might be tough."

"Do you think Tom kept copies of those documents on his laptop?"

Rory scanned through the file index, but didn't immediately see any folders or file groupings that looked promising. "I don't know. If he did, they might be hidden or encrypted. I'll have to spend some time looking, but we may need to get a computer expert to search the hard drive. I'll download the video, and those two spreadsheets I found. If I find anything else, I'll start building a file."

"Rory?" Monica's face was blank. "Do you think Jack found out what Tom was doing and killed him?" Monica grabbed Rory's hand in a frightened grip.

"It's possible. Tom seemed to be worried about your safety. And what was that reference to somebody named Al?"

Monica turned away, then spoke softly. "Al Reilly. He was Tom's mentor at Northrup. They were very close. Six months ago, he died in a car crash at his beach house. Tom was really shaken up about it. It was an accident. He was drunk and drove

DEAD WINNER

his car off the road into the rocks. But I heard Tom once talking on the phone about it. He thought Jack had him killed and staged the accident. He never told me that, or explained why he thought Jack was involved. I never asked."

"I'm thinking it's time to go to the feds now," Rory said. "After what happened today, I'm not sure you're safe, even if Jack's guys got the documents back."

"No!" Monica cried out. "They got what they wanted. I don't have any other documents. You heard what Tom said—that I need to get out of town and hide before going to the feds. Jack will come after me."

"Well, we could certainly report the assault from today."

Monica reduced the pressure of her vice-grip on Rory's hand. "What do we tell them? We can't identify those two guys. We can't tell them what was stolen. You said that the feds could still take all Tom's money, even if we can find it. Oh, Rory, we have to figure out a plan."

"OK. OK. Fine. We have to find the lottery ticket. Those funds are safe. I was sure it would be in the box."

Monica put her hand on Rory's leg. "I have another idea about where Tom might have put it."

"Where?"

Monica looked out the window, toward the river. "On his video, Tom said I had to get away someplace safe; somewhere nobody could find me. If he needed someplace besides the safe deposit box, he might have hidden the ticket on the boat."

Rory furrowed his brow in puzzlement. "What boat?"

135

Chapter 24 – Keeping Secrets

BREONNA HAD NEVER BEEN SUMMONED to Jack Northrup's office before. She could think of no reason why the big boss would want to talk with her, unless it had to do with Tom.

She walked into the executive suite through large double doors made from dark wood. The outer foyer was a semi-circle with four closed doors evenly spaced around the curve, each belonging to one of the senior executives. The space was designed so that nobody had the "corner" office, since there were no corners. A secretarial station guarded each door, staffed by a smartly dressed assistant. Breonna made eye contact with Gwen Simmons, Jack Northrup's executive assistant. She and Gwen were friendly, but not friends. All the executive secretaries occasionally covered for each other and shared resources and gossip, except Gwen, who was treated like the warden's deputy.

"Is he alone?" Breonna whispered as she slowly passed Gwen's desk. She knew Gwen would get in trouble if she gave out any information—if anybody heard her. The subtle head shake from her counterpart told her she was walking into the lion's den with multiple predators. She gave a tiny nod of thanks, then set her feet and pushed open the heavy office door.

In contrast to the artificial light of the windowless outer foyer, inside the expansive office the sunlight made Breonna squint. She halted two steps beyond the threshold. As the door closed with a solid *ker-chunk* behind her, Breonna took stock of

DEAD WINNER

her opponents, as she did when entering the judo circle. In competition, the assessment was of only one adversary. Here, there were three. Behind his desk, Jack Northrup lounged casually in his massive leather throne. His dark suit jacket was draped across the back of the chair, exposing the CEO's blue and maroon suspenders, which exactly matched his necktie. Jack did not need to look mean or intimidating to engender fear.

Facing Jack's desk, three guest chairs formed a semicircle that mirrored the curved walls. The end chair closest to the window was occupied by Northrup Investment's chief operating officer and Jack's second in command, Oscar Lexington. Lexington was on the edge of retirement and was revered as the mastermind of the firm's best investment programs. He had a grandfatherly countenance that made Breonna want to bake him cookies. In the chair farthest from the window sat Buster Altman, the firm's chief of security, who had led the cleaning crew in Tom's office the day before. Buster's smirk told her everything she needed to know. He was overconfident, looking forward to whatever the three men had planned. She had seen the same expression before on the faces of opponents who underestimated her in the judo ring. Mostly men.

The center seat was empty. Breonna fixed a confident smile on her lips and walked straight to the empty chair, her skirt swishing above her knees. She sat and crossed her legs, feeling the men staring. "What can I do for you, Mr. Northrup?" She ignored the other two men and fixed a level gaze at the boss.

"Miss Nelson. Thank you for joining us. First, let me express my sincerest sympathy about Tom's death. It was a shock to all of us, and I'm sure to you also." He paused, inviting Breonna to say something.

"Yes, sir. Quite a shock." Breonna held the older man's eyes, showing no emotion.

137

KEVIN G. CHAPMAN

Lexington then spoke, his voice soft and sympathetic. "My dear, we know this is a difficult time, but it's important for us to know whether Tom said anything to you about why he wanted to kill himself. Did he confide in you about it?"

"No, Sir," Breonna said, turning her whole body sideways to look at the COO.

"Oh, now, let's get past the 'Sir' thing now, shall we? I'm not your boss here, I'm just concerned about the firm. You should be concerned also, young lady. You have a future here, but we all need to protect our interests. So, you call me Oscar, and I'll call you Breonna. How about that, hmmm?"

"Thank you, Oscar, I appreciate knowing you think I have a future here. I certainly would like to stay and work for another investment manager. But as far as Tom is concerned, he did seem unusually nervous and stressed for the past couple weeks. I asked him about it, but he said he was having a bad run and his clients were giving him a hard time."

Jack took back the floor. "Were you aware of the bad run he was having? Did you work on his account records?"

"Well, of course I worked on his accounts. I knew some of his trades had lost money and some of his fund picks were underperforming. I heard him talking to some of the clients, and spoke to them while making appointments for Tom. I knew some of them were unhappy, but Tom had been through ups and downs before. All his clients came out ahead in the long run. It wasn't something that was going to drive him to suicide."

It was then Buster's turn. Jack and Oscar looked at him. The broad-shouldered man walked behind Breonna's chair. She didn't know which way to face—toward the boss, who had called her into the meeting, or toward the man who was clearly going to start talking next. She compromised and sat half-turned. "Miss Nelson, I'm afraid we've found some irregularities in

138

DEAD WINNER

Tom's accounts." He paused, giving Breonna an opportunity to react or respond. She sat attentively on the edge of her chair, waiting for the additional information that was obviously coming.

Buster made eye contact with Jack, then continued. "We have analyzed the reports from Tom's clients and there is a pattern. Relatively small amounts were transferred out of the accounts under a fee code that doesn't exist. It was called 'excise fee.' Do you recall ever seeing line items with that code when you were preparing Tom's consolidated account reports?"

This time, Buster clearly required a response. Breonna swiveled her head toward her inquisitor. "I'm sorry, I don't think we were ever properly introduced. I know you're Richard Altman, the head of security, but I heard one of your men call you 'Buster,' so I'm not sure how I should address you, Sir."

"Buster is fine. Mr. Altman is also fine if you prefer." Buster's voice contained a tiny edge of annoyance. Breonna was stalling, and doing it effectively.

"Well, Mr. Altman, the reports are all computer-generated. All I did was cut and paste the totals into a master spreadsheet for Tom. I can tell you that I never understood why the master sheets couldn't be computer-generated, but Tom wanted me to do them manually for him, so I did. I'm sure I must have seen those entries, but I never pretended to know what all the codes were. I mean, there were service fees and trading charges and transfer fees and a dozen different taxes. If you're telling me that the lines for excise fees weren't real, then I believe you, but this is the first I'm hearing about it. So, where did the money go?"

None of the men answered Breonna's question. Buster charged ahead. "Breonna, we're pretty sure Tom was siphoning off those bogus fees into a personal account. He was embezzling the funds. Did you know? Did he tell you about it?"

139

KEVIN G. CHAPMAN

Breonna turned back to Jack Northrup. "Mr. Northrup, this is a shock. I didn't know anything about this." Then she leaned back and narrowed her eyes. "I hope nobody here is trying to accuse me of being involved."

"Oh, no, no, my dear," Oscar said, sliding forward in his chair and leaning toward Breonna. He reached out his hand and patted her leg, which was much more skeevy than soothing. "Nobody is accusing you of anything. We just need to know exactly what Tom was doing, and we're collecting any documentation we can turn over to the authorities. We're obviously as shocked as you about this."

"You're setting up—" Breonna blurted out, then checked herself. "Setting me up to look like I knew about this. What? You think I'll be a witness against Tom because he's dead?"

The men's silence was as much of an affirmation as Breonna needed. Jack finally filled the void. "Breonna, like Oscar said, we think you have a bright future here with the firm. We appreciate your loyalty to Tom, but we need to see some loyalty to the firm, and to us. Now, the police can't put Tom in jail, so nothing anybody says about him can hurt him. It does seem that he was embezzling funds. Would you like Buster to show you the records, so you can see for yourself?"

"No," Breonna said softly, lowering her eyes for the first time.

"Well, then, while I'm sure you're telling us the truth about not knowing about it—at the time—now that you know, it's possible you may remember how some things he did, or things he said, or telephone calls you overheard, might be pieces of the puzzle. For the moment, we don't want you to say anything to anyone. But the time may come when we'll need you to tell the truth about what you know. So, please think about it, and if you remember anything that might be significant, I want you to reach

DEAD WINNER

out to Mr. Lexington here. After you leave, anything you say about the matter should be in the presence of our lawyers, so it is protected by attorney-client privilege. Do you understand?"

"Yes. I get it," Breonna said tersely.

Buster, still standing behind her chair, reached out and placed his large hand on her right shoulder. Breonna's judo training kicked in instantly and instinctively. She leaned left as her left hand shot up and grabbed Buster's wrist. Then she planted both feet on the carpet and pushed backwards with her hips, thrusting the chair's legs into Buster's shins. In the same motion, she stood, bent at the waist, and pulled the off-balance Buster forward by the arm, flipping him over her back. He landed with a thud and a groan at the foot of Jack's desk, cushioned by the plush carpet.

Looking down at Buster's pained face, she couldn't help thinking about her one and only Olympic games. In the summer of 2016, she had marched into the national stadium in Rio with 554 other athletes, all dreaming of gold and glory. Six days later, she and one of her teammates on the judo squad were in the Olympic Village eating fruit and yogurt cups. Two Russian rowers who were finished with their events had smuggled a bottle of vodka into the athletes' cafeteria and were celebrating—or maybe drowning their sorrows. They noticed Breonna and her teammate, Emily, and decided to introduce themselves.

Emily made it clear she and Breonna were not interested in sharing their vodka, not with their judo matches in two days. The Russians, however, persisted. When Breonna and Emily left the café, the Russians followed. They blocked the path and made the women turn around in order to get away from their unwanted advances. When one of the Russians put his hand on Breonna's shoulder, she reacted and threw the oaf to the sidewalk. Emily took the legs out from under the other guy and pinned his arm

KEVIN G. CHAPMAN

behind his back until a group of Argentinians came by and broke up the "fight."

When the Olympic security force arrived, they refused to take the Russians into custody. When the Russian delegation filed a complaint against Breonna and Emily, the investigation proved "inconclusive," since nobody ever took a blood alcohol level from the Russians and there were no witnesses. The ordeal left both Breonna and Emily emotionally drained. They both lost their first two matches and flew home before the closing ceremonies. It was her one and only Olympics.

Breonna towered over the stunned head of security. "Sorry," she said insincerely. "I don't like it when men touch me."

Buster struggled to a sitting position while Oscar and Jack exchanged a glance of admiration and an amused smile at their ex-cop's embarrassment. Before Buster could regain his feet, Jack told Breonna she could go. "Think about what I said."

Breonna strode to the door without looking back and exited into the secretarial foyer.

"What happened in there?" Gwen asked.

"I'm not allowed to say without consulting the firm's lawyers," Breonna replied with a twinkle in her eye.

In the elevator, she allowed herself to relax, realizing how tense she had been. She was pleased that she had thrown Buster so easily, but knew he was caught by surprise. She had made a dangerous enemy, but it felt worth it.

Chapter 25 – An Unexpected Discovery

STEVE BERKOWITZ EXPECTED the medical examiner to confirm that a self-inflicted gunshot killed Tom Williams. He had already written most of his final report to Captain Sullivan closing the case. It was marked "draft" pending the M.E.'s report and a review of the financial records, for which a subpoena had been issued the day before. Unless something changed, the case was history.

At four thirty, he noticed an email from Nicole, the Assistant M.E., whom he knew had been working on the Williams autopsy. When he clicked, he expected to see a copy of the autopsy report. Instead, he was surprised to see a message asking Steve to call. He frowned and looked up the number on his cell phone.

"Thanks for calling, Steve," Nicole said moments later. "I didn't want to send you the report without an explanation."

"Was there something suspicious about the gunshot?" Steve was puzzled and worried; his closed case suddenly had some life.

"Not really. Everything about the shot is consistent with it being self-inflicted. Of course, it's not impossible for someone to stage it, to place a gun in the victim's hand, hold it up to his mouth, and pull the trigger, but I found nothing to support that scenario. So, I think we have to go with self-inflicted unless your investigation turns up something else."

KEVIN G. CHAPMAN

Steve walked toward George Mason's desk across the bullpen while still on the call. "OK, that's what we expected. So, why did you want me to call?"

"It wasn't the gunshot," Nicole said, "it was the cancer."

"Huh?" Steve said loudly, drawing George's attention. His partner, only a few feet away, raised his head from a stack of paperwork.

"The preliminary toxicology came back this morning and it showed some unusual levels. I went back to examine the body a little more closely and it turns out the guy had cancer of the pancreas. Pretty far advanced."

"What does that mean?" Steve asked.

"It was probably terminal. The cancer was very far along. Pancreatic cancer can do that. It doesn't cause a lot of symptoms in the early stages. By the time it manifests itself, it's often too late to treat. I'll have to get an opinion from an oncologist to be sure, but I'd say he didn't have long to live, and he was looking at a nasty few months with a lot of pain and anguish for his family. I'm not surprised he would have decided to cash in his chips early."

"OK. Thanks," Steve said. "I appreciate the explanation. Please send over the report so I can put it in the file. I think we're about done here."

"I agree," Nicole said. "I'll send it over."

George saw Steve end his call. "What's up?"

"Turns out, not much. Our suicide checks out. The M.E. even got us a motive. Turns out he had advanced stage pancreatic cancer. So I think we're about done."

George frowned. "That's weird."

"What?"

"Well, I just got Williams' account statement from Northrup Investments. He worked for Northrup, right?"

DEAD WINNER

"Yeah."

"So, why would he withdraw most of the money from his account the same day he killed himself?"

"What the fuck? How much?" Steve dropped into the chair next to George's desk.

"Two hundred thousand bucks."

"Do we know where it went?"

"Not yet. We'll need to do some research. Maybe he was trying to hide his assets from the tax man?"

"I'm not sure how that makes sense. I'm no lawyer, but I'm pretty sure the surviving spouse doesn't pay any inheritance tax. Wouldn't he want his widow to get the money?"

George rocked back in his desk chair. "Yeah. And speaking of the widow, don't you think it's a little odd that she didn't tell us about the guy's cancer? She had to know, right? Who's she trying to protect?"

"Well, all this seems inconsistent with the wife killing her husband, eh?"

George let out a sigh. "Yeah. But it means there's somebody else who may have had a few hundred thousand reasons. And it means the widow is lying to us."

"Shit," Steve exclaimed. He could feel his easy case closure slipping away.

Chapter 26 – Anchors Away

ONICA EXPLAINED ABOUT THE BOAT. The longer Rory listened, the more he agreed it made sense that Tom would have hidden the ticket there.

As Monica told the story, Tom had an uncle named Bruce, who was married to Tom's father's sister. Bruce owned a 45-foot sailboat. Three months earlier, Uncle Bruce sold his house on Long Island and moved to Palm Desert, California. Naturally, he needed to get rid of the boat, and when he mentioned it to his nephew, Tom offered to take the boat so he could use it during the summer months. The plan was for Tom to then sell it and send Uncle Bruce the proceeds. Tom rented a slip in the lower Manhattan yacht marina for an exorbitant monthly fee on a six-month lease. The up-front marina fees had put a big dent in their investment savings account, but Tom said it would pay off in the long run.

Tom took the boat out in New York harbor a grand total of six times, three with Monica and several other passengers and three times with his clients but without his wife. While the frequency of sailings would not seem to justify the expenses, Tom invited clients to spend time on the boat while it was moored in the marina. This had proven to be a much more popular activity than actually taking the craft out on the water, which took work and skill.

When Tom's first client asked if he could use the boat for some personal business, Tom was happy to get extra use from his

DEAD WINNER

investment. Within a month, all of what he referred to as his "A-list" clients had a security pass to gain access to the docks and a key to the locked sleeping quarters on board the *Couples Therapy*. It had made Tom even more popular.

Monica had wondered why Tom rented the slip in the name of Uncle Bruce and listed the contact address as Uncle Bruce's now-sold Long Island house. Once he started pimping out the boat, she understood. Nobody at Northrup Investments knew about the boat, except for Breonna, who was the alternate contact person that marina security could call to verify the bona fides of someone seeking access to the love-yacht.

When she finished the explanation, Monica smiled excitedly. "If Tom was in a rush and couldn't get to the safe deposit box, he would have gone to the boat."

Rory nodded, but then asked the obvious question. "Why did you just now think about the boat?"

Monica fixed him with a reprobative stare. "Because we found the safe deposit box key and that was such an obvious place. Since then, we've been a little preoccupied."

Rory nodded and hung his head. "Oh, Jeez. I'm sorry. I'm more stressed than I've ever been. I didn't mean—"

"It's OK, Rory. I get it. I wish I had thought of the boat sooner. But now that I have, don't you think we should check it out?"

* * *

The clouds on the western horizon blazed orange and pink when they reached the security booth at the marina. Monica, who had changed into a pair of white linen pants and a white halter-style top with blue trim, swiped a plastic card and waved at the guard as the turnstile opened. She guided Rory by the hand down a sloping ramp to the floating dock, past yachts of varying sizes. Rory's best attempt at deck attire was a polo shirt, light gray slacks, and sneakers. Several of the floating residents of the marina were so large that they sported tiny two-passenger helicopters perched on their prows. Lights peeked out from water-level windows on a few and a party was loudly underway on a huge floating black bullet, but most of the opulent toys were dark.

Soft lights strung along wires ten feet off the ground all along the dock illuminated their path and cast a pale glow onto the placid water inside the artificial harbor. Monica turned down a small spur dock, then turned left and climbed a narrow metal gangplank to the deck of one of the smaller marina residents. The deck lights allowed Rory to see *Couples Therapy* painted in script letters just above the water line. He carefully followed Monica to the deck, holding onto a thin steel cord and pulling himself up the last step.

Monica switched on deck lights, including a string of bulbs running from stem to stern and another up the main mast. Rory scrutinized what he could see of the craft, impressed since he had never been on such a formidable private boat. But he could also see telltale signs of wear and age. Pits and gouges speckled the teak wood trim, puddles of dark stains marred the deck, and a dull film clung to what should have been shining chrome. The *Couples Therapy* was not in the same league as most of the other yachts in the marina, but nevertheless was a pearl befitting the wealthiest members of New York society. Rory thought Tom's actual income did not rise to the yacht-owning strata, but he had no idea how much cash he had been reeling in as a player in the Northrup Investments embezzlement scheme.

"This way," Monica called out before disappearing down a large hatch at the stern into the interior of the floating condo.

DEAD WINNER

Rory followed, carefully navigating the narrow wooden stairway into the belly of the *Couples Therapy*. In the hours since his emergency room visit, his nose had stopped throbbing. With the help of the pain meds, he was feeling better. He was also no longer actively bleeding.

Lights snapped on when Rory reached the bottom step, illuminating the well-appointed interior space. In front of him, a tiny kitchen lined both sides, which then billowed out into seating areas, including a bar and a table that Rory assumed could be folded down. He suspected the padded sofas on either side could be pulled out into beds. Monica opened a door at the far end, which led to the master suite. He hurried to catch up.

"Do you have any idea where Tom might have hidden the ticket?"

Monica shrugged. "Not specifically. There are a few places I want to check, but I'm not sure. You should start checking the cupboards in the kitchen. The light switch is on the right-hand side inside the door."

Rory agreed and retreated to the open area. The space had a low ceiling but was surprisingly roomy. He opened all the drawers and cabinets. Under one of the sofas, he found compartments with life vests and also a stash of shorts, swimming trunks, towels, and sunscreen. He found no envelopes or containers housing their prize. He even pulled out the hidden mattresses, but found nothing but crisply made sheets and blankets.

When he joined Monica in the master suite, she was on her hands and knees, stretching her arm to reach under a dresser. Rory stared from the threshold. "Can you come shine a light here for me?" she called out, hearing him walk in. Rory used his cell phone's flashlight to illuminate the space, but there was no ticket, nor any receptacle that could be hiding one.

149

KEVIN G. CHAPMAN

"I gather you haven't found it?" Rory muttered. "There was nothing in the kitchen or the common area."

Monica leaned back into a sitting position with her back against the dresser and slapped an open palm against the polished wood floor. "Damn! I was so sure."

"Let's not give up easily. Are there places on the deck he might have chosen?"

A pouting and dejected face replied, "I doubt it, since it's not locked up there, but I suppose it's possible." She struggled to her feet, prompting Rory to offer his arm, which Monica gratefully accepted. He followed her back up the tiny stairs to the deck, admiring her balance as well as the curve of her bottom. She directed him to check the bridge, including the mini-fridge and pantry cupboards, while she checked the storage compartments along the side deck.

Rory found the fridge and crouched down, using his phone's flashlight. He was moving around small cans of soda and mixers when he heard a shriek, followed by the sickening sound of a splash.

"Monica!" Rory dashed away from the fridge. "Monica!" He leapt the two stairs leading down to the main deck and rounded the corner, but saw no sign of her. "Monica!"

Then he heard another splash, softer than the first, next to him on the dock side. He grabbed a rigging rope for balance and leaned over the side. In the semi-darkness, in the small space between the boat and the dock, the water was frothing. He saw a flash of white. "Monica!"

A large balloon-style float, red on top and white on the bottom, bobbed in the murky water, acting as a buffer between the boat and the dock. The marina was calm, causing little motion for the moored craft, but Rory could feel a drift as his weight on the edge of the boat tilted it ever so slightly. The

DEAD WINNER

surface of the dock was three feet above the water, making it difficult to reach from the river. Rory could clearly make out Monica's head. She was unsuccessfully struggling to reach the dock. There was no ladder.

"I'm coming, Monica! Hold on!" Rory sprinted to the gangplank, nearly losing his balance as he rushed down. The thin steel cord cut into his palm when he teetered and nearly fell in himself. A lot of help he would be to Monica if he joined her in the dark water. He totally forgot about any remaining pain in his nose.

Making the dock, he glanced around for something Monica could grab onto so she could climb up. He immediately scolded himself for not thinking to bring a life ring or a rope or pole from the boat. He had been in too much of a hurry. Then he saw the mooring rope securing the *Couples Therapy* to the dock. It had a long length of slack coiled on the dock's planking. He grabbed the end and knelt down above where Monica was treading water. "Here. Catch this." He tossed the rope onto the surface of the river with a splat. Monica grabbed on as Rory held the line taught. He pulled with all his strength, lifting Monica and her soaked clothes until she was able to grab the edge of the dock. He then took her hand and hoisted her the rest of the way until she flopped like a freshly caught salmon onto the wooden slats.

Rory turned her onto her back and prepared to administer mouth-to-mouth resuscitation, but Monica coughed, opened her eyes, and waved him away. Within a minute, she was sitting up. "Rory—You saved me."

Rory pulled her to her feet and guided her in the direction of the gangway. "What happened?"

"I must have slipped. It's what I get for wearing heels on the deck. I lost my balance and fell. I hung onto the rail wire, but

KEVIN G. CHAPMAN

couldn't climb back up. Then I lost my grip and went into the water."

"Why didn't you call out as soon as you slipped?"

Monica tilted her head into Rory's shoulder. He squeezed her gently as they carefully navigated up the gangway in tandem. When they reached the deck again and Monica sat on a cushioned bench, she said, "I guess I thought I could pull myself back up. Then I lost my grip so fast . . ."

"It's alright," Rory soothed. "I'm glad you didn't hit your head on the dock. My God, you could have drowned."

"I know," she buried her face against Rory's chest.

"Let's get you downstairs and into some dry clothes." Rory held out a hand, which Monica gladly took.

Ten minutes later, Monica emerged from the bathroom in the master suite wearing a white terrycloth robe, pulled tightly around her neck. A powder blue towel sat as a turban on her head, giving her the appearance of being taller. She patted the bed, inviting Rory to come join her. Instead, he knelt on the floor and took her hand.

"I'm so glad you're not hurt. No matter what happens from here, I want to protect you and help you . . . if you'll let me."

Her hand found the side of Rory's face, a finger tracing a line to the edge of his mouth. He kissed the finger tenderly. "I'm so lucky to have found you."

"Not lucky enough to find that damned ticket."

"I'm not even thinking about that now. I just want all this to be over. I'm not sure I can take it anymore."

Rory scuttled onto the bed and put an arm around her shoulder. "Don't say that. You're much stronger than you give yourself credit for. You've been much more pulled together than most of my clients going through the death of a spouse. You're handling it. It's not easy."

DEAD WINNER

"Rory, I wish I'd found you years ago." In one motion, she slid her left arm around his neck and kissed him, long and lingering. Her fingers massaged the base of his hairline. She leaned back and fell to the bed, dragging Rory backwards with her.

With both arms around his neck, Monica rolled a half-turn, finishing with Rory under her. She continued to kiss him hungrily, holding his head in her hands and purring softly. When she briefly pulled back, Rory caught his breath, looking at Monica's face in the soft lights of the headboard. The towel had fallen from her hair, leaving her blonde locks wild and damp, falling around her shoulders in thin tendrils. Monica opened her robe and threw it off. It fell away around their legs, leaving Monica's naked body fully displayed for him.

"I must be dreaming," he whispered. His hands caressed the damp skin of her back, sliding upwards. She pulled his shirt out of his slacks and helped him get it over his head. She worked slowly. He drank in the view of her breasts, her smooth belly, her shoulders. He found her eyes, which gazed into his, bringing a mischievous smile to her lips. Moments later, she unbuckled his belt, unzipped him, and began wriggling his pants out from under his prone butt. She snagged his undershorts on the way and in moments he was fully naked and she was perched atop him again, pressing her hips into his fully aroused groin.

"Are you sure?" he asked, knowing after the night before that she was not acting rashly, nor was she drunk. He had decided to assign another lawyer to handle the trust so that Monica would not be his client, although he had not yet formally executed the switch. But it was essentially done. He certainly wasn't going to let that technicality hold him back at this point.

His fingers found her nipples. She threw her head back and moaned, pressing her palms into his chest. Rory apologized in

KEVIN G. CHAPMAN

embarrassment when he prematurely ejaculated at the first touch of her smooth fingers. She responded by kissing him softly, then taking her time nursing him back to health. She guided him through their lovemaking, prompting caresses in her most sensitive places and encouraging exploration with his mouth before engulfing him in urgent intercourse.

They lay exhausted on top of satin sheets, Monica's head resting on his chest, her manicured fingernail tracing circles in his light hairs. "Thank you," she whispered.

"Oh, no. Thank *you!*" he responded quietly. "You have no idea how wonderful that was for me."

She giggled sweetly. "I have a pretty good idea about how amazing it was for me, though."

"You don't have to flatter me. I know I'm inexperienced at this. I'm glad you helped me."

"C'mon, Rory. You must have had tons of women chasing after you. You're a successful lawyer, and you're so sweet. You're a great catch. Why didn't you ever settle down and get married?"

Rory pulled her against him with the arm he had draped around her shoulders. "There were a few women. A few said they wanted to get serious."

"So, what was wrong with them?" Monica propped herself up on an elbow.

"They weren't you." Rory allowed his head to sink into the pillow and pulled Monica's back onto his chest.

Rory felt the gentle motion of their floating bedroom. He lay awake, admiring the smooth skin of Monica's leg, draped over his, and the delicate rose tattoo above her ankle. It didn't seem possible that, less than a week earlier, she was completely absent from his life. As he felt the regular pattern of her breathing, matching the swaying of the *Couples Therapy,* he couldn't imagine his future without her.

154

Chapter 27 – Edging Toward Disaster

BUSTER WAS CONFUSED. Jack Northrup should have been happy that Buster's guys—well, the Gallata guys— had retrieved the envelope full of incriminating evidence from Tom Williams' safe deposit box. His surveillance had tipped them off about the key, then the guys under his direction had tailed them to the bank and extracted the material, apparently without drawing any attention. It had been as clean an operation as Buster could have imagined. And yet, the boss was somehow pissed off.

"You were supposed to have that data locked down!" Jack stalked around his office holding his coffee in a steel vacuum cup with the company's logo emblazoned in red ink on both sides. Oscar Lexington, the COO, and Douglas Melton, the general counsel, sat passively as Jack continued. "How the fuck did he get those documents out of here and into a safe box under your nose?"

Buster faced down the CEO from his chair. He thought about standing up, since Northrup was on his feet, but he figured that would be viewed as an aggressive move. "C'mon, Jack. You know as well as I do that making a copy of a printout is something you can't intercept. We trust our guys, and if they want to look at a sheet on a piece of paper instead of their screen, it's not unusual. We're not tracking in real time whenever a record from a hot account gets printed. It's not possible, unless you want me to hire a personal spy to watch every move every insider makes every day. Is that what you want?"

"Hell, no!" Northrup bellowed.

"So we contained it as much as we could. You trusted Tom. We always knew that if somebody on the inside decided to drop a dime on the operation, we'd all be screwed."

Northrup looked around the room. Nobody was contradicting Buster, or offering Jack any help. "So, how badly are we compromised? Is this a Krakatoa event?"

Douglas Melton removed his spectacles and polished his lenses with a soft cloth he had removed from his jacket pocket. "Now, Jack, let's not jump the gun here. Tom took those documents and locked them away, along with the video explaining what they all meant. He was obviously setting up that stash to be divulged at some specific time—either when he died, or upon some other event. The feds haven't yet burst through our doors with a warrant, so I think it's safe to assume that our boy did not already spill the beans. Why would he have those documents locked up if he had another copy somewhere else, eh?"

Buster picked up on the assist he was getting. Krakatoa was a code word. Northrup would send it out to all the insiders if the operation was blown. Everyone would initiate a plan to destroy all evidence of the embezzlement, inject money back into the accounts from which funds had been appropriated, and substitute in revised account statements that would mask the operation and make it difficult for the authorities to uncover the fraud. Everyone involved would be cut off from the spigot of cash that had been flowing for nearly six years. Nobody wanted to blow it up.

156

DEAD WINNER

"Exactly. I think we got all the evidence. If he was going to send them to the feds, he would have done it. Instead, he gave a key to his wife. I'm telling you she and her dweeb lawyer didn't know what was going to be in that box. I think they expected something else. We got the evidence. I think we're safe."

"I'm comforted by your confidence, Buster," Northrup's sarcasm was unmasked. "I'd prefer some more definite assurances. What if Tom's wife knows? What if Tom had loose lips? I assume they looked at the documents before you nabbed them back, so now she and her lawyer know the score. She might think we took out old Tom because he was going to turn into a rat on us. So now she's probably pissed off enough to go to the feds herself."

"We didn't kill Tom," Buster said calmly.

"So you told me. I suppose I have to believe you. So, what? He killed himself? Why would he do that? He was hoarding those documents, probably as an insurance policy. Why would he eat his gun? I don't buy it. I'm thinking somebody did it for him. Hell, it could have been his little lady. You told me Tom was fucking around on her, right?"

Nobody in the room responded.

"Right. So he probably was. Now the scorned widow knows, if she didn't already, and she has every incentive to screw us over. Do we know where she is?"

"Yeah," Buster replied, adjusting his posture and pulling out his phone. After consulting a text message, he advised the group that Monica and her lawyer, Rory McEntyre, were at the Battery Park marina. Buster's best guess was that the lawyer owned a boat, but his people were checking. "I have a guy on her."

"What about Tom's laptop? What are the chances there's evidence on it she could still give the feds?"

KEVIN G. CHAPMAN

Buster shrugged. "It's possible. The laptop is inside the lawyer's apartment. I have someone checking out the building to see if we can get in there. We're working on it. If the lawyer, or the wife, takes the laptop out of the building, we'll try to grab it."

"Try?"

"We'll get it," Buster returned the phone to his pocket. "If they leave it in that apartment, we'll get inside and take it. One way or the other, that loose end will get wrapped up. Meanwhile, we got the evidence he left behind, which was in a Goddamned safe deposit box. Give me a little credit."

"Fine," Northrup drained the last of his coffee and sat down behind his desk. This was normally a signal that the meeting was over. "Keep me informed. I want an update before the end of the day."

The assembled men pushed up from their chairs and moved toward the door.

Before Buster got far, Northrup said, "Buster, a quick word, please." As the other two men filed out of the office, Buster approached the desk, where Jack spoke softly. "Once you have Tom's laptop, I would like the widow Williams to disappear. I don't want her to be a witness. She saw what was in that box, and she probably read that note Tom left for her. That's too much risk. If her lawyer friend gets in the way again, have our friends show them both the bottom of the river."

Chapter 28 – Following the Money

STEVE BERKOWITZ'S DETECTIVE colleagues often told him to keep it simple. The most obvious suspect was often the guilty party. And when all else failed, follow the money. In the case of Tom Williams, there was a lot of money. The problem was, none of it seemed to lead anywhere.

By the end of the day Wednesday, the detectives had established that the funds from Tom's Northrup Investments account had been transferred offshore. The detectives had requested a subpoena for the receiving Bermuda bank, but the red tape connected to issuing a subpoena to a foreign jurisdiction meant they would not get any records for several days. Steve and George assumed that, if the transfer was indicative of criminal behavior, then the criminals were probably smart enough to use the Bermuda bank as a conduit and move the money out and into some other hard-to-trace location. Or, the hypothetical criminals could withdraw the money via a check in Bermuda, in which case it would be even harder to trace. But as their senior colleague, Mike Stoneman, liked to say, you could never overestimate how stupid a criminal could be.

"If it were me," George said, "I'd use the money to buy crypto currency like Bitcoins. Then it would be totally untraceable."

"It's Bitcoin," Steve corrected.

"What is?"

KEVIN G. CHAPMAN

"The crypto. It's not Bitcoins. No 's'. Any amount of money is just Bitcoin."

"Like you know shit about crypto," George scoffed.

"Yeah, well, apparently more than you."

They huddled in the tiny corner conference room off the bullpen. Printed copies of bank records, phone and text message records, tax returns, credit card statements, and a few other assorted documents were strewn all around the surface of the aged wooden table as they tried to make sense of Tom Williams' financial life.

George gave a summary of their findings when homicide detective Mike Stoneman stopped by to ask how the case was progressing "Tom Williams rented a posh apartment in a swanky building called the Winchester Tower. Tom's wife, Monica, had a much more modest job than her high-flying financial tycoon husband. She worked as a graphic artist for a Madison Avenue advertising firm for a salary less than a quarter of Tom's base pay. Tom was clearly the main breadwinner. He did have a life insurance policy, which would pay off even if he killed himself, but his earnings potential over the next thirty years was tons more than a one-time payment. If the wife had been looking for an exit from the marriage, that might have been a motive, but nothing we've uncovered so far suggests any trouble in paradise."

"The wife had some pretty hefty credit card bills," Steve observed, scanning several sheets in front of him. "Bloomingdales, Saks, high-end restaurants, Gucci . . . she was taking advantage of the cash flow. And they took some nice vacations. There are tickets on the credit card to Nassau, Bermuda, Cancun, and Hawaii. Jetsetters, it seems."

"Bermuda?" George raised one eyebrow.

"I noticed." Steve reached out to grab the investment account report, showing the funds transfer to the Butterfields

160

DEAD WINNER

bank of Bermuda. "Of course, it could be a coincidence. Bermuda is a popular destination."

"It is. But I don't like coincidences. I don't believe in them."

"So, what? The wife set up an account at a bank in Bermuda when they were on vacation, because she was planning on murdering her husband? She then staged it to look like a suicide, even when it would have been much easier to make it look like a robbery? Then, she took the money out of their joint investment account, even though the money would belong to her as the surviving spouse if she just left it alone? That really makes it look like a robbery and becomes a million times more suspicious."

"Maybe she was worried about losing the money if she got caught?" George meekly offered.

"If she got caught, she'd be in prison. Losing her dough would be the least of her problems. It don't wash."

"I suppose you're right. She's got no motive. Plus, she's got a pretty great alibi. Did we get the video from the nursing home yet?"

Steve shook his head. "Nah. Not yet. If she was a serious suspect I'd send a uniform out to look at the video in person. Right now we're waiting for them to upload it and send us a link, but they confirmed there's a record of her visiting her mother Monday afternoon. The surveillance cameras in the place are pretty obvious. Then, she says she took the Long Island Railroad back to Penn Station, where they have cameras that we haven't looked at. The doorman confirms that Tom Williams arrived home that afternoon earlier than normal. If the wife killed him, she had to get into the apartment without the doormen seeing her, kill him when he arrived home, then slip out again unseen, set up her alibi, come back again at nine o'clock, and pretend to find the body. It also means that she intentionally got his blood all over herself and planted her prints on the gun on purpose to

161

KEVIN G. CHAPMAN

cover up any that might have been there from earlier in the day. If she did all that, then she deserves to get away with it."

They all exchanged a somber laugh. Stoneman left and George went to get a cup of coffee from the ancient black-and-chrome heating urn sitting on a rickety credenza in the corner. "If she has an explanation for how she could have not known that her husband had terminal cancer, then she's in the clear. But until then, I still say it's a big black hole in her story."

"I agree. Did you call her lawyer again?"

"Yeah. He hasn't returned my calls. You think he's avoiding us?"

"Maybe. She isn't returning our calls and texts either. Let's give her one more day and if she doesn't come in on her own, we'll send some uniforms out to track her down."

"Fine. Sully's going to want to know why we haven't closed this one out."

Steve tossed a stack of paper into a cardboard box in the middle of the table. "I know. There's something off here. We need to talk to Monica Williams again and get a few answers. Maybe it will all make sense. Maybe not. All I know is that we're not done yet."

Chapter 29 – Getting the Call

ON THURSDAY, Rory had some obligations at the office from which he could not beg off. After untangling on the boat, Monica opted to shower back in Rory's marble-tiled master bathroom rather than shoe-horn herself into the miniscule onboard unit. Rory called dibs on the first shower. The brown and yellow blotches on his face from the day before had blossomed into deep purple. He looked like he had gone fifteen rounds with a heavyweight champ, but he felt better. Monica said the swelling was down quite a bit.

Rory dressed and rushed out, already late. He spent his commute coming up with a plausible story to tell. Monica was luxuriating under the rain-barrel shower head when he closed and locked the apartment door.

He spent an hour meeting with three siblings who haggled over the distribution of their grandfather's estate, with their mother serving as referee. Then he had a will signing for a couple who had recently adopted three children and had to change the distribution of the husband's five-hundred-million-dollar fortune. The firm had a strict rule that the lawyer who met with the client and drew up the will had to be there for the signing. It gave the client a sense of continuity and confidence. After the clients left with a copy of the document in their pocket, the original went into the vault. Years later, when death brought the surviving heirs back to the firm, they would not remember who the lawyer was who held their hand during the signing and would

KEVIN G. CHAPMAN

not care. But at the signing, they cared. It made the clients refer their rich friends to the firm.

Back in his office, Rory took four Advil tablets. His face had stopped throbbing, but he figured some meds wouldn't hurt. Everyone had been impressed by the story of how he had taken on two street thugs and protected his client from harm.

Before lunch, he arranged for one of his senior associates to take over the Williams' trust account. He could still keep tabs on it, but as of noon, Monica Williams was no longer his personal client. His assistant brought him a chicken Caesar salad and a Diet Coke while he caught up on email and phone messages.

Near the top of the pile of message slips, he paused on one from Detective George Mason with the message "Call back immediately." He felt his gut clench. There was so much information he had, but couldn't tell the cops because of the attorney-client privilege and his promises to Monica. But it felt wrong withholding information. The more he knew about Tom's involvement in the embezzlement scheme, the more likely it seemed that somebody did kill Tom. The cops probably weren't even looking for the murderer. Why was the detective calling? He put his plastic fork down in his salad bowl and pushed it away.

Before Rory could gin up the nerve to call back Detective Mason, a knock on his door jamb startled him. He looked into the stern face of the firm's senior partner, Harry Packman. He and Michael Fitzsimmons had founded the firm, but Fitzsimmons had retired, leaving Packman as the lone founding partner. Rory's mouth gaped open for a moment as he breathed, his nose still mostly clogged. Packman had never before appeared in Rory's office. As far as he could remember, he had never seen the senior partner on his floor since the big offices were three floors up, where the walls were linen and the coffee was served in fine China.

DEAD WINNER

"Mister McEntyre, I understand you had quite an adventure." The old man smiled his concerned, grandfatherly smile. Rory had heard that Packman could strike fear into subordinates with his signature scowl. Now, his presence was comforting.

"Well, yes, you could certainly say that."

"Looks like you paid the price."

Rory felt himself blushing with embarrassment in the presence of the big boss. "I'd say you should see the other guys, but I don't think I left a scratch on them. I'm afraid I'm not a natural brawler."

Packman stepped into the office and quietly closed the door. He removed his wire-rimmed glasses, looking down at the seated Rory. "Son, it seems to me that you're into something here that's over your head. The past few days you have neglected your clients, missed appointments, and had junior associates covering your work. You want to tell me what's going on?"

Rory shifted uncomfortably under Packman's burrowing stare. "Sir, I know things have been somewhat muddled this week. I've been working with a new client who needed some . . . special attention. I'm sure things will settle down and I'll be back to my usual steady self."

"Who is the client?"

It was a reasonable question, and despite having an attorney-client privilege regarding Monica's secrets, she and Tom were technically clients of the firm, not Rory's personal charges. Rory couldn't think of a reason to refuse to answer, and doing so would be a risky career move. "Tom and Monica Williams. They're setting up a trust and wills. They've had a personal crisis, and they're both old friends of mine from Columbia Law. I had to help." In New York City, the suicide of an

KEVIN G. CHAPMAN

investment manager was not big news. Packman would not have heard about it. At least, that was what Rory was hoping.

"Well, make sure you take care of *all* your clients, Mister McEntyre." Packman turned and left without another word or a glance back toward Rory.

After exhaling and trying to get his pulse to steady, Rory returned to the message slip from Detective Mason. A glance at the clock confirmed that he was going to miss his weekly book club meeting. The discussion of Lyndon Johnson's biography would have to go on without him. He suddenly had more important things on his plate.

He took three deep breaths, then dialed, slipping on his headset and rising to walk around the small office while he talked. After being put on hold by a receptionist, Rory eventually heard the policeman's voice say, "Mason."

"Detective Mason, this is Rory McEntyre. You left me a message." Rory could have identified himself as Monica Williams' attorney, but he didn't want to help the detective recognize his name.

"McEntyre? Oh, right. I'm trying to get in touch with your client, Monica Williams. We have a few additional questions we'd like to ask her about her husband's suicide. Can you arrange to have her come to the precinct to meet with us? We're on 94th Street."

Rory wondered what kinds of questions the detective had in mind, and certainly had no intention of trekking to the Upper West Side to provide Monica for questioning. He decided to try an aggressive response. "Detective, I don't want to seem uncooperative, but Monica is having a very hard time dealing with Tom's death. I would prefer not to subject her to questioning by the police, and I have a very busy schedule today. Can this wait until Monday?" Then, he added, "And can you

DEAD WINNER

arrange to come to my office? I can get Monica here, but getting us both uptown could be a problem."

The line was quiet. Rory gazed out his office window. He did not rate a river view but the vista of office towers, including the edge of One World Trade Center, was nevertheless impressive. When Detective Mason next spoke, his tone had changed from casually friendly to annoyed government official. "Look, Mr. McEntyre, I'm trying to take Mrs. Williams' feelings into account here, but this is an active investigation and it can't wait until Monday, or whenever *your* schedule is free. I'd like to avoid having uniformed officers find her and bring her in involuntarily, but if that's what you prefer, it can be arranged."

Rory reached out an arm, steadying himself against a support pillar that ran between his two windows. "Well, um, I understand, Detective, but . . . I'm not sure when I can contact Monica. She has been keeping her cell phone off. As soon as I can reach her, I'll call you back and we can make arrangements." He scolded himself for being so easily intimidated. He was a lawyer. His client had rights. "And, Detective, I have to tell you I have instructed Monica not to answer any questions without me. On her behalf, I must insist that you not question her without her attorney present."

"Fine," Mason grumbled. "Call me as soon as you contact her." Mason hung up, leaving Rory standing next to the window with his heart pounding. He was not a litigator or a criminal defense attorney. He didn't negotiate deals. He was never in high-pressure situations, unless speaking at a convention of other trusts and estates lawyers counted as pressure. His hand was trembling as he replaced the headset on its charging base. What was he going to do? The firm's senior partner had just admonished him not to neglect his other work. He couldn't run out on his afternoon appointments to fetch Monica.

167

KEVIN G. CHAPMAN

He sat at his desk and sent a text, letting Monica know he had spoken to the detective, who wanted her to come in to answer some additional questions. Then he said she should not jump simply because the police called. They could talk over dinner that night about when to answer any more questions. The thought of dinner with Monica calmed his shaky nerves.

* * *

After a busy afternoon at the office, Rory ducked out at the stroke of 5:00, which was quite early by the firm's normal standards but which he figured was justifiable under the circumstances. He was still recovering from his beating. He did a great job showing up and working at all. When he opened his apartment door, his mouth instantly began to water, inhaling the scent of pasta sauce, fresh bread, and garlic.

"Did you order in dinner?" he called out, then rounded the corner and saw that the kitchen was fully engaged. Steam rose in spiraling streams from a large pot bubbling over a high flame. A smaller pot half full of dark red sauce simmered on a neighboring burner, the dome of a meatball peeking up from the molten tomatoes. Monica stood in front of the stove, a floral apron covering her front and a wooden spoon stained with sauce in her left hand.

"Surprise!" she brightly responded. "I decided to try cooking for us. I hope you don't mind me making a mess."

Rory broke into a huge grin. "Heavens no! I'm impressed, and pleased. I'll break out a good bottle of wine to go with your wonderful sauce."

"I don't guarantee how wonderful it is."

"Nonsense. I can tell by the aroma. I can't wait to dig in." He gave her a quick kiss, as if coming home to her was a perfectly

DEAD WINNER

normal event. He then opened the door of a cabinet high over the refrigerator, where a rack of wine bottles greeted him. He reached for a bottle bearing the image of curved stitching, like on a baseball. The bottle bore the block letters "GTS" on the label. A minute later, the cork was out and two large wine glasses sat on the table waiting for a pre-dinner toast. Monica served the pasta and sliced the fresh bread. It was an instant loaf from the supermarket, but Rory said it smelled amazing.

Rory extolled the virtue of Monica's sauce while they lingered over the food and wine. Both avoided any discussion of the call from the police, or the still-missing lottery ticket. Eventually, however, the elephants in the room could not be ignored. Pushing his clean plate away and sighing, Rory poured the last of the bottle of cabernet into his glass and leaned back in his contoured wooden chair. "Have you given any thought to the call I got from the police?"

Monica, who had looked contented and calm, morphed into the face of anxiety. "Do I really have to?"

"I don't think they can force you. You do have the right to remain silent. But, if you refuse to talk to them, it may cause them to think you're hiding something. I mean, besides the lottery ticket, and the embezzlement."

Monica flashed a disapproving glare, but then softened. "Yes, well, except for those." She put down her now-empty wine glass and wandered toward the living room.

Rory dutifully began clearing the dishes. He could not see Monica from his position in the kitchen. He heard the television and recognized the cadence of the local evening news.

"This is Ali Bauman, reporting from the New York State Lottery Commission headquarters in Manhattan. I just attended a press conference where Mrs. Barbara Harrison was announced as the holder of the third of five winning tickets from the recent

KEVIN G. CHAPMAN

three hundred-million-dollar Mega Millions jackpot. Mrs. Harrison, a resident of Fort Lee, New Jersey, works in lower Manhattan and purchased her ticket on her way to work on a whim. We should all be so lucky. Coming up next, Otis Livingston has a report live from the New York Jets training camp, where controversial quarterback Jimmy Rydell has been up to some new tricks."

Rory called out loudly, "I'm thinking maybe tomorrow afternoon would be a good time for you to talk with the detective. Late on a Friday seems likely to keep it short and sweet. What do you think?"

When Monica didn't respond, Rory loaded the last plate into the dishwasher and stepped around the corner. Monica was gazing out the window. The low sun shone in Rory's eyes, silhouetting Monica's form. Her right hand was held to her ear, along with her cell phone. When she turned her head, she caught Rory in her peripheral vision, causing her to spin all the way round. The concern etched on her face made Rory rush toward her. She held out an open palm to stop him.

"How do I know this is for real?" she asked whoever was on the other end of the call.

Rory silently mouthed the words, "Who is it?" but received only a hurried wave of Monica's hand as she turned away.

"Are you serious?" Monica turned and rushed toward a glass table next to the sofa, where she dug into her purse while holding the phone against her ear with her shoulder. She extracted a pen and a scrap of paper and scribbled as Rory watched in puzzlement. "Yes . . . Yes . . . I have it, but I'm going to need— . . .Alright. . . Yes." Monica suddenly held the phone away and stared at it, then twirled to stare at Rory, her eyes wide.

"What was that?"

DEAD WINNER

Monica set the phone down in her purse and plopped onto the adjoining sofa. "I—I'm not sure I believe it, but that call was from some guy who says he has our lottery ticket."

"That's great!" Rory burst out, then checked himself. Monica did not seem happy about the news. "So, why do you look like your dog died?"

"Because . . . he's holding it for ransom."

Chapter 30 – Ransom?

RORY DID NOT IMMEDIATELY PROCESS Monica's statement. "You mean he wants a reward?"

"Ha!" Monica spat out a derisive laugh. "You could say that. He says he has the ticket and he'll burn it unless we pay him three million dollars."

"Seriously?"

"That's exactly what I said!" Monica paced around the sofa, flailing her arms as she spoke. "More specifically, he wants one hundred thousand in cash and three million in Bitcoin. Aside from the fact that I have no way to get three million dollars, you know what this means?"

Rory paused, realizing that how he phrased his response mattered. "It means that the guy who has the ticket got it from Tom . . . before he died. And it means that he might have killed Tom."

"What do you mean, *might?*" Monica shot back, now angry with Rory.

"Well, I mean, it's still possible that—" he broke off the point he was going to make when he saw Monica's agonized expression. "You're most likely right. He must have forced Tom to give up the ticket, and forced him to reveal the password to his investment account, and then—" He didn't need to finish the sentence.

All the calmness of the pasta dinner had evaporated. "Oh, this is a nightmare."

DEAD WINNER

"Don't worry. We'll figure it out. Maybe now it's time to bring in the police."

Monica slumped onto the plush sofa. "Oh, Rory, I don't know. What would we tell them?"

"We'd tell them there is a criminal on the loose who probably murdered Tom and he has the lottery ticket . . . that you didn't tell them about . . . and that same person probably stole the money from Tom's investment account . . . that you also didn't tell them . . . about." Rory lost enthusiasm for the argument the deeper he dug the hole. "Well, I can see how that would create some issues."

"Besides," Monica scooted across the sofa's leather, making more room for Rory to sit, "this isn't a human hostage, it's a slip of paper. If this guy gets at all nervous, all he has to do is light it on fire and there's no evidence. We won't have any proof the person is the one who just called me. The ticket can't testify. And we'll lose out on the money. But it hardly matters. I don't have the ransom, and there's no way I can get it. The bastard said he knows he can't cash in the ticket, but he's happy to destroy it if I don't come through with the money. It's hopeless."

Rory was quiet. "If I were this guy, I'd probably do the same thing. He can't come forward to claim the money without explaining where he got the ticket. He knows you would contest its ownership, and as far as he knows the cops would be there to arrest him for killing Tom. If it's a sixty-million-dollar ticket, then three million is only five percent, before taxes. It would make sense to pay the ransom."

"Sure, if I had three million dollars in Bitcoin." Monica's sarcasm and anger were unmasked.

"You don't need to have Bitcoin. You can get Bitcoin if you have the funds."

"Do you own any Bitcoin?"

KEVIN G. CHAPMAN

"Sure. A little bit. I got into it on the early side. I don't have much in it, only a few hundred thousand."

"That sounds like a lot to me."

Rory waved a hand in the air dismissively. "It's nothing. I bought ten Bitcoin at one thousand. Now they're worth twenty times that. I got lucky. But the process is easy. You just have to set up a wallet and go to an exchange and buy them."

Monica leaned over, landing her head on Rory's lap. "This is unreal."

"What did the guy say, exactly?" Rory stroked her hair. "I saw you writing something down, what was that?"

"Just the amounts. One hundred thousand in cash and three million in Bitcoin. He said he would call again tomorrow to tell me where and when to meet to make the exchange. He said I had to come alone, like I'm going to show up by myself with that kind of money and hand it over. How would I even know he was giving me the real lottery ticket?"

"You would have to get the ticket first and examine it before confirming the transaction. The real ticket has Tom's initials on it, remember."

Monica shifted her weight and pulled her legs up onto the sofa. "What do you mean by confirming the transaction?"

"There are a bunch of different ways to transfer Bitcoin. One way is to use a code number. You can also do it with a QR code, so it's one image the other party scans with a smart phone. You can also transfer the funds into an escrow account that holds the Bitcoin until the sending party confirms it with a second instruction. That works like the kind of two-factor verification Tom had on his investment account. I would use that method, if it were me. But at some point you have to trust the other person. Somebody has to have the last action. If you gave him the code before you had the ticket, he could rip it up or throw it in the

DEAD WINNER

sewer or something and you'd be out the money. Or, if he gave you the ticket before you confirm the transaction, you could run and keep the ticket and the money. It would be tricky to make it happen unless you trusted each other, which in this case you obviously don't."

"It doesn't matter." Monica let out a deep sigh.

"What do you mean?"

"I mean I don't have the money, so it's all academic. At least I won't spend my life looking for the missing ticket. Now I know where it went."

"I could front you the money." Rory's words hung in the air.

"What?"

"I mean it." Rory stroked Monica's soft hair as he spoke, building momentum as if afraid to stop in case she interrupted him. "These past few days have been the craziest hours of my entire life, but they have also been the happiest. Since you walked into my office last Friday, all I have thought about is how empty my life has been since you married Tom and I moved to Boston and left you behind. I never told you how I felt about you. I haven't stopped thinking about how my life would have been different if I'd had the balls to fight for you then. Well, damn it, I'm going to fight for you now. I love you, Monica. I always have. I'm not going to let you get away again."

Rory bent down and softly kissed the back of Monica's head. "I don't care if we get the ticket or not. Either way, I'm going to take care of you, if you'll let me. I don't expect you to feel the same way. I know this week has been hell for you. Just give me a chance. You can stay here, with me, or you can go back to your old apartment, or somewhere else. Just, please, let me be in your life."

Rory looked down at the back of Monica's head, wishing he could see her eyes and gauge her reaction. Without any visual

175

KEVIN G. CHAPMAN

encouragement, he pressed forward while he could. "I have money I inherited from my father three years ago. It's socked away in a nice safe bond fund as my safety net. Four million, after I used a million to buy this condo. I haven't needed it. My job is great and I don't spend much. I've always made the safe plays. My father told me I was a loser; that I'd never be a great man because I was afraid to take risks. He pushed me as a kid to play sports I was bad at, to leap off the top of the hill without knowing what was on the other side. He used to call me the cowardly lion—Rory without any roar. Right before he died, he told me he was disappointed in me. He still gave me and my sister the money. I could liquidate three million and turn it into Bitcoin pretty quickly. We could pay off the scumbag who killed Tom and get the ticket. It would be worth it."

Rory could hear the low hum of his dishwasher and the rhythmic pounding of his blood pulsing in his ears. He had made a huge play and spilled more of his heart than he ever intended. He was prepared for the crush of heartbreak when Monica told him that, despite their little fling, she would never want to marry him or even stay with him. When she didn't respond immediately, he removed his hand from her hair and sat back.

Monica gracefully levered herself into a sitting position facing Rory, her legs tucked under her on the sofa. Her eyes glistened. A single tear trickled down her cheek. When she spoke, it was a hoarse whisper. "Rory, that is the most wonderful thing anyone has ever said to me, including Tom." She reached out and grasped Rory's hand.

Rory knew what was coming. The words of encouragement were the preface for the "but" that was bound to follow.

"When I married Tom, I was a different person. Now, I know much better what I truly want from a man. I thought it was Tom, but it wasn't. Tom didn't ever change. I knew who he was when I

176

DEAD WINNER

married him: a hard-driving hustler who would give anything to make money and be successful. He loved thrills and risk more than he loved me. I loved that he was fearless, like a cowboy or a knight of the round table. It excited me for a while, but it wasn't enough. I thought I could change him, but I never had a chance. He was who he was. I came along for the ride.

"What I really wanted was someone to put me first. Someone to rub my feet after a long day and make me tea and curl up with a romantic old movie. Someone to take me on long walks and tell me I'm the most important thing in the world. Tom could never do that. So, I'm starting to think that what I wanted all along was . . . you."

She leaned toward Rory's shocked face, lost her balance as one leg shot out from under her, and fell forward onto him. They laughed for a moment, and then their lips found each other. Rory lost count of how many times they kissed, each more tender than the last. When he felt moisture against his face, he realized that Monica was crying, even while she was kissing him. He pulled back and wiped away the tears.

"It's amazing for you to offer, Rory, but I couldn't let you put up the ransom money. That would be crazy. And like you said, it's dangerous and it might not even work. I'm going to have to let it go. I'll find the money to take care of my mother. It's wonderful that you think you love me, Rory, but it's only been a few days. It takes more than that. I'm so glad you've been here for me and I don't regret making love with you. Maybe I love you, too. I can't think straight. I know I care about you. I always have. I want this—us—to keep going. We don't need sixty million dollars to be happy, do we?"

Rory did not hesitate. "No. I'm happy right now, right here. I don't need anything more than this." He paused. He truly was happier in that moment than he could remember being in his life.

177

KEVIN G. CHAPMAN

But he also knew Monica had loved Tom, the swashbuckling adventurer, the man who made her life exciting. "But you will never get over Tom's death and losing that money if we sit by and do nothing. Maybe we can figure out a way to put the cops on the guy's trail, once we have the ticket. I don't want him to get away with it. Tom was my friend, too, even if we hadn't hung out together since law school. No. I'm not going to take the safe road, for a change. I want to do it. I want to get that ticket. Will you help me?"

Monica leaned into his chest and took two deep breaths. "If you're there with me, then . . . yes."

Chapter 31 – Plugging Leaks

BUSTER TRIED TO FORMULATE a way to put a positive spin on what was generally lackluster news. He had hoped Monica Williams and her lawyer would return to her apartment again, so their surveillance devices could give him some insight into what their targets were planning. More importantly, he wanted to know how much Monica knew about Tom's involvement in the firm's illegal business operations. She probably looked at some of the documents Tom stashed in his safe deposit box, and she probably read the letter he left. He doubted she had watched the video he left on the flash drive. The real question was whether Monica had known about the operation before she opened that box. Did Tom clue her in? Buster had a bad feeling that Tom would not have planned to kill himself without telling his wife about what he had been up to.

His thought process brought him back to the nagging question he couldn't figure out. Why would Tom eat a bullet sandwich? If he was gathering evidence against the firm, intending to turn state's evidence or have his wife claim an SEC bounty, why check out before he dropped the evidence with the feds? It didn't make any sense. Buster might think somebody took Tom out and made it look like a suicide, except the cops didn't seem to be pursuing that possibility. Besides, the only obvious person who would want to murder

Tom was Buster. Since the cops had access to the autopsy and the crime scene, they were in a much better position than Buster to suspect foul play. Until something changed, he would have to assume the suicide was real. He certainly planned to take that position with the boss.

Buster and Dexter entered Jack Northrup's office at 8:35 a.m. on Friday. Dexter, who was decidedly not a morning person, carried a coffee cup with a white lid and sipped as he sat down in one of the chairs facing the senior partner's massive desk. Buster had insisted that he come along to the meeting. Jack might want details about the metadata that Buster couldn't provide. Unless it was absolutely necessary, Buster promised Dex he would not be required to speak.

"Alright," Northrup said the moment Buster's butt hit his chair, "what was so important you couldn't tell me on the phone?"

Since Jack had his office swept weekly for bugs, Buster was confident their conversation was fully confidential. "There are a few things, Mr. Northrup, but the first is that we have finished an analysis of the documents we retrieved from Tom's widow."

Jack did not show any signs of speaking, but nodded slightly to affirm his recognition.

"We've analyzed the metadata on the files on the thumb drive. The drive also contained a video message from Tom. All the documents were from Tom's clients. He didn't have any records from the clients of other investment managers, so that's good. All his evidence essentially incriminates himself. There are some emails that suggest others in the firm knew about the operation, but they all use the standard code words, so it's unlikely they could be evidence. The system is sound."

DEAD WINNER

"Fine, but I'm waiting for the bad news." Northrup sat back in his reclining leather desk chair, his eyes fixed on Buster.

"Not really bad news, but interesting information. Most of the documents were downloaded from Tom's desktop. A few were copied off a different computer, probably Tom's laptop. I'll get to that, but what's more interesting is that some of the documents were copied from the desktop of Breonna Nelson."

Northrup raised his head and sat forward. "What's that mean?"

"Tom probably didn't use his assistant's computer when he had access to all the same documents from his private office. If the documents had been downloaded from multiple computers, like he was trying to disguise his identity, then he wouldn't have used his own machine for the bulk of the files. The only conclusion is that his assistant handled some of the downloading for him."

"Is it possible that Breonna didn't know what she was copying? She was simply executing an instruction from Tom without knowing what the documents were?"

Buster shook his head. "It's unlikely. Possible, I suppose, but it would make no sense why Tom would farm out only some of the copying. It would have been quite a risk to hand over his thumb drive when he could have done it himself. Dexter thinks that downloading all the documents would have taken a while, so Tom might have been in such a hurry that he needed his assistant to do some of it for him, but we don't think so. It's more likely that she knew what she was doing and she was working with Tom. We have information suggesting that Breonna and Tom were sleeping together."

KEVIN G. CHAPMAN

Northrup held up a hand, indicating that Buster should stop talking. He then pressed a button on his phone console. A moment later, his executive assistant, Gwen Simmons, walked in the door holding a steno pad. Gwen was a model of efficiency, dressed in a pressed red pants suit with a cream blouse accented with a blue neck bow. Her hair was swept back into a tight bun.

"Yes, Sir?"

"Gwen, does Breonna Nelson report to you?"

"Yes, Sir. All the EAs report to me."

"How well do you know her?"

Gwen pursed her lips. "She's been here for about four years. I meet with her for her annual reviews and I see her at office functions and such, but I wouldn't say I know her well. Why?"

"We have some information to suggest that Ms. Nelson was engaging in a sexual relationship with her boss, Tom Williams. Do you have any information about that?"

Gwen's stoic face burst into a brief laugh, which she quickly stifled. "Oh, heavens no." She regained her normal professional demeanor. "I mean, no, Sir. I don't think that's— I don't think that's likely."

Buster, who knew that he should keep silent, couldn't help himself. "Why not?"

"Well, um, Mr. Altman, it's just that it's, well, rather common knowledge among the EAs that Breonna—Ms. Nelson—is a . . . a lesbian, Sir. She doesn't like men. In fact, she's rather hostile toward them."

"Oh," was all Buster could say in reply. He contemplated asking Gwen if she was sure, but realized how stupid, and potentially offensive, that question would be. He left it alone.

"Thank you, Gwen," Jack said. "That's all for now."

DEAD WINNER

She nodded, spun on a two-inch heel, and efficiently left the office.

When they were alone again, Jack said, "Well, it looks like somebody's information isn't reliable. We're going to need to change our approach toward Miss Nelson."

"I agree, sir. I'm already making some plans to extract additional information from her."

"Good. I'll leave it to you and your team. You're still using our contractors for this?"

"Yes, Sir." Buster was not excited about needing the Gallata gang's muscle, but the deeper they fell into Tom Williams' tangled web, the happier he was that the Gallata guys obfuscated any links back to him—and the company.

"Alright. I assume the reason he's here is because he's the one who did the tech analysis?" Jack motioned toward Dexter, who shifted nervously.

"Yes."

"That's good work," the boss nodded and gave a tiny smile.

"Um, thank you, Sir," Dexter managed to squeak out.

Jack turned back to Buster. "What was the other thing?"

"The wife, Monica Williams, seems to be shacked up with her lawyer, Rory McEntyre. She hasn't gone back to the apartment, so we don't have any more audio, but we figure she'll eventually have to go there for something, so we're well positioned. The laptop is in the lawyer's apartment with Monica. If they ever leave it unattended back at Monica's apartment, we will grab it, but getting into McEntyre's place has been a challenge."

"I thought you knew all the tricks, Buster?" Northrup enjoyed taking his ex-cop down a peg whenever the opportunity arose.

183

KEVIN G. CHAPMAN

"I do, but the security staff at his building hasn't been very cooperative. I've got a guy working on it, though, and if other options don't pan out, we should be ready to implement a plan there in a day or two."

"What other options?"

Buster smiled. "McEntyre works at Fitzsimmons, Packman & Kronish, so we have a potential pressure point."

"What are you thinking?" Jack asked without any sign of annoyance. Buster was pleased that he was curious and not disappointed.

"We're a client of the firm. The lawyer is holding onto our property. At least, we think there is company property on that laptop. It's actually Tom's personal machine, but we want to get it so we can check for any client documents he might have left there. It's a reasonable request, and one that doesn't raise any suspicion. If the senior partner instructs McEntyre to give up the laptop, he'll have to do it."

"Hmmff," Jack grunted in a way Buster interpreted as a grudging acceptance. "OK, makes sense. I'll give Harry a call, but every minute this lawyer has Tom's laptop there's a risk he might stumble on something, so keep working on getting into the guy's apartment. The sooner we have that laptop, the sooner we can take care of the rest of our business. Is there anything else we need to be worried about?"

"No. All is quiet. We've heard nothing from the SEC or the FBI. We've implemented green protocol, so the relevant accounts are clean. It'll cost us some profit for a month or so, but it's necessary."

"OK. Securing the laptop is our top priority. If everything else stays quiet, we'll stand down for a month and reassess." Northrup nodded to Buster, then looked down at something on his desk, which was the signal that the meeting

DEAD WINNER

was over. Buster left without another word. As he was opening the office door, he heard Jack ask Gwen to get him Harry Packman.

Chapter 32 – Pressure Tactics

RORY ARRIVED AT HIS OFFICE Friday morning fifteen minutes before his first appointment. He had considered calling in sick and lingering in bed with Monica, but Mr. Packman's admonition the day before had stuck with him. Even if they were able to ransom back the lottery ticket and collect the $60 million (less the $3.1 million payment), he would not be quitting his job. Besides, it was Monica's money, not his. As optimistic as he was about a future with Monica, he was self-aware enough to have doubts about the long term. He needed to go about his business, which would also help shield Monica's identity as the beneficiary of the trust.

Monica said she wanted to go to work that morning anyway. She had alerted her boss at the advertising agency about Tom's suicide and had been taking bereavement leave, but she wanted to see some office friends and get back to something like normal. She didn't want anyone at the office to associate her with the lottery winnings. Rory perceived that Monica was feeling more confident that they were going to get the missing ticket. Rory gave her a spare key and alerted his doormen to let her come and go as she pleased. He drew admiring smirks. Rory had never before had a

DEAD WINNER

woman staying with him, and Monica was a head-turner. He and Monica made plans to meet at a restaurant on Greenwich Street for dinner. Under the circumstances, they planned to blow off Detective Mason's request to have Monica come in for more questions. She could apologize on Monday.

After two client meetings and two conference calls, Rory spent a half-hour in his office with the door closed, transferring funds from his trust account, refreshing his Bitcoin wallet, and making arrangements with his local bank branch to get $100,000 in cash. He had an account with sufficient funds, but securing so much cash on short notice was a challenge. The branch manager tried to convince him to take a bank check, but Rory lied that he was going to Atlantic City for the weekend and needed the cash. The manager agreed to have the money ready for him, but he had to be at the branch before it closed at five o'clock.

As soon as he hung up with the bank, his assistant buzzed his intercom, announcing that Mr. Packman was coming in.

Rory had a moment of panic. Two visits from the senior partner in two days? This could not be good. He didn't have time to cycle through all the ominous possibilities in his head before the door opened. Packman stepped through, leaving it open behind him. That was a good sign. If something bad was coming, Packman would shut the door.

"Rory, I got a call from our client at Northrup Investments this morning about their employee—well, former employee, Tom Williams. You told me yesterday you were representing him and his wife and that they had experienced a personal crisis. I suppose the husband's suicide qualifies." Packman paused, waiting for Rory to

KEVIN G. CHAPMAN

acknowledge that he had neglected to mention the suicide the day before. When Rory remained impassively silent, he continued. "Well, I'm not sure if you know that the late Mr. Williams worked at Northrup. They reached out because, apparently, he had a laptop computer with sensitive company information on it. They have been trying to reach his wife, but so far have not made contact. They want us to facilitate the return of the laptop so the firm can clean off any confidential data. Are you in communication with the widow?"

"Um, yes, I'm scheduled to, uh, meet with her later today."

"Good. Well, please ask her to turn over the laptop to the Northrup folks on Monday. They'll give it back once they have cleaned off the company's data."

"Um, Mr. Packman, if I may ask . . ." Rory's brain was churning through several questions, trying to figure whether he could ask without revealing any information that he and Monica didn't want anyone to know. "How did the Northrup guys know to reach out to you?"

"No idea." Packman's reply was terse, indicating he wasn't interested in discussing it.

Rory didn't press the point. "OK. Well, I'm sure I can relay the request when I speak with . . . Mrs. Williams."

"Good. See that you do." Packman turned and exited, leaving Rory to ponder the significance of the request. The Northrup managers must suspect that Tom might have evidence of their account-skimming on his computer. They knew he had the laptop. Maybe the request was as innocent as Packman said. It would be fairly normal for a company to recover data left on the personal laptop of a departing

188

DEAD WINNER

employee. Maybe it was nothing, but he could not shake the feeling that this was no coincidence.

* * *

Over dinner at an outside table facing Seventh Street, Rory told Monica about his meeting with Harry Packman. They went back and forth about whether Northrup Investments' interest in the laptop could be innocent. As Monica sipped on a Cosmopolitan and Rory nursed a beer, they concluded that it was probably very, very bad. They already figured that the thugs who stole the documents from the safe deposit box were working for Northrup. They still couldn't figure out how they knew to be staking out the bank. Maybe they were just following Monica. It didn't really matter, though. Jack Northrup knew what Tom had hidden in the box. They would not be satisfied with merely having stolen back the documents. They would want to eliminate anyone who knew about them and who might go to the feds. That was why Tom wanted Monica to slip out of town and lie low—because Jack Northrup would be looking for her. Now, here they were in plain view.

"The Northrup guys definitely had a motive to kill Tom," Monica said, with less anxiety than Rory expected. He had been thinking the same thing, but didn't want to mention it for fear it would spook Monica.

"Yeah. I was thinking the same thing. But Tom's laptop was in the apartment when he died. If they figured out he was stashing away incriminating documents and killed him for it, they would have taken it, right?"

"Right . . ." Monica said as if she was thinking about it. "And they wouldn't have been worried about stealing the

189

KEVIN G. CHAPMAN

money from his investment account, or taking the lottery ticket."

"Right," Rory agreed, starting to feel better about the laptop request being more probably innocent than ominous. "If they were going to try to make it look like a robbery, they could have stolen your jewelry or other things from the apartment."

"Except that would have been inconsistent with setting it up as a suicide," Monica pointed out.

"Right. It would have been much easier to make it look like a robbery than to try to stage it as a suicide. Plus, why would they contact you and ask for a ransom? That would risk connecting the Northrup operation to Tom's murder. I can tell you for sure that three million dollars isn't enough for them to worry about."

"So, you think the guy who called isn't from Northrup?" Monica seemed excited about the possibility.

"Yeah, that's what I think." Rory sipped from his tall glass. When their food arrived, they settled into more casual conversation. Monica described her day at work and how much sympathy her coworkers expressed to her. A parade of New Yorkers walked past them, happy to be out on a warm Friday evening and looking forward to the weekend. A couple pushing a stroller and walking a dog ambled by, stopping to do some business at a street-side tree. Several people paused to make googly faces at the baby, whom Monica guessed to be no more than six months old.

When Monica said, "Awww," and smiled, Rory asked, "How come you and Tom never had kids?"

Monica's attention snapped from the nearby carriage to Rory's inquisitive face. Her eyes found her martini glass. "Tom never thought it was the right time. We talked about it,

190

DEAD WINNER

but he wasn't ready." She sipped from the delicate glass with a zig-zag stem, not looking at Rory.

"But you were ready?" Rory reached a hand across the wobbly table and groped for Monica's, which she offered after a few seconds.

"I was ready on our wedding day," she said, her voice suddenly distant.

Rory didn't press the point. He was instantly sorry he had asked and kicked himself for speaking without thinking. This was certainly not the time to bring up the subject of children. At best, she would have said that she and Tom mutually decided they didn't want kids. Then, what? Was he planning to say he wanted at least three children and he wanted to get started with Monica as soon as possible? Of course not.

While Rory was mentally flogging himself, their waitress came with their check. Rory's American Express Black card was on the table in a flash and five minutes later, they were walking toward Rory's apartment. Monica was quiet during the walk. They each looked around nervously whenever they spotted anyone following behind them who could be another Northrup thug.

As soon as they settled on his couch, Rory said, "I didn't want to talk about it in public, but I made the arrangements for the Bitcoin transaction this afternoon."

Monica's melancholy expression brightened. "You did? That's great. How does that work?"

Rory launched into an explanation about how Bitcoin were purchased and then transferred, but he saw Monica's confused expression and broke off the technical discussion. "Let's just say that by tomorrow the Bitcoin will be in my electronic wallet. I can transfer them to anyone who has a

191

KEVIN G. CHAPMAN

Bitcoin wallet through my phone. All they need is an account and my encryption code."

"It's really that simple?" Monica seemed impressed.

"Yes. That's the beauty of it. It's extremely simple to transfer even a large sum in Bitcoin. That's why criminals like it. Well, also the fact that it's untraceable and can't be clawed back by a bank or seized by the cops."

"What about the cash?"

"I got it from my bank this afternoon. It's in my briefcase."

Monica's eyes widened. "You mean you were walking around with a hundred grand in your briefcase all evening?"

"Sure. Why not? Nobody had ever tried to steal my briefcase before Wednesday, so why should it happen today?"

Monica reached for the leather briefcase, which Rory had set down on the floor next to the end table by the sofa. She snapped the latch and opened the case, immediately seeing the bundles of hundred-dollar bills scattered inside. After extracting ten bricks of bills, she stacked them on the glass coffee table in a neat pyramid. "OK, we have the cash and you have the Bitcoin. Now, all we need is the where and when."

"And we need a plan for how this is going to go down so we make sure we get the Dingus," Rory added.

"Dingus?"

Rory lowered his eyes bashfully. "The farther we get into this, the more I feel like Humphrey Bogart in *The Maltese Falcon*."

"Does that make me Mary Astor?" She smiled playfully.

"You're much more beautiful than her," Rory said with a playful smile.

DEAD WINNER

As if on cue, Monica's cell phone buzzed. She looked at the screen, which read "Unknown Number". Monica froze. Rory took her hand and said, "You have Bluetooth ear buds, right? I've seen you use them."

"Yeah?" Monica was confused for a moment, then dug into her purse as she tapped the phone to answer the call. "Hello?" She said as she handed one ear bud to Rory. "Yes. Um, hold on a moment. I need to put in my ear buds." She popped a tiny pod into her right ear, while Rory put the other into his left so he could listen in.

A deep, tinny voice spoke. Rory suspected it was being electronically altered. "Don't mess with me, Sweetheart. I'll burn that damned ticket."

"No!" Monica exclaimed, trying to control her emotions. "No. Please. I'm ready now."

"You have the money?" The voice was calm and under control, not that of a desperate or amateurish criminal.

"Well, yes," Monica responded. "I have the cash, and a . . . friend of mine who has a Bitcoin account has made the arrangements for that. I don't know anything about Bitcoin, so I need him to help me. Otherwise, I don't think I could figure it out."

The line was silent. Rory figured the hustler was wondering how this development would affect his plans. "Fine," he finally said, sounding annoyed. "It won't matter. Tomorrow night at ten o'clock, go to the Hudson river walk at Chambers Street. Wait there for a call from me and I'll tell you where to go. No cops. I'll be watching you. If I see any sign of a cop, I burn the ticket and I'll be gone. Understand?"

"Yes. I understand." Rory motioned to Monica and mouthed "proof," which she understood. "Wait. One thing.

I'll need to see the ticket before you get the money. I have to be sure it's real."

"Fine. I'll work that out." The line clicked off into silence.

Rory extracted the ear bud and handed it to Monica. "You did well." He held out his arms and she fell into his hug. Rory was trembling with a combination of dread and adrenaline. He needed the hug as much as he assumed Monica did. "It's going to be all right," he whispered near her ear. "I'm going to be with you. We can do this . . . together."

She squeezed him harder, without speaking. Then she loosened her arms and stepped back. "Rory, I have something else I want to do."

"What?"

She got her purse and pulled out an envelope, then removed a small bundle of papers, handing it to Rory. While he scanned the typed pages with a puzzled expression, she said, "I thought about this last night, and today I typed something up. I want to do this. Don't tell me not to."

Rory looked up from the pages. "Monica, this is totally unnecessary."

"I know. But I want to. I'm no lawyer, but I think it's pretty simple. I want you to be the trustee for the trust, after we get the money. Tom was going to handle the money, but now I need somebody to do it for me. I want you—well, your law firm—to be the trustee. I put in a one hundred thousand dollar per year retainer for your services. Is that enough?"

"Monica, it's probably too much, and it's not the way we normally charge clients for trustee work."

"Well, whatever. It seems fine to me. I signed it so you have it for your firm. I'm sure they'll like you bringing in more work for them. And I want to change my will, like it says. As far as I'm concerned, that's my new will. I signed it

DEAD WINNER

and everything. I even had a guy from accounting notarize it."

"I can't do that. If I'm acting as your lawyer, I can't write a will making me a beneficiary. And it looks pretty odd for you to make me a beneficiary of your estate. And you're not going anywhere. There's no need—"

"I know, but it's what I want. I signed it. I know it's not all legally correct, but it's enough for now. I want to make sure you get your money back if something should happen to me."

"Nothing's going to happen to you."

"I know, but..." Monica's face projected such a profound sadness that Rory couldn't help but tear up a little himself. "...After what happened with Tom, and all this madness, I'll feel better. I have nobody else. My mother is dying. I haven't got any other family I care about. All I know is that this is what I want right now. Please indulge me. It's what will make me happy. If we were married, nobody would think it strange, right?"

Rory's pulse rate shot up. His brain froze for a moment. If they were married? Had she really said that? Maybe it was a rhetorical hypothetical. Or, maybe it was hope that his fondest dream could actually come true. In any case, he had no ability to deny Monica her small bit of happiness. He could always talk her out of it later. "OK. If it will make you happy, then great. But that's for next week, when we're somewhere far away from here. For right now, we need to do some thinking and planning for tomorrow night."

Chapter 33 – Executive Assistance

BREONNA CLOSED HER BROWSER WINDOW as soon as she noticed someone approaching her work station. Without a boss or an alternate assignment, she had no work and was keeping herself amused by reading celebrity gossip online. She immediately assumed an alert and on-guard posture when she saw Buster Altman approaching.

"Good morning, *Breonna*," he said, emphasizing her first name. She recalled specifically telling him to address her as Ms. Nelson at their last encounter, so it was obvious he was trying to get under her skin. Since he had been lying on his back on the floor of Jack Northrup's office when she last saw him, Breonna anticipated that Macho Man would be looking for any opportunity to beat her down verbally, if not physically.

"Mr. Altman. To what do I owe the honor of your visit?"

"A few questions have come up since we last spoke."

Breonna remained passive, looking quizzically at Buster but not speaking. She hoped it would annoy the tough guy, but she also knew he was a former cop, so it was possible he had more patience than she gave him credit for.

DEAD WINNER

"My IT guys tell me that you accessed some of Tom Williams' confidential client files from your computer."

"Of course. It's my job." Breonna flashed her best "screw you" smile.

"That may be, but is it your job to copy those files and download them onto a storage drive?"

Breonna missed only one beat before responding. "Sometimes it is, yes. And I'm curious why you would ask. I was under the impression that there is no electronic record on my computer showing whether any particular document was copied or downloaded, unless the company is monitoring every keystroke and mouse click of every employee. Are you seriously doing that?"

Buster ignored the question. "Do you recall why you downloaded copies of Tom's confidential files?"

"Well, now, let me think. I don't recall that happening often, but sometimes Tom liked to take his work files home with him. He told me he wasn't supposed to transfer those files via email, so he wanted them to be put on a flash drive for him."

"Why wouldn't Tom just access the files directly from the secure servers from his VPN at home?" Buster leaned in, his voice suggesting he thought he had discovered a discrepancy in her story. She guessed that such intimidation tactics worked sometimes on dumb criminals.

"I know. I had the same thought." Breonna leaned back, placing a finger to her lips. "Maybe he wanted to work on them somewhere other than home, where he didn't have access to the VPN. But, you know, I'm just his assistant. When he told me to do something, I didn't tend to question why."

197

KEVIN G. CHAPMAN

Buster scowled. "When did this happen? When did he have you download those files?"

"I'm not sure. What files are you talking about?"

"Could it have been last Tuesday?" Buster pressed.

"Wow. That's a very specific guess," Breonna tried to look impressed. "Maybe you really are monitoring every keystroke. I think you might actually be right. I might have copied some files that day. But I handled so many things for Tom, and transferring a file would have been so routine that I can't possibly remember any particular one. I'm guessing you know, since you seem to have some way of knowing everything."

"Did Tom tell you why he needed those particular files?"

"Like I said, I don't remember the specifics and I'm not in the habit of questioning my boss about why he's giving me an assignment. He gives it to me, and I execute it. That's my job."

"It seems Tom valued you very highly," Buster stated, not really a question. He was changing the subject, which put her on high alert.

"I think he did."

"Is that why he authorized a $25,000 bonus for you last year?"

This time, Breonna did not miss a beat. "I'm sure that's why. Tom told me I had done such a good job for him that he wanted to reward me for my work. I'm very proud of his faith in me."

"Are you that good a secretary?"

"Yes. I'm that good."

Buster pushed against the top of the cubical wall in front of Breonna, regaining a fully upright stance. "Fine. I think

DEAD WINNER

Mr. Northrup may need to talk with you again. I'll let you know."

"I'll look forward to it," Breonna said calmly. She watched for any sign that Buster had another question. He glared down at her with malice. The moment he turned to leave, Breonna shot out her right hand toward the edge of her desk, in the general direction of where Buster would be walking.

Buster flinched and lurched to his left, away from Breonna's hand. Breonna grabbed a black stapler from the edge of the desk, then slammed her palm on top as she pushed a small pile of paper into the teeth of the mechanism, which snapped through its operation with a loud *ker-chunk*. Breonna smiled at Buster, who regained his composure and balance and strode down the hallway, glancing back once to find Breonna watching him.

Chapter 34 – Weekend Plans

ON FRIDAY AFTERNOON, Steve Berkowitz and George Mason were preparing their case reports for the week. Two days earlier, Steve had placed the Tom Williams suicide in the "closed" column, figuring it would be done by Friday. Now, he had to move it back to the "open" column.

"When is the widow Williams coming in?" George asked at 3:30 p.m.

"She hasn't called. Her lawyer hasn't, either. I'm pretty sure at this point that she's blowing us off."

"You are a master of deductive reasoning, Sherlock," George deadpanned. "What's our next move? Do we send a uniform to arrest her?"

"She's represented, George. What would we charge her with?"

George slumped in his chair and tilted his head back. The ancient fluorescent light bulbs overhead in the bullpen flickered. "You're thinkin' she's not behaving like someone who's entirely innocent, right?"

"It's like you know me, George." Steve stared out over the bustling space. "I'd like to get some surveillance on Mrs. Williams; see what she's doing and try to get an opportunity to question her. I'm dying to know why she didn't tell us her

DEAD WINNER

husband had terminal cancer. We were going to return her husband's personal effects to her when she came in, right?"

"Sure, what about it?"

Steve turned around with a mischievous smile curling his lip. "I'm thinking we could arrange to deliver that envelope to the widow. We are, after all, public servants, right?"

"Sully is never going to go for making this into something," George scolded. "You're wasting your time."

"Yeah, you're probably right," Steve sighed. "But I have to try. We can wrap this either way if we put in a little time."

"Just don't make me work the weekend," George called out as Steve walked away.

Five minutes later, Steve was in Captain Sullivan's office, alone. It was Steve's pitch, and George was neutral. Sully was decidedly not neutral.

"Berkowitz, what the hell makes you think there's something so hot going on in this frigid case that you need a surveillance team on weekend overtime?"

"Sully, I don't need a big team and they don't need to be on overtime. I can use the uniforms who are already working. I only need two. We're not chasing some organized criminals here. They don't even know we're tailing them. The lawyer practically wears a bell around his neck. I called the doorman at his apartment building, who confirmed that Monica Williams is living there with him. They're not exactly hiding."

"Sure, so the hot widow is shacking up with her lawyer. That's not illegal. Did you ever trace the money?"

Steve frowned. "No. It's a dead end. We confirmed that it's not in the Bermuda bank where it was sent. The account is closed there and the money was wired to an account in the

201

KEVIN G. CHAPMAN

Cayman Islands, where we don't have a treaty that would honor our subpoena. So, it's disappeared."

"So, most detectives I know would say that whoever stole the money is a suspect in the possible murder of Thomas Williams, if it was a murder, for which you have no evidence, right?"

"Well . . . not exactly," Steve reluctantly agreed.

"Now, if you tell me you have a theory where the widow killed her husband, made it look perfect, then stole her own money in order to make us think it was somebody else, rather than letting us call it a suicide and leave it alone, I'd like to hear it. Do you have one?"

"Sully, I'm telling you something here doesn't add up. The dead husband has advanced stage terminal cancer, but the wife doesn't tell us about it? Why? Then somebody steals basically all his money—their money—and she doesn't tell us about that, either."

"If she knows," Sullivan pointed out.

"Yeah, if she knows. I suppose it's possible she hasn't checked the investment account since he died, and neither has the lawyer who's supposedly managing his estate."

"It's all speculation," Sullivan barked. "I still don't see how surveillance on them over the weekend is going to give us any information we don't already have."

"It's just a hunch, Sir."

"A hunch? You want me to authorize overtime for you and Mason and assign a team of uniforms because you have a hunch about a case you should have closed three days ago? Is that it?" Sullivan's volume, along with the size of the throbbing vein in his neck and the redness of his facial complexion, increased throughout his questions.

DEAD WINNER

"Not for George, Cap. Just me, but yes," Steve responded with as much force and confidence as a paratrooper affirming readiness for the mission jump.

"And what will we do with this case on Monday, assuming that nothing happens over the weekend aside from you getting confirmation that the wife and her lawyer are screwing?"

Steve jumped to his feet, taking the initiative and interpreting the captain's comment as at least tentative permission. "Sully, if we have nothing by Monday, I will talk to the woman, get her answers to the open questions, and then either arrest her or close the case. You have my word."

"Fine. Grab two scheduled uniforms. And tell Mason he's coming with you. I don't want you out there by yourself in case something actually happens."

"George isn't going to be happy."

"Good. I'm not happy either. You can make us both happy by calling it off."

"I'll tell George." Steve grabbed the door handle and pulled, then spun around. "And, Captain, thanks." He left the office before Sully had a chance to respond.

* * *

Twenty minutes later, Steve and George met with a team of three officers, all crowded into their tiny conference room. Monica Williams had not called. One of the female officers, Yolanda Vega, clutched a large padded envelope. Bill O'Dell and Jodi Seibrie sat at attention in their blue uniforms on the far side of the tiny table. Steve paced around the small space between the backs of the chairs and the battered plaster wall. More than a few cops and suspects had slapped, punched,

203

KEVIN G. CHAPMAN

and kicked that wall over the years. A fresh coat of paint would have destroyed its character.

Steve gave the officers a summary of the facts, then gave them their assignments. Yolanda would go to Monica Williams' apartment building and wait for her. Every time they had sent anyone there, the doormen said she was not home. Steve figured that if Monica was really there, she had to come out eventually. If she was staying elsewhere, she was bound to come home at some point. Yolanda's assignment was to deliver her dead husband's property and try to get Monica into a position where she could be questioned. "Think you can charm the widow?"

"You can bet on it," Yolanda beamed.

"Great. Now, O'Dell and Seibrie are going to change out of those uniforms and spend some time on a surveillance assignment. We want you to keep an eye on Williams' lawyer, McEntyre. We're not looking to arrest him. We don't think he's guilty of anything, but we think he's likely to meet with his client, who we want to talk to. We also think we might find the widow and her lawyer together at his apartment."

"What makes you think so?" Yolanda asked.

Steve glanced around the room, finally making eye contact with George. "It's just a hunch."

204

Chapter 35 – Parking Violations

BREONNA PACKED UP FOR THE DAY on Friday afternoon. She kept the door to Tom's office closed so she didn't have to see the sterile and empty interior. She wiped away a tear, scolding herself for being sentimental. She rummaged in a nearby coat closet and found a canvas tote bag with the logo of the local PBS television station. Looking around her work station, she realized how little she wanted to keep, even after four years.

She removed the Olympic Judo Team plaque on the half-wall of her cubicle space. It was solid maple with a metal overlay bearing the interlocking Olympic rings, the symbols of the international and US judo federations, and an inscription. She felt the heft of the heavy token, symbolizing so much hard work and accomplishment. She slipped it into a large mailing envelope and placed it carefully in the tote bag. A small framed photograph of her younger brother standing next to a barn with two cows made the cut, along with the framed *Chicago* poster, signed by the entire Broadway cast. Breonna had been an instructor for the show, teaching them fighting moves that were incorporated into the choreography. It hadn't paid much, but was the most fun she had outside the Judo circle. She also packed the walking

KEVIN G. CHAPMAN

sneakers she used to get in some stair training during her lunch breaks.

At a quarter past five, thousands of pent-up office workers streamed out of the building like lines of ants marching away from their bivouac. Each elevator car was crowded with smiling people heading to their Friday evening dinner, show, or watering hole. It was a summer weekend in the big city: so much to do, so little time before Monday morning would come around again.

As Breonna crossed the cathedral-like lobby and headed toward the row of exit doors, she felt a hand grab her left arm above the elbow. She twisted in the direction of the pressure, the tote bag, in her right hand, swinging into the legs of a woman walking beside her.

"Hey, careful with that!" the woman scolded, reaching down to massage the back of her knee.

Breonna wasn't listening to the stranger's complaint. She was staring into the intense face of a large man with a linebacker's shoulders whose hand was locked on her arm. Behind him, another imposing man, this one Black and bald, watched her. Both men wore suit jackets with dress shirts and cheap neckties, like they were trying to fit into the business office environment. Breonna doubted either one would know a short sale from a short rib.

The Black man spoke with a soft but forceful tone. "Miss Nelson. Glad we caught you before you left. Mr. Northrup would like a quick word before you leave. He's waiting in his car. This way, please." He smiled, gesturing with an arm toward the side of the lobby where a doorway led to the stairs down to the underground parking lot, reserved for important executives. The White guy, with his ham hand engulfing Breonna's arm, pulled her in that direction. Breonna allowed

206

DEAD WINNER

herself to be herded away from the teeming throng of workers, who were too anxious to escape the building to notice Breonna's distress. She considered screaming for help, but wasn't certain these two muscle-men weren't legitimately security staff from Northrup.

The crowd thinned as they approached the far wall and the doorway to the garage. When they reached the threshold, Breonna jerked her arm away from the big man's grip. She thought he looked like a bodybuilder based on the thickness of his neck and the width of his shoulders. He had brown hair cropped in a very short buzz cut, leaving him with a high forehead sporting ridged lines as he furrowed his brows in anger at Breonna's move.

"Excuse me!" she snapped, "I prefer it if you don't touch me." She kept walking, giving the lug no reason to replace his guiding hand. The Black guy walked ahead and opened the door to the stairs, standing aside like a doorman welcoming her into a hotel. She paused at the threshold, unsure of the situation. "Who sent you to get me?"

This time, Buzz Cut answered. "Buster."

Breonna relaxed slightly. These Neanderthals looked like the kind of boys Buster would have on his team. It seemed plausible that the big boss might want to have a crack at her himself regarding Tom's accounts and that Buster would dispatch Beavis and Butthead to bring her down to Northrup's car. But she was on her guard. She definitely wanted to be ahead of them on the stairway, so she marched through the door and hurried down the steps, leaving the two men scrambling to catch up.

After two flights, Breonna pushed through the heavy metal door into the dimly lit garage. Smooth painted concrete snaked away in the cramped space. Expensive,

KEVIN G. CHAPMAN

elegant vehicles waited patiently in spaces barely large enough for their occupants. Breonna saw no people and certainly no waiting car containing the CEO. She dashed to the opposite side of the roadway, where an elevator door marked an escape route, and turned. The two men exited the stairs and advanced toward her. She put her back to the painted concrete wall next to the elevator and pushed the call button behind her back with her right hand, still holding the strap of the tote bag.

"Hang on there, Miss," the bald Black guy called out, stepping forward quickly without actually running. "The boss will be here in a minute."

Breonna wasn't sure whether these guys were for real, but wasn't taking anything for granted. "That's fine. I'll wait right here." She flashed a quick smile, attempting to seem much more relaxed and off guard than she really was. If these two goons were up to no good, she wanted to maintain an element of surprise.

The Black guy stopped three feet from Breonna while his companion circled to the left, cutting off her potential route to the ramp leading toward the vehicle exit. She didn't hear the sounds of any running motors or tires squealing on the smooth roadway. They were alone. The floor was clean and smooth, like it had been mopped recently. A faint smell of gasoline hung in the air, mixed with industrial solvent.

"While we wait for Mr. Northrup, why don't you tell us where your old boss, Tom, stashed the rest of the documents?"

"What documents?" Breonna now knew this was not a friendly conversation and that Mr. Northrup and his car were not likely to show up—at least not soon.

208

DEAD WINNER

"We can do this the easy way," the Black guy took a step forward, then glanced at his partner, "or the hard way."

As he finished, Buzz Cut removed a handgun from inside his jacket. It had a sleek design, all black. The guy held it casually at his side, but made sure Breonna could see it. She wasn't an expert with pistols. Her father was more of a hunting rifle guy, but she had seen and used her share of handguns. She guessed it was either a Baretta or a Glock, not that the manufacturer would make a difference.

"I can't tell you what I don't know," she pleaded, keeping her right hand behind her back. She wondered how long the elevator would take to make the journey down two levels from the lobby.

"Cut the crap," the Black guy said, taking another step forward and looking down from his above-six-foot height into Breonna's eyes. He was intimidating, which was the point. She figured he was used to women being frightened into submission. She glanced at the ground as passively as she could. His right foot was slightly in front, bearing more of his weight. He was either going to punch with his left hand, or slap her with a backhand right from that posture. She was confident it would be the right. A big guy like him wouldn't feel the need to punch a defenseless woman in the face with the first blow. They wanted information, not necessarily blood.

"So, you two idiots don't have a car down here?" Breonna shifted her weight to her left foot and tensed her right arm while preparing for the reaction she knew was coming. The Black man raised his right hand, then sent it in a wide arc toward Breonna's face. She turned her head as the slap landed, deflecting most of the energy. At the same moment, she swung her right arm from behind her back,

209

KEVIN G. CHAPMAN

whipping the tote bag on the end of its long canvas straps. She planted it, along with the heavy wooden plaque inside, against the man's left ear.

Black Guy grunted in pain and surprise and staggered to his right in the direction of Buzz Cut. Breonna kicked out, contacting Black Guy's right kneecap with a sickening crunch. He crumpled to the floor.

Buzz Cut yelled, "Hey!" and raised his gun. Breonna snapped the tote bag around, spinning counter-clockwise to gather momentum before crashing it into the big White guy's outstretched arm. The gun went clattering toward the wall next to the elevator as Buzz Cut cried out in pain, the corner of the wooden plaque having smashed into his wrist.

Breonna released the bag's strap and lunged toward her much larger opponent, grabbing his now-injured arm and pulling as she threw her weight into his midsection, roll-throwing him over her bent back. He landed with an "ooof" on the hard garage surface as the wind was knocked from his lungs. Breonna scrambled after the pistol, grabbed the tote bag, and stood up, panting. The elevator emitted a satisfying *ding* to indicate that her ride had arrived.

She pointed the gun at Buzz Cut. "I'd stay down if I were you. I'm better with a rifle than this little pistol, but I know how to use it." She checked the safety, which was in the off position.

"Get that bitch!" Black Guy groaned, holding his broken knee with both hands.

Breonna stepped backwards into the elevator's open doors, watching Buzz Cut struggle to his feet with malice etched on his square face. "You really need to learn to follow instructions," she said calmly, then squeezed off two shots aimed at the big lunk's right leg.

DEAD WINNER

The first found his thigh. The second tore through his calf muscle. He dropped like a side of beef, crying out in pain and rage. She had been aiming for his knee, but close was good enough.

Black Guy attempted to struggle toward his good knee, prompting Breonna to say, "Nuh, uh, big guy. I'd stay down unless you want to add a gunshot wound to the reason you're headed to the ER."

As the blood from Buzz Cut's wounds puddled on the floor and a torrent of curses poured from the mouths of the two men, Breonna took another backward step into the elevator car and pressed the "L" button. When the doors closed, she sucked in two deep breaths and exhaled slowly, calming her adrenaline rush. There were probably security cameras in the parking garage, but they may not have been constantly monitored. The security guys at the lobby desk probably didn't hear the shots two levels down beneath layers of concrete. She exited the elevator briskly but calmly, rejoining the stream of humanity rushing out of the building.

Buzz Cut and the Black Guy obviously had evil designs, but they were just flunkies sent by Buster. She kicked herself mentally for not taking their cell phones. Assuming they could get a signal down in the garage, she didn't have much time before Buster had somebody else looking for her.

She glanced at the lobby security desk, where one of the officers in a gold and black jacket bearing the building's logo was watching her. Alerting the desk to the carnage in the parking garage would risk exposing herself if either of them were part of Buster's gang. She couldn't go to her apartment. The firm knew her address. She turned west. There was one place she would be safe.

Chapter 36 – Personal Effects

A SATURDAY MORNING IN NEW YORK means different things to different people. For some, it is time for a run in Central Park. For some, it is a bike and a ride across the George Washington Bridge. Some venture off for tennis, golf, softball, basketball, or rolling up the ramps at the skate park. For others, it means sleeping in, then going out for bagels or a boozy brunch with unlimited mimosas. Rory's first choice was normally to jump on his bike. The boozy brunch option would have been attractive, but he and Monica had decided the night before to go for a run by the Hudson River around Chambers Street. They wanted to get the lay of the land in the daylight and think about both entry points and escape routes.

But first, Monica needed to make a quick visit to her apartment to get running clothes and proper shoes. Rory volunteered to accompany her, but she said she needed to face the apartment alone eventually while Rory scouted the river walk via Google Earth.

When Monica breezed through the glass doors at the Winchester Tower, she waved to Edgardo, the weekend morning doorman. She stopped at the front desk, where

DEAD WINNER

Delroy gave her a sympathetic smile and wished her condolences.

"Thank you, Delroy. It has been a rough few days. Are there any packages for me?"

"Indeed, Mrs. Williams. I'll go fetch them from the back."

While Delroy disappeared into the package room, Monica moved briskly to the mail room, where she unlocked the brass door to their box. She was still thinking of it as *theirs,* as if there were two of them. After pulling out a wad of mail that had accumulated over the past four days and dumping it into her purse, she turned back toward the main desk and ran straight into a female police officer, who was clearly waiting for her. The petite uniformed officer looked too small for the bulky belt around her slim waist, loaded down with equipment including her service pistol, nightstick, and radio. She wasn't wearing a hat. Tucked under one arm she held a large padded envelope, bulging with hidden contents. "Mrs. Monica Williams?" the officer asked tersely, obviously knowing it was her.

"Yes?"

"I'm Officer Yolanda Vega. I have the personal effects of your late husband." She nodded toward the envelope without loosening her vice-like hold on the package locked between her elbow and torso. "I'm going to need you to review the items and sign a receipt. May I accompany you to your apartment so we can handle it privately?" She smiled apologetically.

Monica assessed the size of the envelope and did a mental inventory of the things Tom would have had on him when the coroner carted away his body. She wanted to have his phone. The rest was not likely to be important. "Sure. I

213

KEVIN G. CHAPMAN

need to get some packages from the desk first." She slipped past the officer and returned to Delroy, who held out a thin plastic bag, the kind the supermarket put groceries in, containing three small Amazon boxes and one padded envelope. Monica thanked him and carried the bag to the elevator, followed by Officer Vega.

Opening the apartment door, Monica noticed the lingering antiseptic smell of industrial cleaning solution. She dropped the bag on a small table in the entry foyer, along with her purse. "Follow me," she called over her shoulder on her way through the kitchen toward the dining nook table. "You can put it all there."

While Officer Vega poured out and arranged the remnants of Tom's pockets, she said, "Detective Berkowitz told me you were supposed to come in yesterday to answer a few questions. Would you like me to drive you to the precinct after this so you can do that?"

"No—I can't. I have somewhere I need to be," Monica was kicking herself for allowing the officer into the apartment. She had completely forgotten about the detective. "I'm sorry. How about on Monday?"

"Hang on," Officer Vega said. She was smoothing out a sheet of paper containing a list of the contents of the envelope. Monica saw Tom's phone among the debris. It did not appear bloody, which made sense if it was in Tom's pocket the whole time. Then she noticed another cell phone, this one in a thick black case that looked like rubber. Its screen was lighted.

"Berkowitz," the detective's voice barked out through the speaker.

"What?" Monica was angry and surprised.

214

DEAD WINNER

"Officer Vega here, Detective, I'm with Monica Williams."

"Wait a minute—"

"Mrs. Williams, I'm glad I got you. I want to close out this investigation and need to get a little more information from you. The most important thing is whether you knew that your husband had terminal pancreatic cancer at the time of his death. Did you know?"

"Wait. Are you—? You're not supposed to be questioning me without my lawyer present." Monica was flustered and thinking frantically. "I'm not going to say anything."

"Well, Mrs. Williams," Berkowitz sighed, his annoyance coming through the speaker along with his voice, "I'm sorry you feel that way. Like I said, I'm trying to close out this case. You don't have to say anything, of course, and frankly, if you do say anything at this point we couldn't use it against you, since you have mentioned your lawyer. If you make any statements, it's like they never happened. Isn't that right, Officer Vega?"

"That's true, Sir. I would be obligated to testify that Mrs. Williams requested her lawyer and refused to answer."

"Thank you. So, you see, Mrs. Williams, nothing bad can happen here. I just want to know what's going on. I'm sure there's a perfectly logical explanation for everything. But I need you to fill in the blank space for me."

"I really don't think I should say anything. I'm going to call my lawyer." Monica took two steps back toward her purse.

"Wait!" Berkowitz shouted, unable to see Monica, but likely hearing her footsteps.

Monica extracted her phone and dialed Rory.

215

KEVIN G. CHAPMAN

"OK, OK. Fine. Officer Vega, please hang up on me and have Mrs. Williams sign her form and then get out of there. I'm sorry to have bothered you, Mrs. Williams."

The officer hung up and put the phone on her utility belt. She held out a pen toward Monica, who had her index finger poised over her phone's screen, but had not completed dialing. She tossed the phone back in her purse and composed herself. Marching back to the kitchen nook, she congratulated herself for standing firm and not answering questions, exactly like Rory told her.

She surveyed the sad assortment of items on the little table: Tom's phone, pocket comb, a clip with some cash and a credit card, and his ID card from Northrup Investments. After scanning the inventory list and signing the form, she escorted Officer Vega to the door without saying goodbye or thank you.

Ten minutes later, with a small athletic bag packed, she grabbed Tom's phone, leaving the rest on the table. She retrieved her phone and called Rory. "Hey . . . I'm leaving now . . . Sure. I'll be ready to run. It's so smart of you to check out the ransom drop in the daylight so we know what we're getting into later. I'm so lucky to have you, Rory. . . . I know. By tomorrow we'll have the ticket and this whole nightmare will be over. . . . No, there's nothing here for me. I'd rather stay with you. . . . I'll see you in a few minutes. Bye."

She stopped at the door, looking back for a few moments before exiting.

* * *

Steve Berkowitz called George Mason. He had promised not to pull George into the Saturday operation unless there

DEAD WINNER

was something actually happening, despite Sully's instructions. "Hey, George, you got a minute?"

"Don't tell me you want me working, Steve. We're going to the park with the dog in a few minutes."

"No. I haven't got anything hot enough to spoil your Saturday yet. We caught up with the widow this morning. Yolanda got into her apartment with permission and called me. I tried to get a rise out of her about the cancer, but she clammed up and asked for her lawyer."

"Not the typical behavior of an innocent widow, eh?"

Steve chuckled. "No. It's not. I was hoping she would have a good explanation, but instead all we have are more questions. She certainly didn't seem surprised by the news, at least according to Vega. No reaction except being worried about answering."

"So, let's assume she knew, but didn't tell us. We're back to why?"

"Yeah. Same spot. Why would she not tell us? And why now, knowing that we found out, would she still not tell us? You have to figure she has a story that she'll tell if she has to, so why not spill it? Why leave us suspecting that she's holding back? How does it help her?"

"Maybe she was just following her lawyer's orders," George suggested impatiently.

"Yeah. Maybe. It's eating at me, though." Steve sighed again. "I'm gonna keep the surveillance on her and her lawyer. There's something going on here."

"Yeah. Well, if nothing happens this weekend Sully's gonna bust your balls about it for a year, so I hope you're right. On second thought, I hope you're wrong. I do *not* want to work this weekend."

KEVIN G. CHAPMAN

"Fine. I won't call you unless I've got something definite. Enjoy the park."

Berkowitz stared at his phone, trying to figure his next move. He called Yolanda and confirmed that Monica had left the building about fifteen minutes after Steve hung up. She walked back to the building where the lawyer lived.

"Fine. You're done. The surveillance team will take over from here." He stuffed his phone into his pocket, kissed his wife goodbye, and headed for the subway. If he was working, he might as well be in the office.

Chapter 37 – Who Are These Guys?

OFFICERS BILL O'DELL AND JODI SEIBRIE, wearing civilian clothes, sat in the unmarked Chevy issued to them from the motor pool. Since they didn't know how long they would be staking out Rory McEntyre's apartment and they weren't sure where their targets might go if they left the building, they took the car. It made for a relatively comfortable base of operations for their surveillance. O'Dell had spent forty minutes listening to a New York Mets podcast called *National League Town*. Jodi wasn't jazzed to talk baseball with Bill, so he settled for yelling at Greg Prince and Jeff Hysen's commentary on the season.

They were parked in a hydrant zone a block down from where Rory and Monica had disappeared inside the building five minutes earlier. Bill switched off the podcast and turned to his partner.

"You wanna call it in?" Jodi asked.

"Sure," Bill grabbed his phone and put it on speaker. When Berkowitz answered, he gave a summary of Monica's and Rory's morning. They had run to the river walk along the Hudson, then walked north several blocks, then back south several blocks. Then they meandered around Rockefeller

Park, then jogged back to the lawyer's apartment. "So, not much to report on the targets, Detective. But there's something else."

"Yeah?"

"We picked up a couple of dudes who were following our marks."

"What kind of dudes?"

"One really big White guy, one smaller, skinny White guy. Wearing casual clothes—jeans and t-shirts, sunglasses. The big guy is huge, like a body builder or something. We noticed them on the way over toward the river, but made them for sure on the way back. When our targets went back into their building, these two guys waited on the street for a few minutes. Then the huge guy made a phone call and the two of them went into a café down the block. They're sitting at a table by the window with a view of the front of the building, sipping drinks in take-out cups. If they're not tailing our couple, then I will never take the detective's exam again."

The phone's speaker was silent. Bill and Jodi exchanged shrugs, waiting for the detective leading the investigation to give them an instruction. "You get pictures of our two mystery tails?"

Jodi, who was the designated photographer on the team, said, "Of course. You think I'm carrying around this big-ass Nikon without getting images? I'm downloading them now. You'll have them in your email in a few minutes."

"OK," Berkowitz grumbled. "I'll run the photos through the facial recognition database and see what pops up. In the meantime, I'll grab somebody and come down to meet you, unless something else happens. Keep the two guys in your

DEAD WINNER

sights, but don't give up the surveillance on the primary targets. Got it?"

"Yeah, we got it, Detective." Bill clicked off the phone, while Jodi fussed with her laptop and sent the images to Berkowitz in an email.

After she closed her computer, Jodi asked, "What do we do now?"

"Now, we enjoy these comfortable American-made seats and wait for something to happen. Toss me a bottle of water."

* * *

Steve hated the idea of calling Captain Sullivan on a Saturday. It was enough that the captain had given the approval to run the operation on a weekend. Sully would not want to talk about it, and he certainly wouldn't want to expand the scope. But the new information was too hot to keep to himself, so he did the logical thing: he called his partner.

"Aw, Steve, what happened?" George dispensed with any preliminaries after seeing it was Berkowitz calling. Wind whistled into the phone's microphone, indicating that George was somewhere outside. Steve heard distant hip-hop music. "I'm trying to enjoy my Saturday."

"I hate to call, but we've got a wrinkle."

"So, take it to a dry cleaner."

"There's a couple of goons from the Gallata mob tailing our Mrs. Williams and her lawyer boyfriend."

"The fuck you say?" George was suddenly paying more attention. "Hold on, let me put in my buds." Steve waited on hold for his partner. When George came back on the line, the

KEVIN G. CHAPMAN

background noise was gone. "OK, I'm on my earphones. Did you say the Gallata mob?"

"I did. I wish I hadn't, but that's what we've got. The two officers I have on surveillance reported in. Nothing of note about our two targets, but they picked up on two guys who were also following Williams and her lawyer. They got pictures, and when I ran them, they popped up as known muscle for Fat Albert."

"That makes no sense," George said. The Gallata mob was the largest organized crime operation in the city. They were mainly involved in prostitution, drug distribution, and illegal gambling, but also dabbled in extortion, protection shake-downs, and money laundering. The head of the family, Alberto "Fat Albert" Gallata, recently took over the business after his father, "Slick Mick," was murdered. The Gallatas had many tentacles, but why they would be watching Monica Williams or her lawyer was a puzzle. "What connection could our widow have with those guys?"

"I'm not sure," Steve admitted. "Nothing makes much sense about this case. But the widow's husband worked for Northrup Investments. They move a lot of money, and the Gallatas love money."

"Not much of a theory."

"I know. And it's not going to impress Sully when we ask for two more officers to help us with the surveillance."

"Whaddaya mean, when *we* ask Sully? This is your weekend gig, Steve. And I hope you don't think I'm jumping in on this just because two Gallata goons are hanging around your suspects."

"They aren't suspects," Steve corrected. "But, yes, I'd like you to back me up and call Sully with me. We've got two marks now, the Williams woman and her lawyer—well,

DEAD WINNER

actually they're two marks, but we expect them to be together—and now we're going to need to tail these other two guys to see what the hell they're doing there. We can't do it with the team we have in place. Don't you agree?"

"You said *we* again, Steve. That's Goddamned presumptuous. And why do you need me? I know nothing about this."

"You do now, Partner."

"You are going to buy my dinner for the rest of the month."

"Fine. Now, you hang on and I'll conference in Sully." Steve punched the conference call function on his phone, putting George on hold without waiting for confirmation that his partner would wait until he got Sully on the line.

Captain Sullivan was predictably not happy to be disturbed on the weekend, less happy that it involved the Williams "suicide" case, as he called it, and fully pissed off that Steve and George were asking for even more weekend resources to devote to such a "stupid" case. When Steve told him about the connection to the Gallata organized crime family, he totally lost it.

"Are you fucking kidding me, Berkowitz? This was a simple suicide until you got conspiracy theories into your head." Steve and George knew to let the Captain think when the line went silent and not jump in with comments. After a pause, Sullivan asked, "How sure are you about these two guys?"

"Cap, I wish it wasn't certain, but the facial recognition came back 99% positive. One guy is named Ivan. Last name may or may not be Roshenko. He's been one of Fat Albert's main enforcers. We thought he was deported, but it seems he's back. He's a big bald mountain, so he's hard to miss. The other guy is Ricky Newman, who's in our database and also the FBI's as a known associate in the Gallata organization. He apparently used to be a lieutenant in a human trafficking operation that the feds shut down a while back. The database doesn't say where he's been lately, but he's connected, for sure. I don't know why they're tailing our marks, but they are, and that has to mean something's going on here. I know it's inconvenient, but if the Gallatas are following the same people we're following, then something's up and we don't want to miss it. I've got two officers and one car, but now I've got four people to track. If I stay with the wrong ones and we miss something significant, we'll be sorry. So, I want you to have a chance to give the authorization now, rather than be second-guessed by the Commissioner's office later."

Steve knew the only thing Sully hated more than signing off on overtime was being called out by Earl Ward, the police commissioner, for botching an investigation. The commissioner generally didn't care unless the media came sniffing around. If questions got asked and Sully had to admit he had a lead but didn't assign staff to it and missed an important opportunity, he would regret his choice. If Steve waited long enough, he was confident Sully would approve at least one more unit for his impromptu operation.

He wasn't wrong. After five more minutes of fuming and several threats to hold Steve and George responsible if the operation was a bust, the captain finally authorized Steve to call in another unit of two officers.

"Should we alert our organized crime task force?" Steve asked, "or the FBI, since the Gallatas are somehow involved?"

"No," Sully barked. "Until we have something more than two known guys hanging around our suspect—"

DEAD WINNER

"The woman isn't a suspect, Sully. She's only a person of interest."

"I don't give a good God damn if she's a prima ballerina. Just stay on her. If we're doing this, make sure you don't screw it up." The captain hung up abruptly, leaving Steve and George to discuss the logistics. George reluctantly agreed to meet Steve at four o'clock.

Chapter 38 – Warriorsaurus

MONICA AND RORY STAYED in Rory's apartment the rest of the day, looking over Google map images of the area they had scouted. The swelling in Rory's nose was significantly down, although he still had dark circles under his eyes. Rory insisted on talking through different scenarios of how the ransom drop might go. With each different run-through, he became more confident about their chances for success.

"I didn't know you had experience in mission planning," Monica said at one point, admiration and surprise in her voice.

Rory smiled bashfully. "Well, I've planned out a hundred operations like this . . . inside video games."

"Really? What kinds of games?" Monica's question did not contain a hint of reproach or condescension.

"Mostly *Counter-Strike*, but also *World of Warcraft* and some other RPGs."

"Cool," Monica said, standing and walking toward the kitchen, where she poured herself a cup of coffee. "Want a cup?"

"No. I've had plenty today." Rory returned to his laptop screen. He took a screen capture of the map, copied it to a notepad program, and engaged his computer's drawing functionality. Removing a metal stylus pen from beneath the

DEAD WINNER

keyboard, he started drawing circles and lines on the screen. "Come here and let's go over this one." He pointed animatedly at the satellite image, drawing lines to show the route they might take if the man they were meeting instructed them to enter Rockefeller Park. He drew circles for places where the guy might have accomplices hiding or waiting for them, and how they could escape in multiple directions if needed.

"Why would he have accomplices?" Monica asked. "Once he has the Bitcoin and we have the ticket, isn't he just as happy as us to never see each other again?"

"Ideally, yes. But you never know. I want to be prepared."

"I have to say, I'm surprised, Rory. I always knew you were sweet and a bit of a Boy Scout, but I never would have pegged you for such a brave fighter."

"I'm not a real fighter. Ha—" He laughed derisively. "You saw me Wednesday, when those two guys jumped us. I was pretty pathetic trying to fight with them. I do much better when I'm Warriorsaurus."

"What?" Monica chuckled softly, clearly amused.

Rory blushed. "That's my avatar's name in *World of Warcraft*. It's embarrassing, now that I have to say it out loud. I've used it ever since I was a teenager. It was supposed to be a cross between a warrior and a dinosaur, like a T-Rex. It's stupid."

"It's not stupid." Monica lifted her head and gently kissed Rory's lips. "It's adorable."

Rory pulled his head back. "I don't want to be adorable. I want to be . . . heroic. In the game, that's what I am. I charge into battle courageously and attack aggressively. Others fear me—I mean, they fear Warriorsaurus."

KEVIN G. CHAPMAN

"Well, I'm sure I would fear Warriorsaurus, too. And I'm sure you will charge into battle for me tonight, if battle is what we need. But I'm hoping all we need is good negotiating skills."

"Huh!" Rory blurted out. "I can definitely provide that as the real-life Rory McEntyre."

"I know. That's why I'm not afraid of what's going to happen. At least, I wasn't until we started talking about all these worst-case scenarios."

"I'm sorry, Monica. I don't want to scare you. But we need to be prepared for all possibilities."

"OK. I get it, and I'm glad you're trying to be so prepared. I'm worried that, no matter what we prepare for, things will not go the way we think they will."

"You're probably right," Rory pulled his arm back and returned his attention to the screen on the coffee table. "But the more we prepare for different situations, the better we'll be able to deal with whatever does happen." A buzzer sounded from the entry foyer. "That's our Chinese food," Rory announced. "We don't want to go into battle on empty stomachs, now, do we?"

"Certainly not!" Monica replied enthusiastically, getting up and heading for the cupboard where Rory kept his dinner plates.

* * *

After dinner, accompanied by a chilled Chardonnay, Monica said she needed a nap and led Rory to the bedroom. They laid on top of Rory's powder blue comforter for a few minutes in silence, each breathing deeply. Rory was running through more "battle" scenarios in his head, figuring that he

DEAD WINNER

would not be able to sleep. When Monica's lips found his, he startled, surprised that he had actually dozed off. Her kisses quickly became more urgent. He felt her warm fingers slip under the bottom of his shirt, sending electric shivers up his torso as she slid her hand across his chest. When Monica's fingertip found his nipple, he couldn't control the "oooohh," which interrupted their kiss. Her tongue flittered against his open mouth as Monica rolled on top of him, straddling his waist. She pulled his shirt upward, coaxing him to raise his arms so it could slide over his head.

"Let me take your mind off of everything," she said playfully as she slid herself down his torso until her mouth found his belly button with a soft kiss and a twirl of her tongue inside the sensitive indentation. She pushed up onto one elbow, then began unbuckling Rory's belt.

Ten minutes later, they laid naked under a thin sheet. Monica's right leg was casually thrown over Rory's as she snuggled against him, their sweat mingling. Rory took deep breaths, attempting to slow his speeding pulse as he gently stroked Monica's hair. It was a perfect moment, following ten amazing minutes. Ever since he first met Monica, this had been his fondest fantasy. He could hardly believe it was real.

"I have an idea," he whispered, reluctant to break the mood.

"Mmmmm? What's that?" Monica purred, barely awake.

"What if we forget about the ransom drop? We let the guy burn the damned lottery ticket. We stay here, in bed together, forever. I have enough money. I have a great job. We don't need more. Stay with me. I love you. I've always loved you. I don't need anything more than this. Ever."

KEVIN G. CHAPMAN

"That sounds wonderful." She draped a slender arm over his chest and squeezed herself into him. "But we can't walk away from sixty million."

"Fifty-seven million, before taxes," Rory mumbled.

"Sure. I know. But that's early retirement money. That's never have to work again money—at least for me. Maybe it will be easy and we'll just make the exchange and walk away."

"Yeah, maybe . . ." Rory drifted back into his thoughts about how many ways things could go wrong. The perfect moment was over. He had spoiled it. "Promise me that the moment anything looks like it's going bad, you will run and get out of there."

"OK. We'll run. You're coming with me, right?"

"Of course. But if I have to, I'll do whatever it takes to give you a head start. If I say to run, you just go. I'll be right behind you. I don't want anything happening to you. Alright?"

"Alright." Monica didn't lift her head. She spoke into Rory's chest hairs. "Thank you. It's nice to know that, somewhere in the world, somebody is putting my best interests first."

"I'll always put you first, Monica. I promise."

"I know." She kissed the skin of Rory's pectoral muscle, smooth and firm. Then she rolled backwards, away from Rory's warm body. He turned his head to watch her saunter naked to the bathroom and shut the door. The sound of the shower told him it was time to emerge from the post-coital fog and get ready for whatever the evening had in store.

230

Chapter 39 – A Walk in the Park

AT NINE-THIRTY, Monica and Rory left Rory's building and turned left onto Reade Street, toward the river and their rendezvous. They both dressed to blend into the evening. Monica wore black yoga pants, dark sneakers, and a white sleeveless top with a thin, dark blue jacket. She had her cell phone in the jacket pocket, in its case with her credit cards and ID. Rory wore blue jeans, a dark t-shirt, a denim jacket, and his "lucky" Bacardi baseball cap. He carried a shoulder bag with the Emirates Airlines logo, which had been a gift at a legal conference and never before used. Inside the gray bag with its long, silver shoulder strap, one hundred thousand dollars in cash rested comfortably. Rory had tucked one of his business cards into an outer pocket of the bag, figuring their criminal was likely to ditch the bag and some good Samaritan might want to return it.

"Hey, Mr. McEntyre!" called out a British accent from behind the small front desk in the lobby. Rory recognized it as belonging to Imran, one of the friendlier members of the building staff. He always found it amusing to hear his smooth, Sean Connery voice coming from an obviously Middle-Eastern man. "Nice bag. I didn't know you fancied Arsenal."

KEVIN G. CHAPMAN

Rory stopped, puzzled for a moment, then realized that Emirates Airlines sponsored several English football clubs. He assumed Arsenal must be one. He had no actual idea. "Thanks," he waved, placating Imran.

Rory's cell phone was open to his Bitcoin wallet in his jeans pocket, ready to make a three-million-dollar transfer. At least, the Bitcoin had that value the day before when he had transferred the funds. The actual value might be several thousand dollars more or less at this point in time. He assumed the recipient of the ransom would not hold it against him if the value wasn't exactly three million at the time of transfer.

They walked without hurrying. They had plenty of time to get to their designated destination. After that, Rory had no idea what to expect. He held Monica's hand as they strolled down the sidewalk, occasionally needing to disengage to let other pedestrians pass without obstruction. But their hands always immediately found each other again. Within fifteen minutes, they arrived at the corner of Chambers and West. Crossing the street, they both scanned the greenway, teeming with active New Yorkers on foot, bicycles, and various forms of rolling conveyance. They looked over the benches, most of which faced the river, so all they saw were the backs of heads and shoulders. Nobody looked familiar. Nobody was making eye contact, as if expecting them. Neither of them looked behind to see if anyone was following.

When they reached the greenway, Rory scanned north and south, slowly spinning around but seeing nothing but normal New York sidewalk activity. The sky was dark, dotted with the few stars and planets that shone brightly enough to penetrate the ambient light that never allowed full darkness

DEAD WINNER

to fall in Manhattan. Street lights along West Street and ground-level lighting along the pedestrian path gave plenty of illumination to see faces, not that Rory knew what their ransom recipient would look like.

Having no better ideas, they sat on an empty bench and waited. It was several minutes before ten o'clock. Happy pedestrians strolled by, some licking ice cream cones while others sipped ice-filled drinks. On the grassy lawn off to their left, "Grazing in the Grass" was playing on a jazz-lover's boom box. Five silent minutes later, Monica jumped when her cell phone vibrated.

After making eye contact with Rory and taking a deep breath, she swiped up and said, "Hello? . . . Yes . . . Yes, we do . . . I had to. I don't know anything about Bitcoin. . . . He has it and we're ready to make the transfer . . . Yes, we have that, too . . . You have the ticket? . . . We're going to need to see it before you get the coin code thing . . . Sure. . . . OK. . . . How will we recognize you? . . . Fine."

"What did he say?"

"He wants us to walk into the park and sit on one of the benches next to the river by the corner, where the path turns south. He says he'll find us."

"OK, I remember where that is from the map. The big field is right behind the path. It's not bad for us. Multiple escape routes, north and south. Plenty of people around, so less likely the guy will try anything. I think we're in good shape."

"I hope so." Monica stretched her arms and turned toward the path leading along the side of the iron railing that prevented pedestrians from falling into the river. She and Rory walked west toward the corner of Rockefeller Park. She reached for Rory's hand and squeezed it. Rory's hand was shaking, but it steadied once in contact with Monica's.

Chapter 40 – Patience is for Suckers

HAVING WORKED OUT as long as he could stand, Buster showered and changed into his normal Saturday night clothes. He paced nervously around his apartment, waiting for some communication from the two Gallata operatives who had Monica Williams and her lawyer under surveillance. Most Saturday nights, he would be on his way out to the local clubs so he could strut his stuff on the dance floor. He would look for some hot young thing to hook up with. He seldom came home alone. Tonight, he was waiting for confirmation that the two people most likely to mess up his retirement plans were no longer a threat. Then, he would hit the clubs and celebrate.

His guy who was planted outside Breonna Nelson's Brooklyn apartment reported in every hour, but there had been no sign of the girl. He was happy the idiots who botched their assignment to capture her in the parking garage were not his responsibility. It bothered him that he didn't know where Breonna was. He guessed she had run away for good—hopefully without any incriminating documents. If she surfaced, Mr. Northrup would make the call about how to handle her. For now, Buster was focused only on Rory and Monica, and on Tom's laptop.

KEVIN G. CHAPMAN

Patience, however, was not his strong suit. As a cop, it was always noted in his annual performance review that he needed to take his time and be willing to wait for a suspect to make a wrong move, rather than swooping in and making a premature arrest. He hadn't improved in that area since he left the force. He wanted to be involved in the operation, directing the stakeout instead of waiting at home.

He poured himself a generous helping of The Oban Little Bay and spent ten minutes enjoying the smooth single-malt scotch. When his glass was empty, he said, "Fuck this," and stalked to his bedroom. He stuffed his Glock 17 under his belt and fastened the button on his suit jacket to hide the gun. He had a different pistol that was legally registered, but for this excursion he wanted the unregistered piece he had obtained from a drug dealer a few weeks before he retired from the police force. The dealer was willing to hand over his gun, his cash, and his cocaine in exchange for saving Buster the paperwork involved in an arrest. He was about to leave his apartment when his phone buzzed. The text read, "Birds are flying west tonight."

He punched the phone icon next to a contact in his address book listed as "Audubon Society," which connected him to the burner phone of a man he had never met. He said his name was Ivan. He spoke with a vaguely Eastern European accent, maybe Russian, but Buster was no expert. He was told the Gallata team was two men, but he had no information about the other one.

"Where are you?" he barked, without any pleasantries.

"Walking west on Chambers Street. Our birdies are one block ahead, moving slowly. The lawyer has a shoulder bag. There are many people on the street, so we are following

DEAD WINNER

until we have them isolated. Are you worried about what might be in the bag?"

"I'm not sure. You might as well get it to make it look like a robbery even if it's empty. I'm on my way to join you."

"This is not necessary," Ivan said sternly.

"I know. But I'm coming anyway. This is my operation."

Ivan didn't fight the point. "Fine. I will text you when they land somewhere."

"Don't text. Call me. You've got a burner, but this is my actual phone and I'd rather not have to trash it."

"Fine." Ivan hung up. Buster was annoyed. He wasn't being given sufficient respect. He selected another burner phone number from his directory and dialed.

"Yeah?" the voice on the other end was high-pitched, but male.

"Did you see our two pigeons fly their coop a little while ago?"

"Yeah. They left maybe five minutes ago."

Buster didn't try to hide his annoyance. "When were you planning to tell me, shit-for-brains?"

"Relax, Buster. We have it covered. Ivan is gonna let me know when they are far enough away that we have a safe window to get into the apartment. I'm waiting for the green light, then we're gonna get your item and scram. My maintenance guy with the gambling problem is on call tonight. Piece of cake."

"Don't tell me to relax. This is my operation, and I expect you to keep me updated. Get the item and call me when it's secure. You got that?"

"Sure. Whatever." The line clicked dead. Buster scowled at his phone, but let it go. He had somewhere else to be.

237

KEVIN G. CHAPMAN

* * *

Buster saw Ivan standing on the northeast corner of Chambers and West Streets with his companion. Ivan had called with the location and enough of a description of himself that Buster couldn't miss him. The big Russian—if he was Russian—was six-five and a mountain of muscle. His head was completely shaved, making him stand out like a 100-watt bulb on a candelabra. He wore a black t-shirt that strained against his pectorals. A black-and-white windbreaker covered his arms and hid his gun, but did little to mask his girth. Buster experienced muscle envy. He was proud of his work in the gym. This guy was Arnold Schwarzenegger. The other guy was thin and wiry, but looked extra scrawny next to Ivan the muscle man.

Buster thought Ivan was a poor choice for a surveillance operation since he stood out so much in any crowd, but their targets were unaware they were being followed. On the streets of Manhattan, populated by a wide variety of characters, it probably didn't matter much. He walked slowly up to Ivan and spoke softly. A steady stream of pedestrians passed by them, but like good New Yorkers, they paid no attention. "Where are they?"

"Sitting on the bench across the street, on far side of walkway. The girl took a phone call a minute ago."

"You mean, like they came here to meet somebody, and just got the call? Like they have something in that shoulder bag you told me about and they're maybe handing it off to somebody? I don't like it. I don't like it at all. He could have more documents from the asshole's laptop, or maybe even another copy of his stupid video."

"What video?" Ivan asked.

DEAD WINNER

Buster remembered that these two were not filled in on the full story. They didn't need to know. They were muscle, not brains for this operation. He was basically talking to himself. "Never mind. The point is that if they try to hand the bag over to somebody, we need to get it. These two are dog meat, along with anybody they meet with. Understood?"

Ivan nodded.

"What's your name?" Buster asked Ivan's silent companion.

"Ricky." No further explanation was forthcoming. Ricky had no accent Buster could detect, and seemed to be Italian based on his dark complexion and hair. Buster had to trust that he was competent, or he would not have been sent by Fat Albert for this job.

Ivan looked casually in the direction of the bench and saw Monica get up and start walking. "They are moving," he said calmly.

"OK," Buster said, "I'm running this show from here. You guys know I was a cop, right?" The other two men shrugged simultaneously. "Trust me. You do what I tell you. Right now we need to keep that bag in sight. Follow me."

Chapter 41 – Tailing the Tail

STEVE AND GEORGE DISCUSSED whether to abandon their car. George had grumbled most of the evening about being called into Saturday service. He also groused about Steve's surveillance team decisions. He thought they should keep one unit farther back. He also thought it was stupid to give the units code names from Star Wars. But it was Steve's operation, so he didn't try to take over; he just complained.

The R2 unit reported that Monica and Rory were sitting on a bench, seemingly waiting for something. Whatever they were waiting for, unless it was an Uber or somebody else in a car, they were probably going to stick around the area. Before Steve made a final decision about leaving the car, the radio crackled again.

"D2, here, Red Leader. We've got another guest at the party. Our two . . . goons are now a threesome. New guy is another big White dude, wearing a suit jacket and dress clothes. He spent the last several minutes talking to the other two guys and now they're all moving together, following our two targets."

"Thanks, D2. We're leaving our vehicle now. Everybody seems to be on foot at this point. Suggest all units do the same. We'll come in from the south. R2, you follow behind the targets and take up a position where you can keep them

DEAD WINNER

in view, but don't get too close. D2, stay behind the two—three goons. If something happens, I want you to cut off their escape route. Everybody switch to cell phones on the secure conference line." George then switched the channel on the dashboard radio unit. "Dispatch, this is Detective George Mason. We have a suspect under surveillance at Rockefeller Park. Please dispatch two patrol units to this vicinity with instructions to stand by for back-up."

Steve raised an eyebrow. "You really think we need backup?"

"Not yet, but the Gallata goons have called in another guy and I don't want to get caught short." He opened the passenger-side door and stepped out, with Berkowitz right behind him.

Chapter 42 – Getting the Drop

RORY AND MONICA PASSED two benches along the concrete pathway, with the water of the Hudson River to their right. The benches were occupied, so they continued on to the point where the park jutted out and the path turned ninety degrees to the south. At the corner, they stopped momentarily to watch the city lights shimmer off the surface of the water. Two more fully occupied benches straddled the corner, so they made the turn and walked south. Twenty feet down from the corner two long benches faced the river. The first was occupied by a couple with a black Labrador sitting at their feet. Rory and Monica passed by and took seats at the second, as far away as possible from the couple and dog.

They looked out over the river toward New Jersey but constantly scanned the walkway to their left and right, looking for someone approaching. Rory's pulse was elevated, but not racing. A sheen of sweat formed on his bare arms in the humid summer air. He squeezed Monica's hand every thirty seconds, trying to reassure her that he had things under control. He wondered if she was more or less nervous than he was.

DEAD WINNER

More benches a few yards farther to the south were all occupied, but nobody paid the hand-holding couple any attention. Behind them, a line of short shrubs and a stand of trees separated the walkway from a large grassy field, where they had seen a few intrepid teens attempting to throw a frisbee around in the semi-darkness. Several groups sat on blankets, sipping wine and enjoying the remnants of their picnic dinners. The field was hidden from their view, but they could hear jazz music coming from an unseen speaker. It had been a balmy day and the temperature hovered in the low 80s. The air was tinged with the pungent odor of tree pollen.

"Don't turn around." A low, gravelly voice came from directly behind Rory. It sounded like the voice he had heard over Monica's ear buds. It had a mechanical edge to it, even in person, as if coming through a voice-altering device.

Rory turned his head, almost involuntarily, in the direction of the speaker.

"I said don't!" the voice snapped, keeping a low enough volume that none of the people on the nearby benches seemed to notice. Rory had the thought that New York was a criminal's dream because nobody ever paid attention to conversations around them. To do so would drive a person insane, since there was always a conversation going on around you.

"Sorry," Rory snapped his head back to face the water. He felt his pulse pounding in his ears. He was now in a full sweat from the intense adrenaline rush.

He heard footsteps approaching from directly behind him, then the voice spoke again, much closer. The guy must have come through the trees directly behind them. "Do you have the cash?"

243

KEVIN G. CHAPMAN

Now Rory was certain the voice was mechanically altered. It made sense. It would be much harder to identify him, even if they got a look at his face.

"Yes," Monica said when Rory didn't respond. "It's in the bag."

"Put it on the ground behind the bench."

Monica nudged Rory with her elbow. Rory, facing the river, said, "W-we need to see the ticket."

"You will," the voice replied, "but the cash is your show of good faith. I get that first."

"What if you run off with the cash?" Rory asked.

"What if I shoot you in the back of the head and take the money?" the voice responded without apparent emotion.

Rory froze. Being an attorney did not give him any experience with having his life threatened by a criminal who almost certainly had a gun trained on the back of his head. "OK. I get it. Here." He slid the bag off his shoulder and lowered it by its long strap over the back of the bench until it landed on the concrete with a soft *thud*. Rory caught a flash of movement in his peripheral vision as the figure behind them reached out to grab the bag, looping the strap loosely over his left shoulder. Rory heard the zipper on the bag and figured their trading partner was checking the interior to confirm the existence of the cash.

"Now, I'll need the transfer code, please."

Rory was surprised to get the "please." His pulse was still racing. He knew this was the time he needed to be strong. They had discussed it. He wasn't turning over the complete transfer code until they had the ticket. "I'm going to transfer the Bitcoin into an escrow account. Then, you give Monica the ticket."

DEAD WINNER

"OK, but keep in mind that I have a gun pointed at your girlfriend's head, so be very careful."

Rory reached into his pocket to get his phone.

"Slowly!" the mechanical voice warned.

Rory pulled out his phone and held it up to demonstrate it was a not a weapon. It was already open to his crypto wallet. When he pressed the button, the Bitcoin moved into the escrow account. After that, Rory had to authorize the final transfer to the wallet of the mystery man.

Rory stopped. His hand was trembling. In his video games, he never wavered before pulling off a kill shot or leaping off a cliff. Here, where the bullets were real, he could barely move. He held up the quivering phone, which displayed a QR code. Then he attempted to say the words he had been rehearsing in his brain. "N-now, b-before we finish this, we n-need the ticket."

"OK. Here it is." A gloved hand passed by Rory's right ear, handing a thin slip of white paper to Monica. She hesitantly reached for it, then held it in her lap.

"Is that—is that it?" Rory stammered.

"Yes," Monica whispered, "I think so." She handed the ticket to Rory, who took it and examined it by the light of his phone screen. It looked like the ticket he had seen on Tom's video. It had a bar code and the logo of the New York lottery. The winning numbers were there. Tom's initials were there in bold blue ink next to the logo. He was holding sixty million dollars in his hand.

Rory held his phone, screen up, over his left shoulder, without turning his head to look at his trading partner. His hand still shook. Then he heard a mechanical tone, signifying that the man behind him had scanned the QR

KEVIN G. CHAPMAN

code. The escrow account was now ready to complete the transfer. "Now, finish it," their faceless companion said.

Rory handed the ticket back to Monica, who held up her hand. "You carry it, please."

Rory drew back the ticket, folded it, and carefully stuffed it into the front-right pocket of his jeans. He had his phone in his left hand. He pressed the transfer button on his crypto wallet. His screen turned green.

The mechanical voice behind them said, "Thank you. A pleasure to do business. Now, stay put and don't turn around for five minutes."

Rory heard the rustle of clothing backing away. The transaction had gone smoothly, even better than he hoped. He had the winning ticket in his pocket, worth twenty times more than the three million in crypto he had just transferred, even after taxes. The trust he had set up would shield Monica's identity and allow Rory and his firm to manage the money. He closed his eyes and allowed his shoulders to relax. He exhaled, not realizing he had been holding his breath. He reached out his right hand toward Monica, but found only the wooden slats of the bench.

He opened his eyes. Monica was standing, facing away from the river and toward the retreating footsteps.

Rory could not breathe or speak. He heard Monica say, "Not so fast." In her right hand, at the end of an extended arm, she held a tiny silver pistol.

Chapter 43 – Saturday in the Park

STEVE BERKOWITZ LOWERED his small binoculars and let them fall by their black strap against his chest. He and George sat on a bench next to a semi-circular enclosure two hundred feet south of Monica and Rory. The R2 unit officers were with them. After Rory and Monica took their seats on the bench, Officers O'Dell and Seibrie had strolled past behind them and kept walking south until they met up with the detectives. The D2 unit was hanging back on the walkway to the north to keep tabs on the three Gallata goons, who had all gathered near the point of the park and were watching the events carefully, but making no moves.

"The lawyer passed his shoulder bag over the back of the bench to the new guy," Steve relayed the events to his partner. The new guy, wearing dark clothes and a hoodie with a black baseball cap bill sticking out, had arrived a few minutes after Steve and George established their surveillance position. He had apparently emerged through the trees separating the riverside walkway from the grassy field.

Steve had been watching Monica through his binoculars. When he saw Rory flinch, he noticed the new guy standing behind them. Steve couldn't determine his ethnicity or anything else that might help identify him later. He estimated the man to be between five-seven and five-nine with a medium build. There was not much light on the area between the bench and the tree line. The hoodie and hat shaded the new guy's face.

Steve reported that "Hoodie Guy," had reached across the bench from behind their targets, possibly making a transfer of some kind. "It's a weird little dance they're doing."

"Some kind of exchange?" George suggested.

"Could be." Steve kept the binoculars at his eyes.

George spoke softly into his telephone headset. It wasn't FBI-quality private voice communication, but standard mobile phones, Bluetooth earpieces, and a secure conference bridge did the job nearly as well. "D2, what are our three little goons doing?"

"They're just standing and watching," Officer Douglas Shellabarger reported. "They're talking to each other. Wait. Now one of them is walking back toward us. He's turning onto the path that goes behind the trees, heading south toward you. He might be getting into position to intercept our targets if they leave in that direction. Should one of us follow?"

"Negative. He's heading in our direction, so we can pick him up," George said calmly. "Stay with the other two."

George then turned to O'Dell and Seibrie, the R2 unit. "You two move to a position behind the stand of trees, between our targets and the open field. Cut off any escape route through the trees." He motioned for them to follow a curving path that meandered north from their position. "The third guy from the goon squad is heading toward us on the

DEAD WINNER

same path. If you see him, let him pass and we'll pick him up."

When George finished talking, Steve said, "Hold on . . . our new guy is stepping back . . . The widow is getting up. Holy shit! She has a gun."

* * *

Buster and Ivan leaned their backs against the iron railing, facing south. They talked casually, like a couple of buddies enjoying the cool breeze off the river on a warm night. Ricky was facing them without blocking their view of the bench, some hundred feet or so to the south. The light wasn't great, but they could see that somebody had approached the back of the bench.

"That was the shoulder bag," Ivan said. "The lawyer handed it over the bench and the new guy took it."

A few moments later, Buster said, "Shit! Look. He handed something to them. That's the payment, for sure. This is definitely a transfer. We have to get that package."

Buster spun Ricky around. "You two stay here. I'll circle around behind them to the south. We need to cut that dude off and get the bag when he leaves. If he comes this way, grab him."

"What if he don't want to be grabbed?" Ricky asked. The man had not said a word since he spoke his name when Buster first approached. Now, Buster noticed a pronounced Brooklyn accent.

"Do what you need to do," Buster said. "I would prefer that we not call undue attention to ourselves, but if you have to shoot him, then shoot him. But get that bag. Don't wait for me. Get out of here with it and I'll find you later."

249

Chapter 44 – Pulse Race

RORY JUMPED TO HIS FEET. His frazzled nerves had finally relaxed for a few seconds. Now, Monica was going totally off script. "Monica!? What are you doing?"

"This piece of shit killed Tom!" Monica shouted to Rory. Then, turning back to the figure now standing behind their bench, "I hate you!"

"Monica, stop! Put down that gun!" Rory thrust out his hand. "Don't—"

Monica fired the little silver .22. It was not a large gun and had limited range, but at point blank it could kill. The report sounded like a sonic boom in the relative quiet of the esplanade.

The couple with the black lab sitting on the next bench jumped. The dog barked. The woman screamed. The man shouted, "Shooter! Gun!" Although the dog's owner was the first to voice it, nearly everyone who heard the shot immediately knew what it was. They all had the same reaction—to run away as fast as possible. The esplanade was not crowded, but suddenly people filled the path in both directions. The dog charged toward the trees, his owners trailing after on the end of a long leash. The sense of calm and relaxation changed to pandemonium in a heartbeat.

DEAD WINNER

Rory flinched at the deafening *bang* a foot from his ear. When he looked away from Monica, the man in the hoodie, with Rory's Emirates Airlines bag slung over one shoulder, was down on a knee. He bounced up, a black gun four times the size of Monica's tiny Saturday Night Special in his hand. Rory dropped to the ground, reaching out for Monica's arm in an attempt to drag her down with him. Instead of ducking, Monica shrugged off Rory's hand and fired her gun again, but Rory had thrown her off balance and the shot went high. Rory had no idea how many bullets the little thing could have.

Time seemed to stop. The ringing in his ears drowned out all other sounds. He stared at the big gun and at the face of the man who was the object of Monica's rage. It was distorted and lumpy in the dim light, under a black baseball hat. He couldn't see their assailant's eyes. Rory heard another deafening explosion and saw a flash from the muzzle of the black gun. He turned away instinctively, then reached up again. Monica screamed. He could see her open mouth and the anguish on her face. He could not hear her voice over the ringing in his ears.

Monica staggered backwards, dropping her silver pistol, which appeared no bigger than a toy on the ground. Her hands flew to her chest. Another shot blasted through the evening air. Rory heard it clearly, but not as loud as before. His ears throbbed with each beat of his heart, now well over one hundred per minute. He recognized how bizarre it was, calculating his heart rate based on his experience with a heart monitor during fifty-mile bike rides. He could accurately estimate his heart rate up to about 140. The thought raced through his brain in a millisecond as he watched Monica stagger backward again, her arms flying into the air. Her hands were stained crimson. A dark splotch marred her shirt, between her breasts.

"No!" Rory shouted, barely able to hear his own voice. He reached again toward Monica, but she had fallen back too far.

One more shot split the air. Monica lurched to the side, spun by the force of the bullet. She fell face-forward against the iron railing, her upper torso falling limply over the top bar. Then, as he watched in what seemed like slow motion, her feet lifted off the ground as her body teetered over the fulcrum of the railing, having just enough momentum to carry her limp form forward.

As Rory looked on in horror, Monica's head dipped down, becoming nearly vertical. Her legs rose further, then her hips slipped over the edge of the rail. Her torso slid forward, gaining speed until her black sneakers reached the rail and caught for a moment as her toes appeared to clutch at the bar. Then she disappeared from his sight.

He couldn't hear the splash when Monica hit the water. The ringing in his ears drowned out all else. He sprang forward, grabbing the top rail with both hands, and leaned over. He peered into the dark night. The water, six feet below, rolled gently in the soft summer breeze, reflecting the street lamps. Ripples from an unseen source spread out, already mostly absorbed by the ambient surface disturbances. Even as he looked, the concentric circles disappeared. No arms or legs thrashed in the water to indicate someone struggling to stay afloat. No body emerged from the darkness, nor could he see any sign of one underneath the murky water. He smelled a hint of Monica's *Poison* hanging in the air.

DEAD WINNER

Rory realized his phone was still in his hand and fumbled for the flashlight function. Maybe if he could illuminate the water, he would be able to see her. He could still save her.

Before he could activate the light, another shot rang out. He jumped and looked back toward the man who had just shot the woman he loved. He felt rage and sorrow simultaneously. He could charge toward the gunman, or he could jump over the rail into the river to save Monica. Both options were awful.

The gunman fired again. Rory flinched and turned away. The bullet had missed him. He cried out, "Monica!" His voice sounded miles away. His feet felt like lead weights. His pulse pounded. The man in the hoodie raised his black gun again.

Rory ran. He stumbled on his first step, falling on his right knee and grabbing the railing to steady himself. He sprinted south. His ears throbbed, a high-pitched whine drowning out his footfalls and heavy breathing.

Everyone was running. He nearly tripped over a dog, this one a Golden Retriever. He heard another gunshot, causing him to involuntarily duck his head. He passed an older couple struggling to move away from the source of the shots. He whizzed past, immediately scolding himself for not stopping to help them. He should stop. What if they didn't make it? He kept running. They were too far back.

Two men wearing dark jackets passed Rory going the other way, toward the shooter. Maybe they would help the old couple. He couldn't think straight. He ran farther south.

Two more shots. Rory's ears were still ringing, making it difficult to tell exactly where they came from. Was the guy crazy? Why was he still shooting? Who was he shooting at?

KEVIN G. CHAPMAN

As he ran, the pedestrian traffic on the path thinned out. Fewer people were running away here. A quarter-mile from where he started, Rory reached a railing where the path turned to the left, eastbound. He stopped, his breath coming in deep heaves. From this point, he was only a few hundred yards from the marina. He could see the strings of lights marking the docks and the lights on a few of the yachts where Saturday night parties were underway. Without thinking, he scanned for the *Couples Therapy*. He thought he found it, but it was dark and the boat was not lit up, so he couldn't be sure. It had been only three days since he and Monica spent a blissful night there.

Monica! Rory rested his forehead against the top of the railing, sucking air. Despair, pain, disbelief, and anger all broke over him like an emotional wave. He should go back. The shooter was surely gone by now, with his cash and his Bitcoin securely transferred. Rory should tell the police what happened. He could say it was a robbery. But what if they caught the man in the hoodie? The guy had his Emirates bag and the money. How could he explain that? It would be in the press. What story could he tell?

Rory cut to his left, now running back in the direction of West Street. Other people were running on the same path. He passed them by. His hours of bike training kicked in automatically. He settled into a steady pace. He knew he was safe from flying bullets. There were now buildings and trees between him and the site where, only moments before, he and Monica sat holding hands.

Monica! He slowed to a walk, again gauging his heart rate. It was at 130. Even after a long uphill climb at the end of a three- or four-hour ride, he seldom registered a higher number. The ringing in his ears continued. The sounds

DEAD WINNER

around him were muffled. All he could think was that he had failed. He was supposed to protect Monica. Why did she have a gun? He could have jumped in front of her. He could have rushed at the gunman. He didn't. He ran away. He saved himself. Monica was dead. He crossed West Street and continued toward his apartment.

Chapter 45 – All Hell

BERKOWITZ AND MASON EACH DROPPED to a knee when they heard the first shot, then moved forward cautiously, drawing their service pistols. George reached for his police radio and called in, "Shots fired–Rockefeller Park. Officers need assistance. Send in our backup units."

Then the second shot. People ran and screamed. Steve and George took two steps forward. Over the next thirty seconds, there were three more shots. Each explosion made them pause to assess where the fire was coming from and whether the threat level had changed. They were not close enough to see clearly in the dim light. Steve didn't dare try to use the binoculars while shots were being fired. He needed all his peripheral vision available.

Having seen Monica Williams holding a gun and muzzle flashes from that direction, they were pretty sure the shots came from their targets, or maybe from Hoodie Guy. They ducked against the end of one of the wooden benches, where they had a little shelter, now only fifty feet from the bench where Monica and Rory had been sitting. Steve saw a figure wearing a white top fall over the railing into the river. He saw the lawyer rush to the spot, look over, then turn.

Another shot made Steve flinch and duck. That one definitely came from Hoodie Guy. Then another shot.

DEAD WINNER

The lawyer turned toward Steve's location, stumbled, and fell, but got up and sprinted south. "The lawyer's running this way," Steve informed the teams. He and George resumed their approach toward the shooting scene, pushing against the panicked flow of civilians fleeing from the gunfire.

"R2, D2, report!" George called into his phone.

Officer Mike Fidler's voice came through Steve's earpiece. "The two Gallata guys hit the ground as soon as the first shot was fired. They're still at the corner."

"Where's the shooter?"

"Unknown. We don't have line of sight on the shooter."

"Move in!" George ordered, "But keep an eye on those two guys." George took two more steps. "R2 team, where are you?"

"This is R2. We heard the shots coming from the river. We're behind the trees. No line of sight. Should we move in?"

"Negative!" George barked. "Hold your position and make sure the shooter doesn't come your way through the trees. Be ready!"

George and Steve ran forward, fighting the people and a few dogs fleeing the scene. Steve felt like a salmon fighting through rapids to get to his spawning ground. The shooting had stopped. Rory McEntyre sprinted past them, but with an active shooter up ahead and without any reason to think the lawyer had anything to do with it, Steve and George let him go.

They approached the scene and slowed down, not knowing whether more shots were forthcoming. They crouched down at the end of a now-empty bench, twenty feet from the one Rory and Monica had been sitting on moments before. Steve could see two figures in the dim light cast by a street lamp at the water's edge. One was Hoodie Guy; the other wasn't familiar. The new guy was bigger than Hoodie. He looked to be White and had a crew-cut. The new guy was wearing a dark suit jacket against which Steve saw a shoulder bag, its silver strap snaking up toward the guy's head. Crew Cut had his right arm extended.

Steve grabbed George by the shoulder. "Careful! The new guy has a gun."

George crouched down next to Steve. As they watched, Hoodie reached out and grabbed Crew Cut by the arm. Another shot shattered the New York night. Steve and George both ducked. An object flew from Crew Cut's hand as his body flipped over Hoodie's back. Crew Cut landed on the concrete with a muffled thud.

Officer Shellabarger from the D2 team called out, "The Gallata guys are moving toward you!"

"Follow them!" George shouted. Steve and George moved forward carefully, not sure how many shooters there were and wary about the approaching goons. Crew Cut's gun was down, but Hoodie was still an unknown.

The smaller member of the Gallata gang duo, who they had identified as Ricky Newman, reached the area first. Hoodie saw him coming and went into a fighting stance. When Ricky charged forward, Hoodie stepped sideways and grabbed his arm while tripping the attacker with his foot, sending Ricky sprawling forward. Ricky crashed into the iron support of the wooden bench and crumpled to the ground.

The huge bald guy, Ivan, came in next. He stopped five feet from Hoodie, a pistol held in his massive paw. Hoodie turned toward his new attacker. Ricky was down for the count, but Steve saw Crew Cut getting to his knees.

DEAD WINNER

The two officers from the D2 unit ran up behind Ivan. There was so much background noise from people screaming and running that Ivan apparently didn't notice the footsteps behind him. He kept his gun fixed on Hoodie.

Steve stood and stepped forward, raising his gun. George, on his right, called out toward Ivan and Hoodie, "Police! Drop the gun and freeze!"

Simultaneously, Officer Shellabarger yelled from behind Ivan, "Police! Freeze!"

Ivan spun toward the officer at his back, holding his gun in an outstretched arm.

George and Steve both fired. The big man lurched to the side. Then another shot came from in front of them as Shellabarger fired. Steve and George, not knowing for sure who was firing, dropped down again. Ivan toppled. The two officers from the D2 team charged forward, securing Ivan and taking his gun. George jumped up and tackled Ricky; who had regained his senses and was scrambling toward Crew Cut's gun, which had fallen to the ground.

Officer Fidler called in a request for an ambulance. Four uniformed patrol officers, responding to George's earlier call for assistance, stormed around the corner of the park and ran toward the scene.

To the north, at the point of the park, a small group of people huddled. Two were taking video with their cell phones. Everyone else had fled. There was no sign of the R2 unit.

Steve stood and surveyed the scene, then said, "Where's the Hoodie?"

George, with one knee pressed into Ricky's back, said, "And where's Mr. Crew Cut?"

259

KEVIN G. CHAPMAN

* * *

Buster had hurried down the winding path around the back of the stand of trees that separated the grassy field from the bench where Monica and Rory were making their exchange with the unknown guy in the hoodie. When the first shots rang out, he had pushed through the trees, hoping to come up behind Hoodie, who had taken the shoulder bag. His plan was to snatch the bag, or shoot Hoodie if he had to. He had not anticipated shots being fired.

When Buster reached a row of thick boxwoods lining the edge of the paved esplanade, he saw Hoodie Guy's back. The lawyer's bag was slung loosely over his left shoulder. The man's right arm was extended, holding a gun. On the other side of the bench, the woman—Monica Williams—held her hands over her head, near the edge of the path. By the light from a lamppost on the iron railing, Buster saw a dark splotch in the middle of her white top. The man in the hoodie fired again. Williams spun toward the river, fell forward, and flipped over the railing.

Hoodie Guy fired twice more in the direction of the lawyer, who jumped, turned, then ran away to the south. At that point, Buster moved quickly toward Hoodie —and the shoulder bag.

Buster charged through a gap in the shrubbery behind Hoodie, who shoved his pistol into the front pouch of his sweatshirt, oblivious to Buster's approach. People all around shouted and screamed. Several dogs barked excitedly. Hoodie Guy turned, ready to dash into the stand of trees. Buster reached out with his left hand, his gun in his right. He snatched the shoulder bag and pulled it off Hoodie's

DEAD WINNER

shoulder. Buster couldn't make out a face under the black baseball cap in the dim light.

"Don't try it!" Buster shouted, holding out his Glock when Hoodie reached toward the pouch, now holding his own gun. As Buster slid the strap of the bag over his own head, Hoodie's hand flashed forward. He grabbed Buster's wrist above his gun and pulled him off balance, planting a sneaker on top of Buster's shiny black loafer. Buster pulled the trigger, sending a bullet wildly toward the river. He felt himself falling forward and flipping. He landed with a thud on his back. Buster's gun clattered away on the concrete esplanade. He was momentarily stunned, then shook off the impact and looked up to see Ricky careening past him and crunching into the bench. Hoodie's gun fell out of the sweatshirt's pouch and clanged against the pavement.

Buster caught his breath and rolled in the direction of Hoodie's gun. He heard somebody shout, "Police! Drop the gun and freeze!"

Police? How did they get there so fast? Buster abandoned the gun and scrambled toward the tree line, hoping to get under cover before the police moved in.

Three more shots rang out. Out of the corner of his eye, Buster saw Ivan lurch to the side. Hoodie darted toward the trees to Buster's left. Buster dashed after Hoodie, the shoulder bag bouncing against his hip. He leapt over the row of boxwoods and crashed through the trees, stumbling over a root in the darkness. Charging out the other side, he paused for a moment, scanning the pandemonium on the grassy field as everyone rushed away from the shooting.

"Police! Stop right there!" a female voice shouted off to his right. More police? What the hell? He sprinted forward toward the apartment buildings on the far side of the field,

261

KEVIN G. CHAPMAN

the shoulder bag banging against his hip with each stride. He knew the cops would not shoot a fleeing person, so he turned on as much speed as he could manage, regretting his decision to wear clubbing clothes.

"Stop!" a deeper voice called out behind him. He did not look back or slow down.

Reaching the far side of the grassy field, already breathing hard, Buster hung a quick right onto a path that wound through the landscaping between two apartment buildings. He figured it would lead back to West Street. As the path curved, he caught a glimpse of the figures on his tail fifty feet back. He had to believe they were cops, although they had no uniforms. That meant detectives. What the hell?

Buster knew the cops might be calling for backup to intercept him. He needed to lose them and get somewhere he could blend in or hide. Rounding another gentle curve, he saw an elderly woman emerging through a large metal door, pushing a wire shopping basket on four large black wheels. Buster took a sharp turn, stormed past the surprised lady, and caught the heavy door before it closed. Inside, he walked quickly, without running, down a long hallway painted battleship gray. No other residents passed by on their way toward the locked rear door. He was confident the cops would not be following, at least for a while. They would try to get to the front of the building, and maybe call for backup.

Where the hell did all the cops come from? It was a puzzle he didn't have time to solve. At the end of the hall, he turned right, then left, finding himself in the building's lobby.

Clumps of people huddled together near the entrance talking excitedly, no doubt about the shooting in the nearby park. Buster swung the Emirates Airways bag over his head

DEAD WINNER

and dropped it on the ground next to an arrangement of chairs and a sofa at the rear of the lobby. He removed his jacket and left it on the wing chair, tucking his wallet into his pants pocket. Now wearing only his silk dress shirt and slacks, he walked toward the exit doors, holding the bag by its handle like a briefcase.

A cab pulled into the semi-circular driveway in front of the building under a large awning. Buster waited impatiently for the passengers to exit, then popped into the back seat.

As the cab pulled away, Buster unzipped the bag. He expected to find folders, loose papers, or portable digital storage devices. He was shocked to see bundles of hundred-dollar bills, each strapped with a yellow band labeled $10,000. He dug his hand all around the bottom of the bag, but found nothing else. The outside of the bag had two zippered pockets. Inside one was Rory McEntyre's business card. The other pocket was empty. He found no other pockets or compartments.

Money? Payment? For what? Buster suddenly had the awful thought that his real objective might have been whatever Hoodie gave to McEntyre. He muttered, "Shit!"

He pulled out his phone. There was a missed call from the burner phone belonging to his man at McEntyre's apartment building. There was a voice message. It was short. "The item is secure." At least one thing had gone right.

263

Chapter 46 – Stages of Grief

RORY ARRIVED AT HIS APARTMENT dripping with sweat and shaking. His pants were dirty, with a torn knee exposing a bloody scrape. He had hardly noticed. His doorman, Imran, concerned about his appearance and noticing the absence of the Emirates bag, offered to call the police. He thought Rory had been mugged. Rory declined and scuttled to the elevator, trying unsuccessfully to seem composed.

Once safely inside his apartment, he stripped off his clothes and threw them in the trash under his kitchen sink, including the sneakers. Standing under a hot shower, feeling the water trickling down his body and stinging his scraped knee, he tried to make sense of what had happened.

Monica was dead. Dead! All the plans he had imagined about their future together—gone. All the happiness of the past week evaporated in a heartbeat. Why? They had accomplished their goal. The exchange had gone perfectly. Why had Monica brought a gun? Why did she have to confront the guy? Sure, he had murdered Tom and stolen their money, but the plan was to make the exchange and leave without any confrontation. All they needed was . . . the ticket.

Rory burst from the shower, grabbing a towel but not drying off before hurrying down the hallway, slipping on the

DEAD WINNER

hardwood. Ripping open the cabinet under his sink, he pulled out the trash can and extracted his bloody, ripped pants. When he arrived home, he had automatically removed his cell phone from the front-left pocket and put it on the little table in the entry foyer. He thrust his hand into the right-front pocket of the jeans. It was there. He forced himself to slow down and carefully removed the thin white paper, folded in half.

Dropping the pants, he moved to the kitchen table and smoothed the lottery ticket out, careful not to drip water on the precious paper. He stepped back, toweling off on the now-slick ceramic tiles. He began thinking about the future.

He would mourn Monica deeply. When the police retrieved her body from the river, he would organize a proper funeral. He knew the best vendors. It was what he did every week. He would probate her will. He recalled the charitable donations she designated. The trust would claim the lottery winnings. The trust would pay the taxes and the expenses for the funeral and closing up her affairs – and Tom's. Then, the trust would continue, with Rory as the trustee. Monica had made a new will, making him the beneficiary.

That would never fly, he thought. He couldn't claim the money. Could he? The trust could at least reimburse him for the three million he had spent to buy the Bitcoin. What was he going to tell the police? Could they possibly recover his Bitcoin? Surely they had arrested the killer.

He rushed to the living room and turned on the television, channeling to New York One News. What time was it? Nearly eleven o'clock. Had it only been an hour? He switched to channel two, which had local news at eleven. Surely the shooting at Rockefeller Park would be the top

KEVIN G. CHAPMAN

story. Had the local news folks even had time to get there? Would the police give them any information?

He spent the next hour watching every local station. They all reported on a shooting, but none had any details. Channel 4 reported one bystander who said a woman had been shot, but it was not confirmed.

Did the police know who he was? When they found Monica's body, he assumed they would identify her, which would eventually lead the cops to him. Would any bystanders be able to identify him? Would the guy in the hoodie identify him, or Monica? He wondered if the cops had recovered the shoulder bag with his hundred grand. Would he tell them about the lottery ticket, and the ransom demand? Would he say the guy probably murdered Tom Williams?

His mind raced through a thousand questions. Monica didn't want her identity exposed as the winner of the lottery money. No, it was Tom who didn't want to be identified. If he didn't tell the cops about the lottery ticket and the ransom, what would he say about what happened? He could say it was an attempted robbery. Then Monica pulled her gun to protect them. But why did he have a hundred thousand dollars in cash in a bag in the park? He had no explanation. It had to be a payoff. What else could the guy have been holding for ransom? Why would Rory have given him three million dollars' worth of Bitcoin?

He slumped to the floor. It was a nightmare. He couldn't think. He sat there, naked and wrapped in a towel. He thought about the after-dinner lovemaking he and Monica had shared only a few hours earlier. He sobbed softly, his tears dripping onto his bath towel.

Chapter 47 – Open Issues

STEVE BERKOWITZ AND GEORGE MASON were dog-tired Sunday afternoon when they arrived at the 94th Street precinct. They knew Captain Sullivan would be even less happy to be there, but he had to provide a briefing for the commissioner and the mayor. The two detectives were glad to skip that meeting.

In the fifth-floor conference room, away from any stray ears down in the bullpen, Sully had Steve and George summarize what happened. The details would be put in a written report later. The media was saying that the presence of the police on the scene certainly prevented more deaths. Sully, however, wanted Steve and George to explain why they had not apprehended the man in the hoodie, who had shot Monica Williams. Or the mystery man who came out of nowhere, grabbed the shoulder bag, and escaped the scene. The police were not publicizing those bits of information.

Ivan, the big bald man, had drawn a gun and threatened both the mystery man and the responding officers. He had been shot multiple times, but was recovering in the hospital. His accomplice, Ricky Newman, was banged up but also in custody. Neither man was talking about what happened.

"We didn't anticipate gunfire," Steve said. "Nothing up to that point in the surveillance suggested a shoot-out."

KEVIN G. CHAPMAN

"You had four uniformed officers and two detectives split into three units." The vein in Sully's left temple was starting to bulge. "So, how the actual fuck did you let the guy who shot the Williams woman get away?"

Steve and George exchanged eye contact. They had obviously expected the question and Steve had volunteered to fall on his sword. "That's my fault, Sir. We didn't know what we were watching for. We didn't know why the two—then three—Gallata operatives were following our marks. We observed from a short distance on all sides. Williams and her lawyer made some kind of exchange with the shooter, who arrived through the trees. It didn't appear to be anything that could turn violent. I figured we would nab the guy in the hoodie and find out what was going on. If necessary, we could detain Williams and McEntyre. There was no reason for us to expect gunfire." When Sully didn't say anything, Steve took a gulp of air and continued. "We didn't see Hoodie Guy with a weapon until after Williams pulled her little .22 out. We didn't expect her to have a gun, or to use it. When she fired at Hoodie, we were too far away to intervene. We reacted according to protocol—safety first for us and for bystanders. Firing at Mrs. Williams was not advisable given both the distance and the number of civilians who had started to run, which made it too chaotic a scene for us to discharge our weapons."

"Alright," Sully barked. "So, where did the guy in the hoodie go?"

"After the first sequence of weapons fire, two of the Gallata goons—er—men were the closest to the scene, and they arrived before any of our officers."

"Why in blazes would they run *toward* the shooter?" Sully asked nobody in particular.

DEAD WINNER

"We don't know, Sir. There were more shots. We didn't know whether they were directed at us, so we took cover briefly. When the third member of the Gallata group engaged with Hoodie Guy and drew a weapon, we focused on him. Then, one of the others, who we now know was Ivan Roshenko, displayed a weapon. We followed protocol, identified ourselves as police, and yelled for him to freeze and drop his gun. After that, he directed his weapon toward two other members of our team, who had approached from the north. At that point we were forced to fire."

"All by the book," Sully interjected.

"Yes, Sir."

"But you let the original shooter get away."

Steve held his hands out, palms up in surrender. "We did, Sir. The third man, whom we still have not identified, took the shoulder bag and ran. Two members of our team saw him emerge through the trees onto the field and pursued him. In the gunfire and in our efforts to secure the scene, including Roshenko who definitely had a gun, the guy with the hoodie slipped into the trees. We found his outer clothing, including a facial mask and a voice distortion device. He probably mingled with civilians who were fleeing. Since we had no identification on him and none of our officers were focused on him going into the operation . . . we did not apprehend him. The forensics team didn't get any prints off the clothing. We're sending it to the lab to see if we can get any DNA off it, but it's a longshot."

"So, nobody knows what was in the bag, and nobody knows what was exchanged between Williams, McEntyre, and the guy in the hoodie. Is that it?"

"Yes, Sir," Steve responded meekly.

"So we know shit about shit."

KEVIN G. CHAPMAN

"I guess not," Steve responded again.

"That wasn't a question, Detective."

"Sorry, Sir."

"OK," Sully sighed. "I think I've got enough. Try to track down this hoodie guy, of course, and the other one. We had officers chasing him, for Christ's sake. Did they not see where he went?"

"Yes, Cap. We've got two officers down at the building we think the guy ducked into, looking at security cam video. So, we're working on it."

"Well work on it a little harder!" Sully slammed an open palm on the table. Then his facial expression softened. "But I think any damage is contained. I want you two to work the Monica Williams murder case. Hard. Agree? Go talk to her lawyer and see what he has to say."

Steve and George again exchanged eye contact, then both left the conference room feeling like they had dodged a bullet.

Chapter 48 – Assembling the Pieces

BERKOWITZ GOT THE CALL at 11:45 a.m. on Monday that Rory McEntyre was on his way up from the precinct lobby. Steve and George had finally reached the lawyer on his cell phone and had volunteered to meet Rory at his office, but he preferred to meet at the station. They guessed he wanted to keep his involvement in the police investigation confidential, which was fine with them.

Monica's body had not surfaced. In that location in Lower Manhattan, it was possible a submerged body could have been carried out of the harbor by the tide and currents. It was unusual, but had happened in a few known cases—at least they thought so, since they never recovered the bodies. There were other possibilities, and she could still turn up somewhere. For the present, Monica was missing and presumed dead.

The crime scene unit had recovered two spent shell casings from Monica's .22, which had been registered to her three weeks earlier. They had not found the bullets, which could easily be buried in the soft mulch under the stand of trees and shrubs toward which she had fired. The forensics team also found five 9mm shell casings from a Remington

KEVIN G. CHAPMAN

R51, which was also recovered at the scene, presumably fired by the man in the hoodie. There were no prints on the gun and the serial number was ground away. They would try to trace it, but didn't expect it to provide much of a lead. There was also one shell casing from the Glock 17 fired by the man with the crew cut, who was associated with the two Gallata goons, Ivan and Ricky. That gun had a serial number, but was not registered and contained no useful prints.

The two civilians who had taken cell-phone video at the scene sold their footage to separate news outlets. Both videos picked up the scene after Hoodie Guy had fired his first three shots. One of the videos captured Monica falling over the rail into the river, but neither got a clear shot of Hoodie Guy with a gun in his hand. The police obtained the full digital files, but the poor lighting made it impossible to get a clean image of Hoodie Guy. The video did show Crew Cut running off toward the tree line with the shoulder bag, but the images were insufficiently clear to permit an ID.

Ivan had taken three bullets but survived and was in custody, although they were having trouble deciding what to charge him with other than brandishing a gun at the police officers. Ricky was arrested at the scene and charged as an accomplice. The DA had a similar problem charging Ricky, since getting tossed into a park bench by an unknown person was not a crime. Ivan's gun was legally registered, and a high-powered lawyer known to be associated with Fat Albert Gallata showed up to represent both Ivan and Ricky, who were not talking. The lawyer argued that Ivan and Ricky were Good Samaritans, the only people besides the cops running toward the shooter to try to subdue him and save innocent civilian lives.

DEAD WINNER

Monica's blood was on the iron railing. At least it was her blood type, based on information in her health insurance records. Monica's mother granted permission for the police to have access to her apartment, where they got a sufficient DNA sample from a hairbrush. They expected to be able to get a clear match within a few weeks. If the DNA didn't match, they would have a new puzzle, but Steve and George preferred to assume the obvious explanation was true until proven otherwise.

"Maybe the lawyer can help us close out the Tom Williams suicide case," George said with a straight face.

"Sure," Steve replied, "and maybe he's also the Easter Bunny."

* * *

All day on Sunday, Rory had watched the television news reports on the shooting. Late in the day, a spokesperson for the NYPD confirmed that the police had apprehended two men who were believed to be connected to the Gallata organized crime family. She confirmed that an unidentified woman was killed, but would not confirm whether she was the intended victim of the suspects or a bystander. There was no mention of Rory. He was befuddled by the reference to *two* men, rather than just one, and the fact that they were connected to the Gallata mob. Like most New Yorkers, he knew the basics of Fat Albert Gallata and his murdered father. But Rory could not figure out how the guy in the hoodie was connected to them or how the mobsters were involved in the ransom demand? It didn't make sense.

Monday morning, Rory called in sick to work and called a criminal lawyer he knew from another firm, Ned Racine.

KEVIN G. CHAPMAN

Ned's father had died a year earlier and Rory had handled the processing of the estate. They discovered a mutual interest in cycling and had bumped into each other at several local races. Ned was the only criminal lawyer Rory knew outside his own firm. He wanted to keep Mr. Packman and the rest of his colleagues out of this. It was bad enough that he was taking another day off. None of the news reports about the shooting included his name and he was not on any of the video clips. It seemed like he might avoid being connected to the shooting, but he knew the cops would eventually want to talk to him, and he knew enough to want a real criminal lawyer.

During his initial meeting with Ned that morning, under the cloak of attorney-client privilege, Rory spilled out the whole story. Ned said he believed it because it was too crazy to be a lie. Rory insisted he had done nothing wrong. Ned nevertheless advised him to say nothing to the cops about the real reason he and Monica were in Rockefeller Park. Rory, however, had decided to face the music and take responsibility for his actions. He was confident he had done nothing illegal and had nothing to hide. He might be embarrassed, but he wanted to cooperate fully. If it helped catch Monica's killer, he could stand the ridicule of being the lawyer who let his client go to a ransom drop without police involvement where she was shot and killed. He would even admit to financing the ransom.

Ned shook his head, but had to agree to his client's wishes.

* * *

DEAD WINNER

When Ned and Rory were seated in the fifth-floor conference room, George decided to dive into the most difficult issue right off the bat. "Mr. McEntyre, we understand that you had an attorney-client relationship with Monica Williams. We can get into a theoretical discussion about why a dead woman can't assert an attorney-client privilege, but we're hoping you will cooperate and help us figure out exactly what happened and help us track down the guy who killed Mrs. Williams."

Ned interjected, "We all want that, Detective."

"Great. So, Mr. McEntyre, why don't you just tell us in your own words what happened?"

Rory took a deep breath, then calmly gave the two detectives the whole truth, except for the part about him having sex with his client. The detectives sat in silence, absorbing the information and trying to reconcile it with the facts they thought they knew. He finished with the revelation that somebody–presumably connected to Northrup Investments–broke into his apartment while he and Monica were at Rockefeller Park and stole Tom's laptop. Nothing else was taken. He didn't bother telling the detectives that he had copies of the two spreadsheets. He couldn't prove where they came from and without the other account records, they didn't prove anything.

When the story was done, Rory said, "Did you get my Emirates bag back from the guy? I read in the paper that he was shot and captured. I'd like to get my bag back."

Steve looked at George. "No. We didn't find the bag."

Rory dropped his head. He was out three million in Bitcoin, but he had been optimistic about recovering the hundred thousand in cash, even if he had to wait until it was no longer evidence in a criminal case.

275

KEVIN G. CHAPMAN

Steve and George stepped out of the room to confer, leaving Rory and Ned sitting in silence for five minutes. There was nothing to say, and they assumed the room was monitored.

When the detectives returned, Steve's first question was, "So, the guy in the hoodie gave you the lottery ticket?"

"Yes."

"I assume you still have it?"

"Of course."

"It may be evidence. We'll want to dust it for prints."

Ned assured Berkowitz that they would produce the original lottery ticket for inspection and forensic analysis, but doubted there would be anything useful and insisted that the police could not keep the original, which they needed to turn over to the lottery commission on behalf of the trust established by Monica and Tom Williams. The detectives reluctantly agreed.

"So, you have no idea who the guy in the hoodie is?"

"None," Rory truthfully responded.

"And you have no idea why three guys from the Gallata crime organization were following you and Mrs. Williams?"

"Three? I heard it was two? But, no, I don't. I could speculate about how they might be connected to the Northrup Investments embezzlement scheme, but I really have no knowledge."

"Did you know that Mrs. Williams had a gun with her?"

"God, no. I didn't even know she owned a gun. I would have told her not to bring it. There was no need. The guy was going to give us the ticket. If she had just let it go down like we planned it . . ." Rory bit his lower lip.

"Thank you, Mr. McEntyre," Steve said. The interview seemed to be over.

DEAD WINNER

"Detective," Rory asked, "how much of my story are you going to share with the media?"

Steve exchanged a glance with George. "I don't think any of this needs to be public, at least not for now. We'll be investigating. There are at least two people involved who are still at large. We don't want to let them know what we know—for now."

"Thank you," Rory said. "I'm sure you can imagine that I'm not excited about all this becoming public."

"Keeping in mind that Mr. McEntyre did not do anything unlawful," Ned interjected.

Steve pursed his lips. "There was some information withheld from us during our investigation."

"Which was protected by an attorney-client privilege," Ned pointed out.

"Maybe," Steve conceded. "We'll brief the DA and let him decide whether to bring charges."

George then stood, signaling definitively that the interview was ending. "I'm sorry for your loss. It looked like you and Mrs. Williams were pretty close."

"Yes, well, we were old friends from school. Her husband, Tom, was a good friend of mine back then. We had just reconnected when Tom . . . died. So, yes, it has been quite traumatic to lose them both."

"One thing," Steve pushed his chair back from the table with a grinding squeal, "I'm sure you knew Tom had terminal pancreatic cancer. Do you have any idea why his wife didn't mention that to us the night he killed himself?"

Rory was totally unprepared for the question and made no attempt to disguise his shock, surprise, and confusion. "What?" was all he could say.

"So, you didn't know?"

KEVIN G. CHAPMAN

"I—well—I really can't discuss information my clients shared with me in confidence."

"Your clients are both dead." Steve stared down his witness.

"Well—you apparently already know about Tom, and I have no idea why Monica chose to keep that information private."

"Are you sure?"

Rory paused, then said, "I'm quite sure."

"OK. Thank you. If you think of anything else, please give me a call." Steve handed Rory and Ned business cards, then he and George left the room.

* * *

Rory spent a busy afternoon in the office making up for work he had neglected over the past week. He checked in with the associate who was now handling the Williams trust to confirm that everything was in place. He also extracted a flash drive from his briefcase, addressed it to Detective Berkowitz, and dropped it in the outgoing mail.

At the end of the day, Rory took the train to visit Monica's mother in her nursing home on Long Island. He didn't have to, but he wanted to help her deal with Monica's death. Mrs. Bettger was only occasionally lucid, but she understood that her daughter had died.

Rory noticed several large envelopes on the nightstand next to Mrs. Bettger's bed and saw that one was from an insurance company. After asking permission, he examined the envelope, which contained a life insurance policy on Monica. It had been sent to Mrs. Bettger because she was a beneficiary. As he scrutinized the policy document, he was

DEAD WINNER

puzzled that there were two beneficiaries. Monica's mother got half the insurance proceeds. The other half went to Bruce Frommert. Mrs. Bettger did not recognize the name and could not say why Monica would leave any of the life insurance money to "this Bruce person." She was not particularly coherent and Rory doubted her memory about most things, but the reference to Bruce rang a bell that he couldn't immediately place.

On the Long Island Railroad train back to Manhattan, Rory's thoughts drifted to his father. Since Monica came back into his life, he had made some different choices. He had taken risks. His father was wrong about Rory never being willing to take a chance. He had taken a huge one. Now he was out three million dollars. But he still had the ticket. The trust was set up to claim the money. He was designated as the trustee. He had decided he could not try to probate the informal will Monica had drawn up. It wasn't ethical. He would have to be satisfied serving as the trustee and using the money for charitable purposes consistent with what Monica would have wanted.

He ran through the week-long whirlwind with Monica in his mind. He tried to remember each moment, especially the times they made love. In his apartment. On the boat. Then Rory remembered why "Bruce" seemed familiar. Instead of going straight home, he rode the subway an extra stop south and walked to the marina. He remembered Monica explaining how Tom had acquired the *Couples Therapy* from his uncle Bruce. Tom was supposed to sell it and send Bruce the proceeds. It made sense that Monica would want to make sure Bruce got his money.

He was unable to convince the marina security guard to let him in. He walked around the exterior and found a

KEVIN G. CHAPMAN

vantage where he thought he could see the slip where the *Couples Therapy* was moored. He had only been to the boat once; he might not have remembered correctly. But by the time he finally gave up and walked away, he was pretty sure the boat was no longer in its slip.

Chapter 49 – Dodging the Bullet

ON SUNDAY AFTERNOON, Buster reported to Jack Northrup about the events of Saturday night in Rockefeller Park. Douglas Melton and Oscar Lexington were also there in Jack's office. They pieced the story together from the press reports, Buster's eyewitness account, and information Melton had been able to secure from the Gallatas' lawyer. The consensus was that Monica and Rory had paid off Hoodie Guy for something—possibly information. Monica was pissed off, either because the item wasn't delivered, or the information wasn't what she and Rory wanted. Whatever the problem, it made her angry enough to draw a gun. Or, maybe Monica was pulling a double-cross and wanted the cash back.

Buster happily reported that his guys had retrieved Tom's laptop from Rory's apartment. Dexter had combed through the machine and determined that there were no particularly damaging documents on the computer. Tom's video message was there. Dex couldn't say whether it had been viewed. Tom also had two spreadsheets that, if somebody knew enough, might show the skimming of money from Tom's accounts. Buster explained that Rory McEntyre had apparently found those spreadsheets. They had overheard him talking about them. But the sheets showed skimming only from Tom's accounts. Those documents would implicate Tom but not anyone else. Even with the spreadsheets, the feds would have a hard time linking anything to the rest of the participants in the operation.

Jack instructed Buster to maintain their cleansing program. He was not ready to declare a Krakatoa situation. Yet.

Tom Williams' assistant, Breonna, submitted her resignation by email. Dex and Matt Gallante reviewed her files and did not find anything significant. They still thought Breonna had been involved with Tom in copying and downloading the documents that were on Tom's thumb drive, but it did not seem like she kept any copies. At least, not on her work computer or in her emails.

"If she's smart," Buster said, "she'll go find a new job and keep her mouth shut."

"Have you tried to find her?" Jack asked.

Buster had expected the question, but hoped he could evade it. "We've tried, Sir, but so far, we've come up empty. We don't have the ability to track credit card charges or airline ticket purchases like the cops do, but we've staked out her apartment and questioned her neighbors and a few of her friends here in the office. Nobody has heard from her. Her social media accounts have all been shut down. Her cell phone is disconnected. It looks like she's hiding."

Jack nodded. "Anything else I need to know?"

Buster shook his head. The meeting was over. All things considered, Jack was pretty happy.

* * *

DEAD WINNER

Jack's uneasy calm was shattered three days later when Gwen buzzed him to say that two NYPD homicide detectives were on their way up from the lobby. Jack called Douglas Melton, who hustled over from his nearby office. They called Buster, who arrived a few minutes later.

When Detectives Mason and Berkowitz entered and introduced themselves, they paused upon seeing Buster seated on a cushioned chair. Buster did not stand to introduce himself, since he and the detectives were already acquainted. Steve Berkowitz said, "Mr. Northrup, we're here to talk with you about one of your employees, Richard Altman. We didn't expect him to be here for this meeting. I'm happy to have him stay, but that's up to you fellows."

Jack, Douglas, and Buster exchanged glances and nods. "At least for now, Detectives," Melton said, taking the lead as the company's lawyer, "we'll all stay."

"Suit yourself," Steve answered, dropping onto the plush sofa against the wall with a view out of Jack's ten-foot windows. "You may have heard about a shooting Saturday night in Rockefeller Park, not too far from here."

"Sure," Melton said with a solid poker face.

"Well, then you must know from the news reports that one of the people involved was shot and killed, a woman named Monica Williams. She was the widow of one of your employees, Tom Williams." Steve paused to look around the room. None of the Northrup men showed any sign of speaking. "Tom Williams, as you know, committed suicide a week ago Monday."

Melton spoke up. "It's a tragedy for the family, of course, Detective, but what does that have to do with us?"

283

KEVIN G. CHAPMAN

Steve motioned to George, who brought a large envelope out of his saddle-bag briefcase and slid out an 8x10 photograph. He passed the print to Jack Northrup, who showed it to Melton. Melton looked at Buster, then handed the photo back to Jack. It was a grainy color image, obviously an enlargement.

Steve let the men absorb the image before speaking. "This picture is from the lobby security camera of an apartment building that abuts Rockefeller Park. We ran it through our facial recognition database and it came up a likely match for Richard Altman, former NYPD officer and current head of security for your company."

Everyone in the room looked at Buster, who remained placid.

Steve turned back to Jack. "We're going to question Mr. Altman about this privately, but we wanted to talk to you first. You see, when we found out that Mr. Altman lives in the same apartment building as Tom and Monica Williams, and that he is head of security for the company where Tom Williams worked, you can imagine how it piqued our interest to find this image on that security camera."

"It's certainly an interesting coincidence, Detectives," Melton replied when he thought the detectives expected some reaction, "but I fail to see the significance."

"The significance is that when Monica Williams was shot Saturday night, a man fled the scene carrying a shoulder bag that belonged to a lawyer named Rory McEntyre, who was there accompanying Mrs. Williams. Two officers chased this man across the park and saw him disappear into a rear service door of the apartment building from which this security image came. The man who fled the scene fits the general description of Mr. Altman. This image was time

284

DEAD WINNER

stamped a few minutes after the suspect went through the rear door of that building. So, we're wondering what Mr. Altman was doing in Rockefeller Park Saturday night, what interactions he had with Monica Williams and Rory McEntyre, and why he ran away from the police carrying Mr. McEntyre's shoulder bag. Can you understand why we might be curious about those questions?"

Jack, Douglas, and Buster remained silent.

"The other thing," Steve pressed forward, "is we received an anonymous tip that Tom Williams participated in a fraud scheme here at Northrup that involved skimming profits from clients and funneling them into—what did they call it, George?"

"A dummy slush fund account," George quickly responded.

"Right. A dummy slush fund account. Now, I'm going to assume you gentlemen are surprised to hear about this. We're not entirely sure how this might be connected to Mr. Altman's presence at the crime scene last Saturday night, but we thought it was only proper that we should let you know, Mr. Northrup, seeing as how it's your company and you are in some sense responsible for any illegal activity that might be going on here."

After a deafening silence that lasted fifteen seconds, the general counsel said, "Detectives, would you give us a few minutes in private?"

"Sure," Steve calmly agreed. "But, when you're done, we're going to insist on spending some time alone with Mr. Altman." The two detectives left the office, closing the door loudly behind them.

When Buster started to speak, Jack held up a hand. "Don't. Don't say anything." After hushing Buster, Jack

285

KEVIN G. CHAPMAN

turned to Melton. "Call Harry Packman and have him send one of his white-collar guys over here right away. Buster's going to need one."

"Boss—" Buster said, but was immediately cut off.

"Don't!" Jack shot back, pointing his right index finger at his chief of security. "Shut up, Buster. Don't say a word. As of this moment, you are suspended. When the lawyer gets here, you're going to do whatever they tell you to do. The firm will pay the tab, but we need to get some distance from this. I won't fire you—for now. You keep your mouth shut and your head down and we'll see how this shakes out. You stay here and wait. Douglas and I are going to his office. We'll tell the detectives that you are waiting for the arrival of counsel. I'm betting they'll wait. I'm going to have Oscar send out the Krakatoa message to the team."

Chapter 50 – Claiming the Prize

THE THURSDAY AFTER the ransom drop, Rory saw a news report that the fourth person who won a share of the $300 million jackpot had come forward. Rory contacted the Lottery Commission to say he represented an anonymous client who was the holder of the fifth winning ticket and that he would be making a claim on behalf of a trust established for the benefit of the winner. The commission administrator told him how to get his claim perfected.

That afternoon, Rory reported the situation with the lottery ticket to his department head, Norman Reid. He explained that he, and the firm, would be the trustee for the lottery prize, and would be due a $100,000 per year retainer for administrative expenses according to an agreement Monica signed before her death. Reid was quite pleased. Mr. Packman later sent Rory a congratulatory email and reminded him about returning Tom Williams' laptop computer to the folks at Northrup Investments.

On Friday morning, Rory, a paralegal, and the firm's public relations administrator marched into the offices of the Lottery Commission and presented the winning ticket. After a half-hour delay, the Commission's chief administrator,

KEVIN G. CHAPMAN

Robert LaCaze, called Rory and his team into a conference room. He advised Rory that the ticket he presented was not authentic.

"What do you mean?" Rory's face suddenly turned as white as the bread-making table at a bakery.

"It means, Mr. McEntyre, that this is a fake ticket."

"Fake? It can't be a fake."

"I assure you it's a fake." LaCaze placed the ticket on the cherry-wood surface of a conference table. The white rectangle had been marked with a date stamp bearing the Lottery Commission logo when they first arrived. Rory had initialed the stamp before allowing the ticket to leave his possession. The ticket on the table was unquestionably the same one Rory brought in. "You see here," LaCaze pointed, "the ticket has a bar code, which includes the information about the date, time, and location of purchase, as well as the numbers. The numbers are also printed for the benefit of the ticket holder, but the bar code is the official record. This prevents any tampering."

"Are you telling me the bar code numbers don't match the printed numbers?" Rory was becoming agitated, but was doing his best to keep his composure in the presence of his paralegal and PR chief.

LaCaze gave him a sympathetic grimace. "I'm afraid it's worse than that. The bar code is completely invalid. It doesn't contain any authentic information at all. No date, no location, no numbers, and the ticket is missing a watermark from the ticket machine. There's supposed to be printing readable only by our scanner that authenticates a ticket and it's not here. I'm sorry, Sir, but this ticket is a fraud. It's not a real winner. It's worthless."

288

Chapter 51 – Turn the Page

RORY STARED GLUMLY across the conference table in the office of his criminal defense lawyer, Ned Racine. Detective Berkowitz had not called Rory to ask any more questions, but he felt compelled to ask some difficult questions of his own. Rory explained that the lottery ticket was a fake. He had some theories to explain what had really happened. The more the story spewed from his mouth, the more embarrassed he became.

"Under the ethics rules, it wouldn't be a violation of my obligation to my client if I reported the criminal fraud, right?" Rory pleaded for confirmation.

"You mean Tom Williams' fraud?"

"No, I mean Monica's fraud."

Ned looked at the ceiling, trying to recall the specifics of the rule. "I'm not an expert in ethics, Rory. We would have to research that. But why would you want to go public with this nutty theory of yours?"

"I'm thinking about filing a claim against my homeowner's insurance policy for my three million loss. I'll need to file a criminal complaint in order to do it. I can do that, right?"

"It might be ethically viable," Ned shook his head, "but it will trash your reputation. If you try to turn in your client, you will have trouble getting new clients. Let's face it, you

KEVIN G. CHAPMAN

represent rich people who have lots of secrets, including pension funds involved in shady investment strategies. Nobody is going to want to work with a lawyer who snitched on his client, even if the snitching is technically allowed because the client is dead."

"If she's really dead," Rory spat out derisively.

"You said you saw her get shot. The cops found her blood on the railing."

"They never found the body. I'm pretty sure the boat is gone. I have my doubts." Rory fought to maintain control of his temper. Rory had gone through the early stages of grief, but had stopped on a combination of denial and anger. Rory was convinced that Monica knew the ticket was a fake. She played him. He had taken the bait without thinking; at least, without thinking with his brain. How could she do that to him?

Ned took a deep breath and leaned forward, placing his forearms on the conference table. "Let's pretend that Monica Williams is alive, that she faked her death, and that she and the guy in the hoodie were somehow in cahoots to defraud you out of three million dollars. The question is, did she lie to you in order to induce you to give your Bitcoin to the guy in the hoodie?"

"Of course she did!" Rory pounded his fist on the table.

"What lie did she tell you?"

"She told me she and Tom had a winning lottery ticket."

"When did she do that?"

"Well, she and Tom came to my office and showed me the ticket, and the video."

"The video that Tom made, on Tom's phone, right?"

"Sure."

"The video you don't have?"

290

DEAD WINNER

"Right. Well, if I needed to subpoena the phone—"

"And who's going to hack into an iPhone for you to find this video, if it's even still there?"

Rory was silent. He was tech-savvy enough to know that, without the password or cooperation from Apple, it was virtually impossible to force information from an iPhone.

"Well," Ned wrote something on his legal pad, "was it Monica or Tom who said there was a winning lottery ticket?"

"It was . . . it might have been Tom."

"Do you have any proof that Monica knew the ticket was a fake?"

Rory opened his mouth, then closed it without speaking. After a pause, he admitted it was theoretically possible that Tom lied to Monica and Monica actually believed the ticket was real.

"What else did she tell you that wasn't true?" Ned pressed.

"She told me she got a call from somebody asking for the ransom."

"And what evidence do you have that she didn't get such a call? Didn't you say you listened in to one of them?"

"Sure I did, but the guy had to be in on the scheme."

"Let's say he was. Did Monica ask you to put up the money to pay the ransom?"

Rory puckered his mouth. "Well, not exactly."

"What happened, exactly?"

"She was so distraught. She didn't have the money. I thought there was a sixty-million-dollar lottery ticket in play. So, I offered to front the ransom money. But she knew it was a set-up."

"Assuming that the guy who had the ticket knew it was a fake, and assuming Monica knew who it was, and assuming that he didn't actually shoot and kill Monica, right?" Ned raised an eyebrow.

"Right," Rory said, but without conviction.

"Was there anything else she lied about?"

Rory turned his head to look out the window. He could see the top of One World Trade Center and the blue sky beyond. "She told me she loved me."

"Rory, if that's a crime, then there's a whole world of people who should be in prison. Besides, how do you know it wasn't true?"

"She wouldn't have done this to me if she loved me."

"Assuming she's not dead?"

"Right."

Ned closed the cover of the leather folio holding his legal pad and replaced the top on his Cross pen. "Well, I have to tell you, if I'm the insurance company, I'm suspicious of *you*. If you're right that Monica faked her death, I might think you voluntarily gave her the money and now you're trying to defraud the insurance. I might even think you were in on the whole supposed scheme all along and as soon as you get the three million, you'll fly off and meet Monica, wherever she is now."

Rory opened his mouth to protest, but didn't say anything.

"You knew Monica and Tom from your school days, right?"

"Yeah, but I wouldn't—"

"I'm not saying I'd believe it, Rory, but you have a complete lack of evidence. What about the information you say you found about fraud at Northrup Investments? Why don't you turn that in to the SEC and be a whistleblower?"

DEAD WINNER

"I don't have it anymore," Rory admitted. "After the cops told me there were three guys from the Gallata mob following us that night, I figured they had to be connected to the embezzlement scheme. It's the only possible connection. They might even have killed Tom. I sent the evidence to the cops. I hope they all go to jail, but I'm done with them. No bounty is worth looking over my shoulder for the rest of my life.

"Plus, Northrup Investments is a client of my firm. I can't be a whistleblower against one of the firm's clients. Even if that weren't an ethical violation, I'd get fired and what firm would ever hire me?"

"Well then, maybe you should put this whole thing behind you and move on. I don't see how getting into a fight with your insurance company is going to end well. If you go down that road, it will stain your reputation as a lawyer. Right now, nobody knows what happened. Nobody knows you lost three million. All anybody knows is that you and your girlfriend were robbed and the robber shot and killed Monica. You escaped. There's no shame in that. You can mourn her and move on. You start telling everyone about your conspiracy theory and people will think you're either crazy or the most gullible man in the world—or both."

Rory hung his head. He knew Ned was right. "So that's it?"

"Yeah. Pretty much." Ned came around the side of his desk and moved toward the door.

Later, as he walked down Broadway toward his office, Rory reflected on the past two weeks. He had fulfilled his fondest dream and had his heart broken. He had been beaten up and shot at. He had neglected his clients and been admonished by the firm's senior partner. Did he wish it all

KEVIN G. CHAPMAN

had never happened, or would he do it all over again? He remembered the smell of Monica's skin when she stepped out of the shower, and when it was sweaty after their lovemaking. Would he pay three million dollars to have the feelings he had with Monica for six days, knowing that it would end?

He walked through the elevator lobby toward his office. The receptionist, Heidi Hottinger, waved to him. She rose from behind her desk and intercepted him before he reached the archway leading to the inner offices. "Hey, Rory, are you alright?" she asked with genuine concern. The black and blue circles under his eyes had mostly receded, but he still looked fairly bedraggled. She placed a slender hand on his arm. "I heard you were mugged and your client was shot. It's a miracle you survived." She squeezed his biceps, gazing with concern at the remnants of his injuries.

Heidi had worked at the firm since before Rory arrived. Tall and lean, with golden hair flowing around her shoulders in soft curls, Rory noticed her on his first day. She had always been professionally cordial toward him, but had never shown any special interest, and certainly had never touched him.

"It wasn't that bad." Rory shrugged off Heidi's attention.

"I would be so freaked out I couldn't work for a month. You must have nerves of steel. Must be from all your bike races, huh?"

Rory gave her a modest smile.

"I'm riding in the five boroughs on Sunday. Maybe we could ride together?"

Rory was surprised and flattered by Heidi's attention. He certainly wasn't going to tell her any of the details of his encounter in Rockefeller Park. "Sure. I'd like that." Rory

DEAD WINNER

pulled away as Heidi allowed her hand to slide down his arm and across the back of his bare hand.

"I'll call you," she called out as he walked away. He broke in to a smile. For the first time in more than a week, Rory wasn't thinking about Monica Williams.

Chapter 52 – Sunny Days

BRIGHT MIDDAY SUN REFLECTED off shimmering blue water. Beyond the gentle swells of the little cove, a sliver of white sand adorned the shoreline like an earring. Dots of sunbathers sprinkled themselves across the beach, with others splashing in the soft waves. A line of palm trees stood sentry over the beachgoers and their brightly colored towels and umbrellas. The salty breeze rustled the palm leaves and the thatched roof of a tiki-style bar at one end of the crescent beach.

Bobbing in the azure sea, a boat relaxed at the ends of twin anchor ropes. Below the prow, its name was written in script letters: *Traveling With Bruce*. On the front deck, two women lounged in reclining chairs, their skin soaking in the sunshine. The tall Black woman on the port side wore a yellow one-piece swimsuit pulled up above her hips, displaying long, muscular legs. On her right, a White woman with short black hair wearing a white bikini stretched her arms above her head luxuriously. She reached for a nearby bottle of water, splashed some on her deeply tanned legs, and watched the drops flow down toward the rose tattoo on her left ankle. Beneath the rose, in thin script, was the word *Tom*.

"Congratulations," Breonna said, "as of yesterday, Monica Williams is officially dead."

DEAD WINNER

Monica turned her head. "For real? How do you know that?"

"I saw a few interesting items on Facebook this morning," Breonna jack-knifed into a sitting posture, keeping her legs suspended in the air. Her toes remained pointed, working her abs.

"You need to be more careful about using the internet," Monica scolded.

"You know I never log in, and I'm pirating off the bar's wi-fi on a burner phone. How much trouble can I get into?"

"Knowing you, a lot," Monica laughed, splashing water from her bottle onto Breonna's torso. It left dark streaks on her yellow suit and caused her to drop from her half-pike. "I'm still surprised you didn't get us both caught, leaving your gun at the ransom drop."

"It's been six months. If the cops were going to trace it to me, they'd have done it by now. I think that ship has sailed." She leaned back in her lounge chair.

"You should be more careful, but I'm happy to know that I'm dead."

"Tom's Uncle Bruce will finally get paid for this lovely boat, and we won't have to use any of the investment account money for that. I'm happy to let it sit in the Caymans account for a few years before we have to tap it."

Monica smiled. "Yeah. It's too bad I can't send Uncle Bruce a note and explain it to him. I could send a picture with the new name. I'm sure he'd approve." The two women exchanged a muted chuckle. "I'm actually surprised it happened already. I thought it would take longer. But with my blood at the scene and so many witnesses, the authorities must have been willing to make it official."

KEVIN G. CHAPMAN

"That bystander cell phone video didn't hurt, either. That was lucky."

Monica rolled her head back to a neutral position, staring at a long-tailed sea bird meandering across the sky. "It was brilliant of you to suggest rigging up a blood packet in my bra. You should have been a film director."

Breonna laughed. "Thanks. My Broadway friends are always good for any favor, even an exploding blood pack. They probably never figured anyone would use it with real blood. Of course, I never figured there would be anybody there using real bullets."

"Yeah. I'm glad that worked out." Monica held up her nearly empty water bottle. "Here's to the final and official death of Monica Williams!" She tipped back the bottle and drained the last ounce. "I only wish Rory had gotten some of his money back, like we planned."

"Hey, you had no way of anticipating that the firm's goons would be on you so fast and grab those records." Breonna sat up and reached across the small space between their chairs, placing a hand gently on Monica's arm. "The plan was solid. Rory should have been able to claim a huge bounty. I'm still shocked that the Northrup guys found out about the safe deposit box."

"I know. You and Tom had all the evidence tied up with a bow. I only wish Tom could have . . ."

"Don't," Breonna reached out and squeezed Monica's hand. "Tom's cancer was just awful luck. He did his part, and took care of both of us. At least it looks like some of the Northrup bastards are going to go to jail. Hey, things don't always work out perfectly. We're lucky that those guys didn't blow up the whole thing. If I hadn't been able to handle those

DEAD WINNER

two idiots they sent for me, I wouldn't have made the ransom drop. Then where would we be?"

"True. I'm happy it worked out for us. I sometimes still feel a little guilty about Rory. Tom knew Rory was an easy target. Hell, all I had to do was bat my eyelashes at him and he would have jumped off a bridge for me. Tom knew he had the inheritance from his father, and knew he was an expert in forensic accounting. All we had to do was plant a little evidence and then let Rory run with it after I was gone. It should have worked, I know. I just didn't expect Rory to be so . . . so sweet."

"Well . . ." Breonna released Monica's hand and swung her legs toward her, sitting up in her lounger. "There was one other interesting thing in today's internet news. It's about Rory."

Monica turned her head again, without otherwise changing her posture. "Why do you watch him online?"

"Because I feel sorry for him, too. And because I have a guilty conscience, I guess. I was worried he might kill himself when you broke his heart."

Monica rolled on her side, facing Breonna. She reached her hand out and gently stroked her leg, swirling a finger around her kneecap, where a scar from long-ago surgery carved a shallow trench. "Both our hearts got a little broken. So, what did you read?"

"He's engaged."

"Aww. That's nice." Monica smiled and propped herself up on an elbow. "Who's the lucky girl?"

"He called her Heidi in the post. They have a date set for the fall. He seemed pretty happy, obviously. I'm glad for him."

KEVIN G. CHAPMAN

"Me, too." Monica rolled to her back, holding up a hand against the sun. "I'm glad he's moving on with his life."

"Did you think he would mourn for you forever and die an old, sad man who never loved again?" Breonna was joking, but Monica didn't laugh.

"No. I want him to have a happy life. He really was good to me. He tried to be my knight in shining armor. He was never up to the task, but he did try."

"You had two men who would do anything for you. That's pretty lucky."

"And one woman," Monica smiled.

"Sure. But I would not have killed myself for you."

"And I wouldn't have asked you to," Monica reached out her hand and softly squeezed Breonna's. "I wouldn't have asked Tom to do it, either." She felt a tear form and spill down her cheek. Despite the passage of time, she still got emotional about it. "I agree with you about feeling bad for Rory. I thought it would be easy, to take his father's money and leave him mourning me. It turned out to be pretty fucking hard."

"You gave him the best sex of his life. Now, he's getting married. I venture to say that if you hadn't had your affair with him, he might not have been able to move on and make some other woman happy. So, you're even."

"No," Monica looked past the rail of the *Traveling With Bruce* at the deep blue water. "I think I came out ahead on the deal."

THE END

DEAD WINNER

Thank you for reading *Dead Winner*. I truly enjoy hearing from readers about their reactions to my characters and stories. I welcome critical comments and suggestions that can help me improve my writing and urge every reader to **please leave a review**. Even a few words will go a long way and I will be grateful. Post on Amazon, Goodreads and/or BookBub to let other readers know what you think. And feel free to send me an email directly at www.kevingchapman.com to tell me your thoughts about this book.

And please tell your friends (and book club leaders) about this book. As an independent author, I need all the word-of-mouth plugs I can get. Keep reading books by indie authors; there are a lot of great writers out there just waiting for you.

Kevin G. Chapman
November 2022

About the Author

Kevin G. Chapman is, by profession, an attorney specializing in labor and employment law. He is a past Chair of the Labor & Employment Law Network of the Association of Corporate Counsel, leading a group of 6800 in-house employment lawyers. Kevin is a frequent speaker at Continuing Legal Education seminars and enjoys teaching management training courses.

Kevin's Mike Stoneman Thriller series, five full-length novels (so far), features NYPD Homicide Detective Mike Stoneman. The series includes *Lethal Voyage*, winner of the 2021 Kindle Book Award, and *Fatal Infraction*, winner of the CLUE Award as the #1 police procedural of the year. You can preview the series by reading the award-winning short story, *Fool Me Twice*, available free on most ebook retailer websites or you can get it directly from Kevin's website.

Kevin has also written a serious work of literary fiction, *A Legacy of One*, originally published in 2016, which was a finalist for the Chanticleer Book Review's Somerset Award for Literary Fiction. *A Legacy of One* is filled with political and social commentary and a plot involving personal identity, self-determination, and the struggle to make the right life decisions. You can learn more on Kevin's website.

Find Kevin on Facebook at Kevin G. Chapman Author.

Book Club discussion questions for *Dead Winner*

1. What was your impression of Rory? Did it change as you read through the story? How?
2. Did your impressions about Monica change over the course of the story? How?
3. How long did it take you to figure out that Monica was not being entirely truthful with Rory?
4. Were you surprised to learn Breonna's role in the real story?
5. Did you guess (be honest) what really happened to Tom?
6. Tom appears (alive) only in the first chapter. Despite that, did you feel like Tom was an important character throughout the book? Did your feelings about Tom change by the end?
7. In the end, is Rory a Hero, or a sap?
8. In the end, is Monica a villain? Do you think she really had feelings for Rory?
9. Did you pick up on the name Ned Racine? (The lawyer, played by Ted Danson in the movie *Body Heat*.)
10. Who predicted the ending? (Really?)
11. For readers who have read the Mike Stoneman Thriller series, did you enjoy the appearance here of a few characters who crossed over from those books?

If your book clubs would like to read *Righteous Assassin*, book #1 in the Mike Stoneman Thriller series, please contact me for information about how your group can get discounted or free copies of the ebook and/or audiobook to get you started. Send me a note via my website at www.kevingchapman.com or by email at Kevin@KevinGChapman.com.

AUTHOR'S NOTE & ACKNOWLEDGEMENTS

As always, I must credit my wife, Sharon, for keeping the story coherent and for being the architect of all the romance and the subplots. Sharon has a fantastic vision for where my characters are going.

I also thank my brilliant editor-daughter, Samantha (Samanthachapmanediting.com) whose careful reads, great ideas, and willingness to tell me when I was off-track helped put the book over the top. She's the editor that every author wants. And kudos again to my cover designer, Peter from bespokebookcovers.com. Peter outdid himself with this eye-catching cover. Also kudos to Jiawie "Peter" Hsu from Fotolux in Princeton Junction, NJ (my local photo shop) for making me beautiful prints for my publicity posters.

My beta readers provided me with invaluable perspectives and ideas as the book was in development. Thanks so much to, Kay Hagan-Haller, Kim Hines, Roxx, Mike "Laz" Lazarine, Matt (M.C.) Thomas, Mimi Bailey, Gayle Wilson, and the amazing Joanna Joseph. Everyone contributed something to the final product.

I also thank Amy Vansant at AuthorsXP.com and her band of Typokillers, who combed over the finished manuscript and rooted out the last few errors, large and small, to make the final text as clean as it can be. (But, if you find a flaw, please let me know so I can fix it.) All authors should use the typokillers. Thanks to Judith Dickinson, Sue Martin, Nancy Harrison, Lynn Feinman, and Jerilyn.

Other novels by Kevin G. Chapman

The Mike Stoneman Thriller Series

Righteous Assassin (Mike Stoneman #1)
Deadly Enterprise (Mike Stoneman #2)
Lethal Voyage (Mike Stoneman #3)
Fatal Infraction (Mike Stoneman #4)
Perilous Gambit (Mike Stoneman #5)
Fool Me Twice (A Mike Stoneman Short Story)

Stand-alone Novels

The Good Girl (coming in 2023)
A Legacy of One
Identity Crisis: A Rick LaBlonde Mystery

Short Stories

The Car, the Dog & the Girl

Visit me at www.KevinGChapman.com

Connect with Kevin:

Kevin's website: https://www.KevinGChapman.com
Sign up for Kevin's Newsletter
Facebook page: Mike Stoneman Thriller Group
https://www.amazon.com/gp/product/Bo8BZMDSVT

Email: Kevin@KevinGChapman.com

Made in the USA
Middletown, DE
04 October 2022

11476159R00187